Ma Polinski's Pockets

**Praise for Sara Sheridan's début novel,
TRUTH OR DARE**

'a thriller for a new generation . . . Sara Sheridan will
go far' *Harpers & Queen*

'a fast-moving, action tale of two girls intent on living
life to the full. Libby and Becka stumble upon a set-up
while squatting in a smart London flat. The owner, an
up-and-coming banker, is missing. After eaves-
dropping on her answering machine, they realise they
have taken on more than they bargained for . . . this is
a story of friendship, bad money and lies. It made me
laugh out loud, but it also reduced me to tears'
Sunday Express

'darkly comic and compassionate' Mike Ripley,
Daily Telegraph

'in a genre where we usually find polemic, melodrama
or worthy-but-predictable tragedy, Sheridan has
written a proper, character-driven novel instead . . . a
pessimistic exploration of how ordinary and even
good people, once locked into a certain mind-set, can
do blatantly evil things yet think them good and right
. . . so well written you never notice the writing'
Glasgow Herald

'poignant, exhilarating, funny' *Time Out*

'written in a snappy, quick-witted style, this urban
odyssey looks set to gain many admirers'
Edinburgh Evening News

Sara Sheridan was born in 1968 in Edinburgh. She studied English at Trinity College Dublin and then went on to live in Galway for eighteen months before returning to her native Scotland. She now lives in Edinburgh with her daughter, Molly.

Her first novel, *Truth or Dare*, was published in 1998 to great critical acclaim and is now being developed for film. She has recently completed her third novel, *The Pleasure Express*, which will be published by Arrow in the year 2000.

As well as writing novels, Sara has a keen interest in cinema and, in 1998, co-wrote a short film, *The Window Bed*. She is now working on her first feature-length screenplay.

Touted as one of *GQ*'s BritLit talents of 1997, she has also been nominated for the 1999 Young Achievers of Scotland award.

Sara Sheridan

Ma Polinski's
Pockets

ARROW

Published by Arrow Books in 1999

3 5 7 9 10 8 6 4 2

First published in the United Kingdom in 1999 by Arrow

Arrow Books
The Random House Group Limited
20 Vauxhall Bridge Road, London SW1V 2SA

Random House Australia (Pty) Limited
20 Alfred Street, Milsons Point, Sydney,
New South Wales 2061, Australia

Random House New Zealand Limited
18 Poland Road, Glenfield
Auckland 10, New Zealand

Random House South Africa (Pty) Limited
Endulini, 5a Jubilee Road, Parktown 2193, South Africa

The Random House Group Limited Reg. No. 954009
www.randomhouse.co.uk

A CIP catalogue record for this book is available from the British Library

Papers used by Random House are natural, recyclable products
made from wood grown in sustainable forests. The manufacturing processes
conform to the environmental regulations of the country of origin

ISBN 0 09 940977 1

Typeset by SX Composing DTP, Rayleigh, Essex
Printed and bound in Great Britain by
Cox & Wyman Ltd, Reading, Berkshire

Thanks are due to lots of people, but this book is only dedicated to two – Ron and Kate Goodwin, my parents, who provided inside information, top antiques tips and some rather great dinners.

The thanks go to my chums, who read drafts of *Ma Polinski's Pockets* and told me what wouldn't wash, and to the archaeologists in Calainis and in Edinburgh. So many people help you when you are trying to find out the details you need that it is difficult to fit everybody in, but I do want to thank the police press officer at Fettes HQ and the cemetery officials who took the time to give me all the information that I needed. Chats with my uncle Clive Lindley were (and are) always illuminating because he's so knowledgeable. Thanks, Clive, and thanks to all the Lindleys, because Maureen and Libby have also been great. I also owe a lot to the Society of Authors and the K. Blundell Trust who so kindly supported me in what I wanted to do. And a final thank-you goes to my daughter Molly, who despite having German measles gave me a bit of space each day to allow me to write when I was just finishing the book.

Prologue

It starts in Edinburgh. A dark, old city. A great big black bastard of a city where there are ghosts of all kinds. Banshees and spirits, bad and good. It's a place where the past weighs heavily on the present, the dips and the valleys between its seven hills all brim-full of history. It laps up against you as you move on through it. It clings to you once you've left. We were brought up in Edinburgh, though only once did my brother and I ever see a ghost. I'll never forget it. We were very little and we had crept barefoot out of bed through the hallways of our solid, stonebuilt family house and down the carpeted stairway to the kitchen where plump, sweet Italian grapes, champagne grapes, we called them, were to be had. We guzzled them under the kitchen table where the musty smell of teapots and roasting ovens had sunk to the ground. The juice ran down our chins. And then we crept upstairs again silent as little shadows to where the grown-ups were asleep. We were very small, I must have been four or five, I suppose, and Simon was two years older. I remember our smooth, thin, white, little feet on the dark carpet. For some reason that sticks out in my mind. Him leading. Me following. The way I'd always assumed it was supposed to be. When we got upstairs again, skipping lightly over the creaky board at the door to Mum and Dad's room, half delighted, half afraid, we sat on the footstool at the bottom of the bed and watched as if what we saw there was normal. As if we had expected it. There was a calm, light cloud around my mother as she slept, safe in the forest-green quilting of her mahogany bed. It was as if it was tending to her, stroking her beautiful face. Simon and I often sneaked around at night together but we'd never seen spirits before. It didn't scare us. The radiant cloud hovered over our mother's head and curled around her shoulders. It wasn't scary at all. It was normal. It was to be expected. It's a strong memory for me, that dark night, and it sets the tone for everything really. Everything which came after. Because of that I suppose I should have realised among everything that happened later on, that my mother was the centre of things from the very beginning. My mother, who was tended by her ghosts. Anyhow, the cloud of light faded slowly away until the bedroom was dark again and my father shifted over and laid his arm around her and we knew it had been a spirit, one of many. Only normally we didn't see them. That was all. We didn't see them. My mother's ghosts, Edinburgh ghosts, our normality, always there in the background, unspoken and unnamed. Strange noises, which, as if we had antennae, we picked up when we were small. The boy who banged his drum under the city chambers. Some evil woman wailing as she hovered outside the tolbooth. And, well for me, anyway, there was Ma Polinski. For me alone. Not that Ma Polinski was ever noisy. In death or in life. She was a quiet woman, strong, I think, and very orderly. Outspoken and determined too. And, as it turns out, she was my parents' best kept secret, the skeleton in their closet, and they had plenty of secrets, like a moat around their castle. Something to divide my brother and I from them. Something to draw us in and also keep us out.

I remember finding out about Mum. It was the first

secret I, Rachel White, ever cracked. We were sitting in the conservatory and it was springtime. The yellow-green trees outside cast dappled shadows over us. I was fifteen, I suppose, and she let it slip, and now I can't remember what we were talking about. The subject of our conversation slips my mind completely. I only remember three words. The words, I suppose, which made me realise that we weren't a normal family. That there was a dark heart to our daily lives. A shadow which I must have suspected but of which I was never sure. Three words which were the key to everything:

'In the camp.'

'What camp?' I asked her, the hairs on the back of my neck beginning to prickle.

And then there was this uncomfortable silence as she made the decision whether to roll down the bridge and let me come over to the battlements.

'The concentration camp.'

I looked at her, just staring wide-eyed in amazement. I hadn't ever suspected that, you see. It hadn't ever occurred to me and I couldn't quite believe it. It seemed such a serious thing to come out of nowhere. My mother didn't even stop sewing, you know. It was as if she hadn't said anything. I looked at her arms. I stared. She was wearing a T-shirt. It had short sleeves.

'I was only a child,' she said. 'I was just there for a few months.'

'A few months? In Auschwitz? A few months?'

'Dachau,' she corrected me. 'I don't like to talk about it.'

I reached out and I touched her forearm. There was a scar there. She'd said before that she had fallen out of a tree when she was a child. There was an old treehouse at my Great-Aunt Petra's place where she had been brought up. We weren't allowed to climb up there because it was so rotted with age but my mother had played in it with her cousins. They had loved card

3

games and had sat up in that treehouse in all weathers playing gin rummy and whist and the occasional illicit game of poker. I'd always thought that she had fallen while she was climbing up there and that was where she had hurt herself. I'd always believed that my mother had had an idyllic childhood full of innocent, summertime games and post-war sweets with shiny foil wrappers. I had gone for everything she had told me. Of course I had. My heart was fluttering. Mum still hadn't looked up. Her pale skin seemed very white in the sunshine and strands of her hair fell down and covered her eyes. And I was transfixed by the familiar scar on her arm which I had seen every day and never understood.

'I had the number removed as soon as I had stopped growing,' she said nonchalantly.

'Why didn't you tell me?' I whispered.

Mum shrugged. She didn't like to admit she was wrong. In fact, looking back on it, I don't think I've ever heard her say that she was wrong. Ever. It's true. I've never heard my mother apologise for anything. A sure sign of a guilty conscience. A sure sign of someone who survived.

It was that day, I suppose, looking back on it, that history really came alive for me. I had seen the footage of wartime newsreels, all grainy and black and white. I had seen the devastation of the night-time bombing raids in London and Bristol; come to think of it, I had seen that it was just as bad in Hamburg and Berlin. I had seen the American troops liberating Auschwitz, those still lucky enough to be alive standing skeletal, too shocked even to smile as the iron gates of the camp were laid open on the atrocities of the Third Reich. *Arbeit Macht Frei*. But I hadn't realised, you see, I hadn't realised because I was so young, that my parents had been alive through that time, I hadn't connected that the war could have touched their lives at all or

4

really changed anything. Up till then history was a separate thing to me. History was the past. The day I found out about Mum my world expanded, my ideas changed and I realised, among many important things, that the awkward movements of the near corpses on the newsreel were once as fluid as my own movements and that meant those Resistance fighters who had risked their lives every day didn't live in a history book, that they had rough, rosy cheeks and shaking hands, and hearts which beat fast whenever they passed a uniform. It meant that they weren't just historical icons to me any more, they were alive. From that moment on, whenever I read a history book I didn't just think about political or philosophical or economic reasons why things had happened, I thought about the people who had lived then. I thought about not having enough to eat or not being allowed to vote, or what it would feel like if your beliefs were made illegal by a hostile church or a repressive government, and I imagined all the anger I could harbour, or the fear or the desperation. I read everything I could about the war. Everything. It became my teenage obsession. My specialist subject. I was voracious. The children they used for target practice. The lampshades made from human skin. The mountainous piles of gold teeth removed after, or sometimes before, each murder. Whole villages kneeling naked beside an open pit, waiting to be shot in the back of the head, one by one. Waiting. I used to cry at night unable to find words for all the unimaginable things that they did. Noticing that my mother still lived in the shadow of the Holocaust, the dimness populated by the dead. Seeing even her happiest moments defined by it. Seeing small signs in her and in myself. Fifty years on, you see, and well, the history was still alive. And it was a combination of that realisation, I suppose, and my childhood background in unravelling secrets, and living in Edinburgh too maybe; yes, it was all of that along with the other things that happened which meant that I decided to become an archaeologist. I decided to dedicate myself to history. Not 'dead' history. Not 'dusty' history because really, you see, those things are never over. But to the past as a way of understanding the present. I chose a career, I suppose, which was all about me.

Chapter One

I grew up around old things, things made with great skill, pieces of astounding beauty. Relics and debris. My father is an antiques dealer, you know. If it wasn't for him, if he hadn't been so good at it, I'd have never met Ma Polinski at all. Dad learnt his stuff on the market stalls in London in the forties. In those days there were still Fabergé enamel picture frames and De Lamerie silver bullet teapots doing the rounds for less than fifty quid which, even counting inflation, is still half nothing. Dad grew up around all of that and he took it all in. He must have been a bright kid all right. I'll say that for him. Nowadays you can't get your hands on that kind of stuff for ten thousand pounds, never mind fifty – it just isn't around in quite the same way any more. Dad got trained up at just the right time. Luck and talent. A devastating combination, and Dad, well, he made a mint. A fortune. He has a real antiques dealer's memory – you can go into his office and pick up some tiny little ornament off a shelf crowded with dusty bric-a-brac and he can remember the day he bought it twenty years ago and exactly what he paid for that small, shiny speck in his great big stock-book even though he probably won't have touched it, thought about it or seen it since. Ma Polinski was like that too. I think that's why she took a shine to Dad because she wouldn't deal with just anyone. More dealers had been bundled hastily out of her shop on that old close off the High Street than she had out of date copies of the phone book to chuck after them in her rage. The antiques trade is kind of different from what you might call a 'normal business'. It's full of characters, it's impossible to franchise and it's very individual. There is a limited supply of goods, and supply is getting steadily more limited all the time, so it's really down to how good you are at finding stock and buying it in. Ma Polinski had a huge range of stuff. Her shop was a really magical place but, like I said, she wouldn't sell to just anyone. You had to be on her right side. Dad used to take me in with him which was kind of a smart move because I was a really cute five-year-old, although I say it myself. There are lots of pictures of me smiling in the sunshine in flowery dresses with a mass of tiny, blondey-brown ringlets framing my sun-kissed, small-featured, five-year-old face. My own idyllic childhood. I don't really remember looking like that but I do kind of remember going to Ma Polinski's shop. She and I really hit it off and it was because of that, I suppose, that I remember it quite well. I mean, I can't remember school until I was about eight, but I can remember those visits I made with Dad all right. The place smelled very dusty and it was very, very dark. The small, medieval windows faced northwards out towards the high-ceilinged, wide-windowed, Georgian houses of the New Town on the other side of Princes Street. The High Street was mostly slum housing around that time although in the sixties they had begun to knock a lot of it down and move the ten-a-room tenement families out to Craigmillar, then the newly-built vision of the left-wing town council, now the worst housing estate in Europe. The Old Town has been refurbished, cleaned, done up and polished half to death since then, but it was still pretty grim when I used to go there with Dad, which would have been around the middle of the seventies, I suppose.

Ma Polinski used to sit in the silty gloom of her office, drinking her tea out of an old jam jar, surrounded by treasures of breathtaking beauty which were stacked right up the walls. Those walls glowed with colour. I remember that much. There were gold plates and canteens of silver cutlery and porcelain carriage clocks and seventeeth-century Venetian glass ornaments the colour of blood. Lying around the floor, all over the place, there were wooden boxes and old leather suit-cases just brimming over with silverware and jewels. And it was a big shop. I mean, that was only one room of it. Dad was truly one of the blessed because she used to take him downstairs to the basement. Now, at first, the basement didn't look quite so good. There were just rows of old grey filing cabinets and a couple of huge safes. But say Dad was looking for a special kind of diamond necklace for a very special customer. Just say that – he was on a commission. Well, Ma Polinski would go to a specific filing cabinet and pull open one of the drawers and inside there would be diamond necklaces sparkling all the way back. Maybe twenty or thirty of them. And then you'd realise that all those rows of filing cabinets were full of gemstone necklaces and bracelets and earrings, each cabinet catalogued according to which stones were in it and then each and every drawer carefully organised according to progres-sion of age. I never saw myself what Ma Polinski kept in the safes but let's face it, it must have been pretty spectacular. Not what you would have expected at all.

She was a small, sturdy old woman. I remember that. She had greying hair which she pulled back into a bun, and a stretched old, grey cardigan which she must have knitted herself. She also had very smooth skin, although then I suppose she would have already been in her sixties, and she smelled just like my mother did, of Helena Rubinstein face cream. Honey and lavender. It gave her face a translucence, I think. Most of all, though, I remember her hands, all white and pink, with fingernails which seemed to have been dusted in white powder. She used to reach up to a shelf and bring down a curiosity for me to look at – a Meissen figurine, or a cast brass Punch, or an odd pewter teapot with an ivory handle. Strange, isn't it, the snippets you remember? Whenever he'd take me to her place, Dad would sit me up on the green leather inset of her mahogany desk and Ma Polinski would go into the cupboard she used as a kitchen and come out with an unaccustomed smile on her face. Usually she looked very strict, I always thought. Kind, but still strict. After she came out of the kitchen, though, she'd smile.

'So, Rachel dear, do you know what I have in my pocket?' she'd always ask.

I just nodded with a stupid, little-kid grin. She always had a biscuit with pink sugar icing on it. She always hid it.

'So which pocket is it in?' she would challenge me.

I used to take this game very seriously. It was, after all, a very serious matter. There were six pockets in Ma Polinski's grey cardigan. It was a lottery as to which she might use for the biscuit. This was a real game of chance. Ma Polinski didn't play poncey kids' games with clues and stuff. She played to win. Most times I got the biscuit. Well, that's the way I remember it anyway: I always got the biscuit and, along with it, the feeling that this daunting old lady liked me. That I'd done well.

'Pretty little thing. Smart too,' Ma Polinski would say. 'Are you going to train her?' she'd ask my dad.

I suppose he probably just shrugged his shoulders because he wouldn't want to say no to Ma Polinski when there was a deal on the cards.

It's not that I wasn't bright enough. It's not that I'm not hard-nosed. But despite early indications that he would let me be involved in his business dealings, the tantalising glimpses afforded by my childhood, it turned out that my father never had any intention of training me up. And apart from the truth about my mother, that was the other big thing I learned when I was fifteen.

It was a year of sobering shocks and realisations for me. A year when the murky shadows of my childhood lightened out a bit and I could start to see some of the things that had been hidden. It was 1988. That summer holidays my friends and I bought drinks underage in a bar up on Morningside Road and I got drunk for the very first time to the strains of Robert Palmer's 'Addicted to Love'. Halfway through the summer I had my unruly brown hair cut into a tight, chic little bob, and I walked from Princes Street Gardens up to the baked potato shop near the Tron Kirk with Andy MacCaskill, the hero of that year's first fifteen at rugby and one of the youngest players on the team. Both of us were laughing in the sunshine, both of us barefoot. I remember I couldn't stop smiling, I was just so happy to be with him. It was a summer of revelations like I said. And it was late on that holidays, just before it was time to go back to school and take my O grades, just when everything was going really well and I felt really confident, that I discovered that Dad wanted the business to go in its entirety to my brother Simon. It really upset me that, it shocked me a lot. It had never occurred to me, you see, that I wouldn't be allowed to work in the business. Not only because of the money. Not just that. But I loved jewellery. I was fascinated by it. Still am. I used to make little brooches when I was very small. Proper claw and clasp ones with old bits of paste and crystal and gold wire. I wanted to please my father, you see. I had always seen myself working for him eventually. I had always thought there'd be a place in the shop for me. I suppose up till then he'd been my hero. I hadn't expected him to shut me out. Originally, when we were really small, there were tax breaks to be had if Simon and I both had shares in Dad's shop. They cleaned up all those loopholes in the early nineties, but we'd had it sewn up for years by then. Anyhow, a few months before I was going to be sixteen, the age of legal responsibility, Dad brought home a sheaf of papers for me to sign. I knew what I was signing. I was signing my shares in Dad's business over to my brother and I can't say that I didn't resent it. I'd worked on Saturday afternoons in the shop with him, and I knew I could sell stuff just as well as he could. It felt, I suppose, like Dad didn't really love me or have faith in me. It felt like he didn't value me at all and, worst of all, it didn't feel safe. All my life that business had been part of my family. It's a beautiful little shop and ever since I could remember it had made all that money. Everything we lived on. I didn't know what other kind of life there was, and in a funny kind of way our family has always been so closed, we've always stuck so closely together, that I couldn't see what on earth I could do. I was spoilt, I suppose. I was middle class and fucked up and spoilt. But I wanted to die when I signed those papers. I really believed that Dad must have hated me. There was no question of compensation and no question of not signing either. It was totally unfair. But I signed the damn papers anyway, cursing myself for my bad luck at birth – the only reason that Dad wouldn't train me up, he said, was because I was a girl.

It wasn't really an issue for Mum and Dad, being even-handed, I mean. That didn't come into it at all. There was no question of hard work counting or giving someone a chance. 'Just wouldn't work out, angel,' Dad explained. 'Seen fathers try it too many times.' And it really didn't irk Dad that it was illegal, to say nothing of unjust. If you'd said to him 'that's unfair' he would have just shrugged his shoulders and told you that it was perfectly fair. That was just the way that it worked and it had worked just fine for a very long time. Which is true, I suppose. Male antiques dealers don't cut in their womenfolk. They're experts in their field, members of a very exclusive boys' club. You can see them all at the back of the saleroom, which is where you get the best view of who's buying what. They stand up there at the back and they don't bid against each other ever because it's easier and cheaper to sort everything out between themselves afterwards. All the men. I've seen my dad bid so subtly that he hardly moved, it was a quiver, a mere twitch of his finger, but the auctioneer picked it up, of course, along with anyone else in the trade. Most of the public don't have a clue. They sit far too far to the front to see the way that the dealers communicate with each other across the back rows of the saleroom. It's faster than any video game I've ever seen. The ones on the left will tell the ones on the right what's going on with a bat of their eyes and vice versa. Men only. No women up at the back. Not at most of the sales, anyway. And if you tried to get in there and they turned on you (which they well might) they could bankrupt you in the space of one sale. My brother always says you need a hundred thousand pounds behind you and the goodwill of the boys. So anyway, Dad cut me out and no one said a thing about it, but that summer after school, Simon smugly bought his first Hugo Boss suit and went into the shop full-time.

I remember just how furious it made me. I remember exactly what it felt like. I was so frustrated that I hit out at the walls of my bedroom one night, boxing at the shadows cast by the moonlight through the trees. Then I took a penknife and ripped the wallpaper all around my bed. That was kind of satisfying because it was so illicit. I did terrible violence to the wall – the paper was an ivory colour with red, open roses twining upwards here and there. It felt really good to hit out at something so traditional and so beautiful. My brother had the

13

walls of his bedroom papered with a discreet, dove-grey and white pinstripe. I had the roses because I was the girl. I remember that I was so angry that I was possessed by it completely. I couldn't think of anything else. I had the roses and Simon got the shop. For a long time it just got worse and worse as it sunk in. For weeks and weeks I was very confused. I never really told my father how angry I was about it, though he must have known. I did try to tell my mother one day, but she just said that things were the way that they were and I should try to accept them. And that made me angrier still because I thought to myself that she ought to have been on my side, that she ought to have stood up for me. But she didn't say anything really. Just a few platitudes and then silence. And that scared me at the time, because I was only fifteen and I had nowhere else to go and if they'd cut me out of the shop, well, to my mind, home might have been next. We were all so certain in our insecurities. Victims one and all. So in the end, without anyone saying anything really, the marks on the wallpaper were silently repaired while I was at school one day and I kind of knuckled down.

They'd always controlled me that way. By not discussing things. Not letting themselves be drawn into conversation but then, to be fair, to see both sides, I suppose I wasn't the only one who was afraid in my family that summer. I was growing up a lot. I had been growing away from them and I reckon at the back of their minds Mum and Dad really didn't want me to be independent, they didn't want to see me with independent means, and that's what those shares would have given me. If I'd had that kind of capital I might not have needed them and, they reasoned, I'm sure they asked themselves, what was I going to do with the shares anyway when it was out of the question that I'd ever be able to deal. I was fifteen going on sixteen and I was beginning to have my own life. I was interested in boys and I was beginning to leave home, to go to stay with friends for the weekend, to talk about going to college and getting a place of my own. It must have seemed to them that my departure was very close. They were afraid, I think, though they'd never have admitted it, that in the next year or two they would lose me completely. I was the one, you see, who spoke out. I was difficult. Ideas interested me too much and they could see me fading out, leaving home, going away, and they couldn't bear it. Mum's never been good at things being taken away. That runs quite deep, I guess. She can't quite believe that something which goes might well come back. Shoes, spectacles, parents. My mother had lost enough people already and I suppose they thought that they had one easy means of control. One thing which would keep them in my life for good. They were so messed up they thought I only needed them for their money. Crazy, isn't it? Scary. Especially now. But wealthy people can be like that and as for people who came out of the Nazi death camps, well, a deep-seated need to keep your family close to you is pretty easy to understand. I didn't realise until recently how guilty I have always felt about hating them for their lack of trust. My parents are such good providers and whenever you complain it sounds so spoilt, so petty. The whole of my family was a trap, though. A kind of a cage. A closed, controlled kind of love and I bought right into it – I had been brought up to. A nice little allowance from my impenetrable parents. Another little secret here and there and well, we all felt very secure among the emerging shadows of the past. We were all very close together.

It's weird. I mean, it's taken me a long time to start to figure that one out. Years of Simon toeing the line and me not quite playing the game, and a profound feeling that although my life was lovely, although I'm middle class and my family's rich, although I went to a nice

school and on to a good college, although I had everything I could imagine, that things were not quite right.
I remember so much laughter in my childhood. So
much fun. I remember the smell of the food, pots and
pots of food. I remember coloured lights playing on to
my wall, creeping over the yellow coverlet of my bed.
Socks warmed on radiators. Cocoa after snowball fights
in the street. And my mother clinging on to me and me
feeling guilty because I had gone too close to the boiler
in the laundry room at the back of the house, and Mum
had screamed and screamed and pulled me back and it
was only later that I understood that the old boiler
looked like a furnace. They burned the bodies in
furnaces, you know. You can't imagine the guilt someone carries with them after escaping that. You can't
imagine your skin hanging off you and your vision so
blurred you can't even stand. You can't imagine
looking down at your sick, tiny body and wondering
'why me?' when it's so obvious you should have died.
And I realise how guilty I feel too. Me. Then and now.
Child and adult. I wasn't ever there. I didn't even know
what had happened until later. But I grew up guilty.
The whole of my life at home with my smug, well-
behaved brother, my mother the Holocaust survivor
and my father who loved to be needed. The perfect
couple with the perfect family, all wound around each
other, so that we were like a ball of string. My mother
as she'd always been, at the centre, then my father and
Simon, and me, well, I was the loose end so I got tucked
in tightest of all. I felt like a real second-class citizen
because of that, but well, that was the plan.

So when I hit sixteen, Dad handed the business lock,
stock and barrel over to Simon. He was a safe bet, my
brother. And that's how he became a millionaire, and I
became pissed off. You have to understand there was a
lot of money involved – it wasn't all just principle.
1988. Strangely enough, it was earlier that same year

that the subject of Ma Polinski came up again, I mean, that's the first time I remembered her after all those years. It's like she was watching over me, I suppose, because she was long dead even by then. She was my guardian angel if you like. My own spirit emerging in glimpses and when she came up, well, it was fleeting, but in retrospect it was portentous. If there's one thing I've learned, if there's one thing she's taught me, it's that you can't pussyfoot around your memories. You have to face your past and when Ma Polinski came up that day, looking back on it, it was like a hint from beyond the grave that if I stood up and faced things honestly, well, what had happened to her wouldn't happen to me. Ma Polinski, you see, had got lost and I think if it hadn't been for her that I would have got lost too.

The débâcle with the shop had happened the week before, and I kind of resented having to even go in that day because I couldn't figure out why Dad had got me to work on Saturdays all those years when he had no intention of, well, you know. He'd already said that when I left school that was it. Not even a sales job, but he made me go in anyway and I just didn't know why I was there at all. Anyhow, I had decided to take a really long break from work. Too long. A contentious kind of break. I was downstairs in the basement at Dad's curled up in one of the old, green velvet armchairs and I was reading my *Jackie* magazine. I can even remember what I was wearing, you know. Everything about it is still very clear in my mind. I was kind of young and kind of cute, I suppose. It's cheesy but I used to wear my school kilt in the shop, especially in the summertime because the tourists loved it and that year there was a late summer and it was still quite warm even at the end of September, so I was wearing the kilt (which was Black Watch tartan – dark blue and dark green) with a pair of sandals and a short-sleeved, white cotton shirt. So there I was all curled up on the old armchair with steely determination, reading my magazine, which I used to buy on the way down there every week as a treat. That day I was all set to read it cover to cover at least once so that I would have to be called back upstairs to work when they realised I had been gone for an hour. Usually I paced it better. On my first break I'd turn straight to Cathy and Clare and read all the letters on the problem page which was, by today's standards, pretty innocent – you know: I'm fourteen, should I kiss my boyfriend and should I use tongues to do it? That kind of thing. I suppose I was naive, I was just a kid, though, and I was way into all of that stuff – I had, not surprisingly, a real passion for inside information and on account of Cathy and Clare, if Andy MacCaskill ever made a move, I was going to be ready. I loved the problem page. By lunchtime I had usually moved on to the photostory. I used to figure that if I read the magazine slowly, bit by bit, I could make it last for the whole weekend. Anyhow, this particular day I had only just settled down to read the thing all in one go and hence Make My Point, when something slightly unusual happened. Billy came downstairs.

Billy had worked in the shop for years. He used to clean the silver and set the windows and take the repairs over to the workshop on Causewayside every morning at eleven o'clock. Dad had taken him on when some old antiques shop went bust and Billy was probably in his late forties by then. He'd worked his whole life cleaning and restoring silver and plate in other people's shops and his skin was absolutely ingrained with the smell of the Blenheim's Caustic Silver Dip which he used to miraculously remove the tarnish. There was a great big bathful of it downstairs in the basement, which is where Billy spent most of his day, dipping the greying items into the chemicals and cleaning them off with Fairy Liquid, warm water and a toothbrush. He looked like he could use a bit of a dip himself: his grey hair never shone and his steely eyes were kind of dull and bleary. I was only fifteen and he seemed absolutely ancient to me at the time although I suppose then he would have been around sixty. He was a kind old man and although he'd worked in the trade all his life he'd never actually developed any skill in valuations. Valuation is the most important thing because without it, of course, you can't buy. So that's what you get trained in. 'It's easy to sell in any business,' my dad would say sagely if you ever got him on to the subject, 'the trick is in the buying.' Billy had never bought, but he didn't seem to mind that. I on the other hand had just been told I would never get the chance to buy and I bloody well did mind. I was hopping mad.

'You OK, Rachel?' Billy asked.

Well, I was only fifteen, I was pissed off with my father and, I have to be honest, I wasn't discreet.

'Nope,' I said. 'I've the wrong genitalia.'

Billy looked wistfully up the stairs. At the time I thought maybe he was thinking about nipping out and getting me some new genitalia, because he was terribly amenable about running errands. Maybe Billy doesn't know what genitalia are, I thought. But really, I suppose, well obviously, he was wondering if he could get away.

'Dad won't train me,' I said.

Billy sat down on the other faded, green velvet chair and lit himself a cigarette.

'No point,' he said. 'No point in that. The other dealers won't cut you in. If he trained you, love, you wouldn't be able to buy in the trade anyway.'

It was stating the obvious, but it was way too much for me. I slapped my *Jackie* down on the table and raised my voice. 'That's ridiculous. If you've got the money, how can they refuse to sell to you? How can they?'

Billy took a deep draw and shrugged his shoulders.

'Come on,' I almost shouted, because I hadn't been able to take it out on anyone yet, 'there must be female antiques dealers. There must be.'

'Junk shops,' Billy commented.

'No,' I remembered. 'No, there was one. An old lady. Dad used to take me to her place to buy when I was little.'

Billy was shaking his head. 'Just junk shops.'

'She was really old and she used to give me biscuits. She had a sign outside that said "No Tourists, No Browsers" and I remember trying to read it. The shop is gone now.'

'Oh,' Billy smirked, 'you mean Ma Polinski.'

'There,' I said triumphantly. 'Ma Polinski, what about her?'

'One-off,' Billy chortled. 'Ma Polinski. Must have been dead about ten years now. What a woman.'

'Antiques dealer,' I pointed out. 'She had good stuff, didn't she, Billy?'

'Oh, but they wouldn't deal with her. No one here ever sold stuff to her. Except your dad occasionally. Ma Polinski got her goods from private customers or she got them abroad,' Billy grinned at me. 'I was in the saleroom one time, oh twenty, thirty years ago now, and she was trying to buy this set. Victorian teapot it was. With ball feet. Had a creamer and a sugar bowl in silver. Anyway, she bid it right up and still the other dealers wouldn't let her have it. She paid ten bob over the top for that teaset, just on principle. But there had been some kind of a mistake and there was a velvet box for it which was in with a different lot. She had balls, that old lady, she walked right to the front of the saleroom, and in front of forty or fifty people, not just the dealers, mind, the public too, she said, "If you bastards bid against me on that box, I'll see to it that you never get a lot cheap at auction here again. I swear it. I'll sit here for the rest of my life and bid every single item right up to its limit." '

'And did they?' I asked, breathless at someone who'd stood up to it.

'What?' Billy asked.

'Let her have the box. Did they bid against her?'

'Course not. You could have heard a pin drop in the saleroom when the bidding was started on it. She got it for two shillings or something. Bought it straight off. Hell hath no fury, you know. That's why no one really wants to deal with them.'

I nearly screamed because it was so unfair. I couldn't read another word of the photostory.

The following week I hit the museum. I went to look at the cases of porcelain at Chambers Street one day after school. I think I had some crazy idea that maybe I could educate myself. That perhaps if I just studied the stuff in glass cases for a while, if I read up on things, then I'd be able to surprise my dad – impress him enough to make him reconsider. But the porcelain room was closed that day and instead I went into a big exhibition all about the Bronze Age and, well, that was when I knew that instead of fighting to impress my father, which frankly has been a bit of a losing battle for the whole of my life, I was going to pre-date the bastard. I was going to go and study things which were so old that only museums would buy them. It was one way to get trained up for a job in valuations and, I figured, it was just about the only way that I could prove him wrong on that particular point.

Chapter Two

The next time the subject of Ma Polinski came up was last year when I was twenty-five. The biggest year of my life so far. The year I sorted so many things out, realised so much which had been obvious all along. Ma Polinski. She's kind of like one of those natural cycles, I suppose – something that turns up every ten years or so. What she has in store for me in my mid thirties I don't know but, heavens, it'd have to be quite something to top what happened last year. I wouldn't want to go through all that again. I had taken my first real job in artefacts, in Glasgow at the Royal Museum. I have kind of branched out in that particular direction because, well, I discovered in my first year at university that I have what for an archaeologist is a really weird ethical belief that it is absolutely wrong to dig up human remains. It's odd, I mean, because out of all the professions which have to deal with dead bodies archaeologists probably treat them with the most respect, really. I mean, have you ever seen what they do to corpses at autopsy, for example? For a few months at college I had this boyfriend who was a medical student and I used to pad around after him, go to his lectures and stuff. Stephen. He was sweet. Anyhow, it really shocked me how little respect the doctors of the future have for the dead, and after I went to this autopsy with sweet Stephen, well, it was more like a class in butchery if you ask me, I threw up. In comparison, we archaeologists are saints. At least when we disinter a body it's done with painstaking care. But one way or another, even when I started out, it always struck me as the wrong thing to do. It's so invasive. The spirits of my childhood were still with me, I guess. As far as I know I'm the only archaeologist who has that particular belief, the only one that I've ever met anyway, so I suppose that I had better explain where it came from.

It was the summer after the first year of my degree and I had gone off on this dig in Israel and I was really, really excited about it when I got there, because it was a huge, big deal for me. They had recruited students from all over the world and the idea was that it would be this big international effort, though, of course, when we got there, it was more like the Tower of Babel because there were people from everywhere and very few linguists. I was so excited – I had never been on a dig before. Not a real one – just the odd weekend field trip here and there. But Israel was astonishing, foreign, exciting and dangerous. And we were out in the desert so it was absolutely silent, and the sky was wide and clear at night and there were no mod cons. It was very romantic in a way. Everyone had to sleep in army surplus tents and every day these dry, dusty trucks would arrive with food and water and sometimes you'd see a camel. When I arrived I remember thinking that it was just like *Indiana Jones* though, of course, archaeology stopped being like *Indiana Jones* some-where in the sixties and moved from the adventure of the treasure trawl to a measured and careful recording of the material past. There is masses of legislation about it nowadays. Rules and regulations for everything. But there, in the desert, I at least felt close to the spirit of the early pioneers – the tomb raiders and the adventurers.

There was permission to dig there for a year, I think, before the bulldozers were going to move in and new housing was going to be put up, so we laboured hard all summer against the clock – and it was hot. We tied our hair up in lengths of cotton and we wore tiny T-shirts and shorts which were drenched with sweat long before midday. The men worked topless. I remember my lips were dry and my skin was smeared with sand and I was just beatific with delight at being able to work there, on my first ever dig and somewhere so exotic. When I got home I was absolutely golden. The sun had got to my hair despite the turban I had been wearing and it had lightened right out and my skin glowed. Israel, well, that was an experience in itself. But whatever crazy things happened, however many soldiers with machine-guns I saw, or beautiful sunsets I watched later on when I was staying in Haifa in the fragrant haze of the orange groves, well, the thing that will stay with me is digging up the dessicated corpse of a 2000-year-old woman. Perhaps if we hadn't been in the desert it would have been different. But it was so dry, and she was so well preserved that you could still touch the wisps of her dark hair and kind of make out the thick features of her face, skin and bone as it was. Even the winding sheet they had used to wrap her was still there, though it was in shreds. She was kind of beautiful, kind of individual, absolutely unique and I was the one who found her. I was the first to clap eyes on her in two millennia. And I knew what we would have to do to her, and I knew that digging her up was wrong. We shouldn't have done it. Not just for the academic exercise. Not without a real reason. If I had found a skeleton I might have got over it, but it was too easy to picture her being alive – her face jumped up at me out of the sand. She just wasn't dead enough to be an object that I could detach myself from, a skeleton rather than a corpse, so as it was I had nightmares.

It took us two weeks to dig her up, you know. People don't realise just how long tomb excavations can take.

The whole thing had to be recorded step by pains-takingly slow step as we uncovered her. Most of the archaeologists on site, especially the more experienced ones, were absolutely nonchalant about it. Almost bored in the extreme. I suppose they knew how long it was going to take to get her out. Tiny trowelful of sand, by tiny trowelful of sand. Bone by skin-clad bone.

I didn't tell a soul what it was doing to me, that excavation. I had friends there all right, I mean, that's where I got to know Nina first of all. But I didn't tell anyone. I used to dread going to sleep, I used to lie in the absolute darkness of that big green tent long after everyone else had succumbed to their fatigue, and try to keep my eyes open, but it was impossible. Working in the heat was exhausting. I had to sleep. So for the rest of the time I was there I had this dream which started out OK – I was living in a tribe in the desert and I had the kind of life which has gone on for centuries unchanged. I don't know what time I was living in. It could have been almost any period in history. I made bread, I milked the goats, I shaded myself from the sun. I had two children in that dream. My life was settled, and then my ancestors started to raise themselves up out of the ground, and at the same time as their dried-out forearms were beginning to reach up out of the darkness and into the light I was getting smaller and smaller and I was being sucked down into a place which smelled of death. I just kept thinking that things weren't happening in the right order any more. Things were out of kilter. And as it went on I got so small that I disappeared into the sand completely, and I was coughing because the stench was in my lungs and I was frozen with terror until at last I slipped down between the grains and I was caught, covered, terrified, and climbing out all around me were these dried-out corpses, perfectly preserved, just like the woman we'd found at Shan Yat. I could feel them walking high above me on the surface, but I couldn't move. I could hear the screams of my children and I was too small to do anything for them. I was trapped. I was tiny. I was helpless. My arms and legs held in place so I couldn't even struggle. It seemed to go on for hours and hours and then, at long last, I would wake up in a sweat, my heart pounding and my limbs jerking in the cold, clear desert night. And I was gasping for clean, fresh air.

I've never dug where there was any reasonable chance of finding human remains since. Not professionally in any case. So I made the decision to look for curatorial work, to stick with artefacts, and I just kind of accepted that it was going to put the dampers on my career a bit – I'd never be a top-class field archaeologist. But I knew that I couldn't have excavated tombs even though they'd have paid me, and that was that. The following summer I went on a field trip to the Outer Hebrides and I dug old blackhouses out of the wet, peaty mud for six damp, windy weeks certain in the knowledge that all I'd probably find, apart from rough hewn stone, was some old pottery and maybe a few well-preserved odd shoes. It was miserably cold and bleak on the island – there was almost nothing there. The main source of excitement was watching the black-faced highland sheep roll over the cattle grids set into the road to stop them from straying. Seriously. That was it. And despite what everyone says about the Highlands, well, I never found the island we were on all that scenic. From time to time you'd find a beautiful beach, like up at Bosta, or a hill with a great view, but generally the place wasn't what they sing about in folk songs. I remember writing to my mother that the low, patchy hills looked like they could do with a bit of a hoover. But at least I didn't have nightmares and sitting around the fire at night, with my friends, well, that was great fun.

After my degree, I got myself a PhD and I got lucky

and bagged this job in the Royal Museum in Glasgow and I moved away from Edinburgh and into a flat in the West End off the Byers Road. I was pretty excited about it. The Royal Museum, it has some important collections and, besides that, my best friend Nina – she's from the west coast originally – had just moved back to Glasgow too. Her flat was ten minutes round the corner from mine and it meant we could hang out a lot, go for meals and hit the odd late-night movie or go dancing. I helped her to paint her place all in white one long weekend, and she helped me assemble the Ikea bathroom units I bought, and hang the brightly-coloured, muslin curtains I traded for the landlord's old, heavy, brown velvet ones. Nina and I had a blast and I think it's maybe because she was there that Mum and Dad could just about cope with my new address out west. I was so used to babying them that I hardly noticed the fusses they made. I was forty-five minutes away on the train, just over an hour by car for goodness' sake. You'd have thought I was moving to New York or something. But I babied them through it all the same. When I first moved in Dad went to the museum and the way he shook my boss's hand, poor Bob Morris, it was like he was handing over the day-to-day reins to him. It was like he was relying on Bob to look after me, which was a bit mad because he's one of those hare-brained professor types, besides which, all along I hardly ever saw the guy. But well, it made Dad feel better and in the end Mum and Dad coped with it OK really. There was a lot for them to deal with and Mum spent a lot of time crying, and Dad blustered around quite a lot saying 'you can't do it like that', no matter which way I faced the bed, or how I set up the TV or what I did with the bins to store them until they were ready to go out. In between helping to unpack Mum stood in front of the mantel in the living room and fingered the good-luck cards which had been sent by friends from college and

27

the couple of mates from school I still saw, and arranged and rearranged the flowers Simon had sent over to meet me on the doorstep when I first arrived. Red and yellow roses which Mum had put into an old, Brighton-blue glass vase. Nina was a star. She arrived with gin and tonics all through that first week at nine thirty on the dot, which is when Mum and Dad left to go home. Every day.

'Do you think you should have got somewhere swankier? Then they could move in. It would save them all the travelling,' she joked.

But we both knew that they were to be humoured. They had a lot to cope with after all. Extra stuff on top of any parent's normal anxiety when their kids leave home. It was a big deal, but in the end they managed; though I had to struggle a bit for even that small freedom, I was aware that it was worse for them than it was for me. I was moving forty-five miles away. A lot to expect them to accept. Given the fact that my mother can't get on to trains because that's how they took her to the camp. Given that she can't even go to pick people up at the station. It's too much for her. Given that I even saw Dad crying as he got into his big car and drove off in the direction of the M8 the last day of the week that I moved in. Given all that, they coped. We all did. We'd chat on the phone together every two or three days after that and at first I'd come home about once a month and stay for the weekend. I know it's odd. I mean I was twenty-four. But my family isn't what you could call normal by any stretch of the imagination. The way we coped with me leaving Edinburgh, well, that was the least of our strangeness. It was a good job at the museum, though, and that was the main thing. In fact, Mum and Dad were as proud of me as I'd ever seen them and things were going really well. They still had me on the payroll so to speak. Mum and Dad. They hadn't given up on that. They still paid a lot of my bills.

Nice clothes and holidays. Close ties with the past. And so, well, they still had some of the control. Or so they reckoned. Nina used to tease me.

A couple of weeks after I'd settled in, Mum and Dad drove through to Glasgow to take me for lunch one day and I took them on this magical mystery tour all around the museum and told them all my best historical stories. They were really into it. Not like they are into Simon, who makes Dad as proud as punch because he has one hell of an eye for diamonds and can spot even a really tiny one of those cubic zirconia at a hell of a speed. But still, they were proud enough. Dad kept calling me 'Doctor White', and Mum kept saying, 'Oh Charlie, she isn't a real doctor.' And I stood my ground, because, fuck it, I had done my seven years, medical doctor or not, and in the end even Mum conceded and called me 'Doc'.

'I hope this means that you'll be able to support yourself now, young lady,' Dad grinned at me over lunch. We were settled down in one of the brown velvet and satinwood booths at Rogano's. Mum and Dad both loved going to Rogano's whenever they were in Glasgow. Dad had ordered some enormous fish which came whole and he was pulling the steaming white flesh off the bone with deft cutlery. I grinned right back at him.

'Certainly not,' I quipped, 'what else are you making money for? I don't want to leave you enough capital spare to allow you to develop vices, and that's all you'll do. You earn far too much as it is. It's a miracle you're so perfect, and it's all down to me.'

'You are so good, saving us from ourselves,' Mum sighed with mock exasperation, even though it was the answer they were looking for. It gave them a stake in me, you see. It let them know I still needed them. It told them I was moving where I lived. I wasn't leaving. And after that we all felt quite comfortable because we'd said what we wanted to without really saying anything.

I have never been particularly great with money, it's true and well, if things hadn't transpired as they did, I would probably still be relying on Mum and Dad that way. I probably never would have broken free of it. They've always been very generous with money if not with information. Thinking about it, I suppose they made a decision way back that they were going to enjoy life. They were going to have a good time and surround themselves with beautiful things. Their house is lovely – it's so colourful and, I don't know, it sounds stupid, but it's such a joyful place too. There is a real sense of it being run for comfort. A real sense of it as a retreat. There is a whole side to my family which is wonderful. It's close and warm and safe. There are parties every summer in our garden. There are fireworks on Guy Fawkes. There is champagne at midnight on the first stroke of our birthdays. We sing out loud. We dance in the kitchen. In between the shadows there is blinding, bright light because somehow you have to recover. I'm sure Mum saw some terrible things – the sort of things you can't tell your children, because how do you find the words for torture or murder or rape? How can you say those things in front of your own little ones when the memory of it haunts and terrifies you in all its horrible detail? She lost all her closest family, you know. But she was young, and when she came out of Dachau her mother's elder sister, who had married a guy from the Borders, went over to Germany to try to find her. It had taken months in the confusion which followed the liberation of the camps, but Great-Auntie Petra had persisted in the dogged belief that despite the rotting, starved bodies piled up by the communal burial pits, despite the devastation and all the evidence to the contrary, something still remained of her family. That someone was alive. When she found my five-year-old orphaned mother, she was overjoyed. She brought her back to Scotland and just showered love on her, bringing her up in her own home with her own children, though, I suppose, the special circumstances dictated slightly different treatment for the tiny, wide-eyed, frightened, German-speaking skeleton. On her very first day in Edinburgh her cousins came running downstairs in the morning to meet her and my mother screamed, lost it completely, because one of the little boys was wearing blue and white striped pyjamas, you see, just like the uniforms in the camp. Mum panicked. Well, you can't really blame her. Great-Auntie Petra ripped the pyjamas right up and told Mum to do whatever she wanted because it was over and she was free. Poor Mum went up the stairs and wouldn't get out of her bed for the rest of her first two months in the country. Not at all. But slowly and surely Great-Auntie Petra made her believe that she was safe. She taught her to speak English with a soft, lowland accent and patiently held the child as she cried. Weeks of crying. Months. Years. They say that you never really get over it, that you spend the rest of your life afraid, that whenever you meet someone you don't see a face, you just see their spirit and how strong they are, because you're always trying to figure out who would have survived. I think that's true. But then, after a while, I've heard from lots of people that you just learn to put all of that to the back of your mind and although it's always there, there are always things which affect you, you don't really notice it so much. It just moves back. And well, that was the pulse of the rhythm of my childhood. It beat away behind everything else and until I was a teenager I never knew what that rhythm was. I saw the light and I ignored the shadows, if you will.

My mother met my father in 1956 when she was only sixteen and Great-Auntie Petra handed her over to him on their wedding day. He took on all the responsibility of my mother's history and dedicated himself completely to taking away all of her pain and all of her nightmares. I think it started then. Those silent rules, beating away, setting the pace in a really practical way which impinged on everything. They didn't go on a honeymoon together because Mum can't bear packing. Suitcases give her the shivers. Dad, to this day, never pushes her on that so we have never been on a family holiday together. We've never moved house. Dad is so patient. I've seen him stroking my mother's hair, silently, for hours as they sit in the big bay window of their living room staring out at the green lush garden which they planned and planted together. She nuzzles him like a lapdog from time to time. I like to think, you know, that he cured her, helped her through it. That he sat up with her at night in the midst of all of her nightmares. That because of him perhaps now she doesn't even consciously think about it every day. That she doesn't wake up with thoughts of death. Of starvation. Of fear. The memory of the smell of the gas oven, the sickly, cloying stench of rotting bodies lying in the sun waiting for burial. Now Mum has this light-heartedness about her, which she is really committed to and, of course, she has Dad so she's very lucky. I grew up feeling left out because they are so close. Thinking about it, it wasn't just the strong, secret bond between my parents which made me feel so small and unimportant, but also a lack of my own history, the part of their story which is mine and which they never told me, that made me feel excluded. I never knew, for example, about my grandfather and my grandmother. My mother's parents. She didn't talk about them at all. She wouldn't tell us anything. For that matter, I don't know anything about my father's background either. The drawbridge always went up really quickly if you mentioned anything about any of that. But it's difficult to complain when you're so privileged. When your parents take you to the muted, yellow-lit safety of Rogano's for lunch as a matter of course. When you aren't really sure what your problem is anyway. When everything seems to be just fine.

The story really starts then, I suppose, once I'd grown up, when I had settled in Glasgow and I'd been working in the museum for about six months and it was all going really well, like I said, and I was quite settled, working hard and seeing my friends, when I got a letter from the lawyer. Mr Williams. It was quite a curt letter, I suppose. He asked me to come and see him because he had something to my advantage. It was a bit of a mystery and when I phoned up he wouldn't spill the beans. He just insisted that I come to see him. It was Thursday.

'Look,' I said, 'I have a job here. I can't just come through to Edinburgh in my lunch hour or whatever.'

'I'll open for you on Saturday morning. Ten thirty OK?' he asked and I should have known then that it was something kind of special. Kind of special is an understatement in fact. That whole day is really clear in my memory now. That Saturday. I can recall all the minutiae of everything that happened, everything he said. It's a day as big as when I found out my mother came out of Dachau, a day as big as the one which started when I uncovered the face of the woman at Shan Yat. The day it all started. The day Ma Polinski broke cover and began to change me. The first day of my journey right to the heart of things. I'll never forget it.

Chapter Three

The train from Glasgow to Edinburgh runs right through the low undulations of the green central belt of the country and I sat there for the whole of the forty-five-minute trip, ignoring the fields as they flew by me and making a list of all the things that the guy could possibly want to talk to me about. I was kind of cross, I suppose, at being summoned and was all ready to create hell if it turned out to be something a bit mundane, and a waste of time, which was, of course, what I was expecting. I was ready for it though, ready to complain with conviction. I had even worn my most respectable clothes – a pair of navy linen wide-cut trousers and a fitted, white cotton shirt with a dark red jacket over the top. That stuff really suits me now, you know. If I whack on a string of pearls and a ring or two, I instantly look like a very expensively kept woman. When I was first at college I used to live in jeans and big jumpers, just like everyone else. If I'd tried to wear something upmarket or mature it would have looked ridiculous. We do have a couple of photographs where I had obviously tried – family parties and a few weddings where I just look like I borrowed my mother's clothes. Recently though, well, that's changed. Perhaps it's because you grow into it or something, but now I seem to be able to really carry it off. Last year, at a family friend's wedding, Simon teased me that it was because of my flat hair and my big, blue eyes, but those clothes and that jewellery, well, they are just like a uniform and in the last couple of years I've really taken to suiting it for some reason. Maybe it is just my age. Anyhow, I was ready.

The train got in to Waverley just before ten. The station was under repair and the place was full of scaffolding. It was a bright, clear April day, so I put on my sunglasses and I walked along the east end of Princes Street, cut up past Jenners, strolled westwards along George Street and then turned right down the hill, perusing the grey-stoned Georgian buildings of the New Town all the way down to Heriot Row where I rang the brass bell beside the imposing black door of the lawyer's office, ready to make my complaint even before I knew what the whole thing was about. I was sure the guy was wasting my time. I watched my shadow, the edges of it quivering very slightly because there was a tiny breeze coming from the west which made my clothes move about me. It wasn't cold though and I didn't have long to wait anyway because the lawyer came to the door straight away and opened it himself. There was no-one else in the office that day – I could see behind him the empty chair at the reception desk in the hallway – and I sensed immediately the cavernous silence of the old house. He caught me off guard really because he was young and he was kind of good-looking. I had expected a grey-haired, disapproving, older guy – that was how he'd sounded on the phone. And it didn't feel like it was an office either, not with the chairs all empty and everything silent, although it did smell of a mixture of industrial cleaning fluid and reams of blank paper.

'Mike Williams,' he smiled at me as he proffered his hand.

'Rachel White,' I smiled back and I took off my dark glasses as I stepped inside the shady, flagstoned hallway.

'Please come in. Follow me,' he said.

He led me into an interview room on the ground floor which looked out on to the back of Northumberland Street. It was so green out there – the trees were budding and it had been very rainy in the early springtime so things were really lush that summer. The summer last year – the summer that never was, because the weather was pretty dreadful right the way through. Mike Williams had a funny walk. It was like he was already old. I've noticed that before in lawyers and accountants. It's a peculiarly Edinburgh thing. Sometimes with the young ones it looks like they are dressing up because they seem so old-fashioned. He wore a faded old cardigan over his bright-blue Next shirt and tie. I decided that he was a man with divided loyalties. We each took a seat.

'Miss White, have you any idea why you're here?' he asked.

I looked into his eyes. They were cobalt. His hair flopped down over his forehead and the way he moved his head to draw it back again was kind of boyish. He didn't look so old now he was seated.

'I haven't a clue,' I said.

'Well,' he smiled. 'You have been left quite a considerable amount of money.'

'Sorry?'

'A bequest. A trust fund.'

And my reaction was immediate. I always know when something is really important, really big. I seem to have this sixth sense and when it happens my body always reacts before my mind can, and as soon as Mike Williams said the words 'trust fund' my fingers were weak suddenly and my spine was tingling. And any thought I had of complaint about time-wasting evaporated. I knew that I had been wrong and that I was on to something big.

'Who would do that?' I asked and I suppose my first

thought was that I might find something out about my family. A crazy old uncle, or a grandparent who had watched me grow up from a distance. Someone out there that Mum and Dad had held back on. The lawyer lowered his eyes.

'Mrs Molly Savage,' he read the name from the buff file in front of him.

'I don't know anyone by that name,' I said.

'Well, she must have known you. The bequest was left to you over eighteen years ago, to be kept in trust and undisclosed until your twenty-fifth birthday.'

'Two weeks ago,' I said.

'It's over eight million pounds.'

The room swam. It had these eggshell blue walls and a black, wrought-iron fireplace and it smelled of old books. I took a deep breath and then I laid my hand on the smooth, lacquered table, but it just wouldn't stay still. My fingers were jumping as I trembled. The lawyer went to fetch me a glass of water and he opened the big sash and case window up on its hinges. I breathed the air in deeply a few times and tried to collect my thoughts. I could hear a faint hammering somewhere off in the distance further down the hill wafting up towards Heriot Row on a south-westerly breeze.

'Eight million,' I repeated.

'Yes, plus two rather substantial properties which have lain vacant since she died. A shop just off the High Street and a house out near the Pentlands.'

'Oh my God, it's Ma Polinski,' I realised and I tried to sip on the water, but I just couldn't stay still enough to manage it. I got up and began to pace around the room with a sinking feeling in my stomach as I moved. 'What happened to her?' I asked him. It seemed only polite to find out.

'Not my client, of course,' he replied. 'Originally, my uncle was her lawyer. He's retired now. But she died in a car crash in Brazil in 1978 if that's what you mean.

They brought back the remains though and buried her according to the terms of her will. In the countryside, somewhere in East Lothian. I can look it up if you like.'

'I should visit her grave,' I mumbled and then my knees gave way and I fell down unconscious. And not because of the money either. It's a lot of money. Sure it is. But it was more a kind of predestined thing than that. I blacked out because I knew that there was a story behind it, even then. I knew that there was more to it. There had to be. I have a hell of an instinct for that. Over the years, I suppose, I've had to develop it. I can spot a secret miles off. She didn't have to leave me eight million to point it up. Eight million. Wow.

When I came to, the lawyer had put a small cushion behind my head and was gently slapping my cheek. I felt like some kind of crazy Mills and Boon heroine.

'How're you doing?' he asked.

'I'm OK, I think. It's just a bit of a shock.'

That was putting it mildly – I had been out cold for five minutes, I suppose, and I'd never fainted before ever. Total shutdown. Absolute blackout. The one and only time in my life.

'Does it say why she left it to me?'

'No. No, it doesn't.'

'Why didn't someone know before?' I asked. 'Why didn't anyone tell me?'

The lawyer shrugged his shoulders as he bent over me. 'It's a lot of money,' he replied. 'Sometimes it's considered better that it remains undisclosed until the recipient is old enough to spend it wisely. It's not very unusual.'

'I can only scarcely remember her,' I said. 'Just about and no more. My father used to take me to visit her and she used to give me biscuits.'

He helped me up slowly. 'I have a key to the gardens over the road,' he offered. 'Perhaps if you took a little walk. We could sit over there. It's a nice morning.'

'Thanks, Mr Williams,' I said.

'Call me Mike,' he smiled.

I pulled my jacket back on and we slammed the big front door behind us and went to sit down by the lake. It felt like we were in the middle of the countryside, really. I had never been into Queen Street Gardens before and I didn't realise they were so all-encompassing. So huge. There were a few children playing with a football but they were quite far off, further along up the slope, and apart from them there was no one.

'Tell me everything you know about it,' I asked him.

Mike looked perturbed. He didn't want me to pass out again in public.

'It's OK,' I reassured him. 'I think I'm getting over it.'

'Well, she didn't have any children. She must have been fond of you. She left you everything. Her husband died with her.'

'And if he'd survived her?'

'He'd have had a small pension. Actually, twenty years ago, it wouldn't have been that small. Fifteen thousand a year or so. Something like that.'

'I didn't even know she was married,' I murmured. 'I don't ever remember there being a man.'

'Oh yes. She had been married twice.'

Ma Polinski didn't strike me as that kind of woman and the information kind of shocked me. I mean, she just wasn't a sexual object. She was an old lady. I tried to imagine her at twenty, but that saggy old cardigan got in the way and I just couldn't visualise it properly. In my mind she had always been old.

'Do you have any photographs of her?' I asked.

'Yes. We do. There is a box of personal effects in the safe. There was some jewellery.'

I remembered the diamond necklaces in the basement.

'Did your uncle know her well?' I asked.

Mike shrugged his shoulders. 'He was her lawyer for years. Her husband's lawyer before that. Her first husband that is. He died when she was very young. Scarcely married in fact.'

'Eight million,' I mused to myself again.

'Yes, you're a very wealthy woman now,' and his voice had so many questions in it. I suppose he was wondering why I wasn't just jumping up and down with joy.

'Let's go and look inside the box,' I said.

He wouldn't let me into the room with him while he was opening the safe so I sat down again back in the eggshell blue ante-room and I waited for him to come out. It was the weirdest feeling. I just kept wondering why she'd done it, why she'd left everything to me. Don't get me wrong – I was delighted. But it was just kind of mysterious. I mean, I know I was a cute kid, and yeah, I was an antiques dealer's kid too. But she must have had someone closer – cousins, friends, anyone. She'd even left it to me over her husband and I found that really strange. Mum and Dad were so different from that. They were an inseparable force and they always put each other first. They were a unit. Leaving your fortune to someone other than your husband would have been out of the question for my mother. I remember Dad telling me one time that when Simon and I were born he had given the doctor specific instructions that if it came to the crunch he was to save my mother rather than save their baby. 'We could always have made another baby,' he had explained. That's devotion for you. That's what I mean. It was naive, of course, to expect everyone to live in the same way as my own parents, but they were my role models in that respect and this differed so greatly from the way they operated that the whole thing seemed alien. She had a husband she lived with and yet she had left everything to me – a child whom she scarcely knew. It was perverse. It was a mystery. And I knew straight off that there must have been more to it.

Mike Williams came back into the room with a keen but respectful expression on his face. He was carrying the box. I had expected it to be kind of special. Something in leather perhaps or, like a treasure chest, carved out of wood. But it was plain brown, thick cardboard with a label on top which the lawyer must have pasted on to it when I was still a child. Mike put it down on the table in front of me, and I opened the lid gingerly. The photographs were on top. She was just as I had remembered her, but with a thick woollen jacket pulled on over her cardigan and a black hat perched on her head.

'She was a councillor,' Mike chipped in. 'She sat on the local authority.'

I hadn't known that.

Further down in the pile the pictures of her became more faded as she got younger. The first one was her in a wedding dress next to a plump old man, who I assumed at first was her father, but it turns out was her first husband, Tom Savage. Under the photographs there was a box which contained a big diamond ring. It was a beautiful, cushion-cut, single stone. It must have been early Georgian and I reckoned just looking at it that it had to be over five carats in size. I picked it up by the shank and then scrambled around in my bag for my eyeglass. Yeah, I know. It was a weird thing to do. I always carry it though. When you're checking the way that stones have been cut, it's invaluable for dating items. I use it at work. You can tell a lot under times ten magnification. This time though, I drew it to my eye just to check the colour of that beautiful stone. It was pretty perfect. Absolute clarity, no colour, and beautifully cut given the technology of the time. Totally authentic. Everything you look for in fact. When I raised my head Mike Williams was staring at me quizzically.

'It's one hell of a ring,' I commented. 'Worth forty or fifty thousand pounds to a dealer. A lot more in a shop.'

'We had everything valued at the time. I can show you the document if you like,' he said.

'Did she leave this stuff specifically? I mean, I never saw her wear this ring. I never saw her wear jewellery at all. Did this just come out of the shop?'

'No. My understanding is that these items were her personal property. These items were specified. The contents of the shop were sold at auction shortly after she died.'

It was weird. I went back to the box and dug down further. Under the ring box there was a black leather case with a yellowing, creamy velvet interior. Inside there was a necklace of flat-cut Colombian emeralds. Below that there was a jade and diamond bracelet. Mid Victorian. Top quality. I checked it all myself, stone by stone, section by section.

'Looks like you know your stuff,' Mike commented from the other side of the room.

I didn't answer him. I was still ferreting about inside the box. Stuck in at the side there was a little, red-gold chain. I picked it up on one finger and dangled it in front of me. It was strange. I mean the rest of the stuff was worth maybe a hundred thousand pounds, or not far off it anyway, and along with all that was this thin chain which you'd be lucky to get a tenner for. Unusual colour of gold, I grant you, but pretty worthless nonetheless. I didn't get it. I raised my eyes to Mike but he shrugged his shoulders and just smiled politely. 'Another little mystery,' I thought, and I put the chain around my neck and tucked it down under the collar of my shirt.

At the bottom of the box there were her papers. A British passport, two marriage certificates and her birth certificate all bound together by a faded blue ribbon and after I'd read them I put all the papers back in the box and I shut the lid, but I put the rest of the jewellery into my bag. I realised that I should have been happier. I should have been dancing around and cracking open champagne. It didn't seem appropriate though. It just seemed weird.

'What do we do now?' I asked.

'I have the keys for the properties, if you'd like to go to see them,' Mike offered and he gave me a paper to sign to relieve him of any responsibility for the stuff I'd taken away.

He drove. He had a pristine, silver-grey Volvo estate which smelt of marzipan and he put his handbrake on whenever we stopped at a crossroads. I began to wonder how old he really was. The Saturday crowds were out in force as we made our way across to the other side of the city centre and as we drove up the Mound people just spilled off the pavement at the bus stop beside the Royal Scottish Academy. Edinburgh was booming. It took us a long time to get parked up on the High Street, but eventually we found a space and Mike backed his car perfectly into the smooth recess cut into the kerb.

'It's down here,' he said, leaving the tarmac of the main street behind and walking down a tiny, cobbled alleyway with the keys dangling down between his fingers.

I trailed behind him. This was really familiar. The blackened stone, the low raggedy archways, the cobbles. The old wooden door up half a dozen steps and the glossy black railings I got told off for hanging down from because it wasn't a play park. Mike didn't notice me getting apprehensive. He opened the door and switched on the mains power first and then the lights. It was smaller inside than I remembered even though it was empty. The rooms were very dark and here and there there were floorboards lying stacked up against the wall. We had to pick our way across the floor so as not to fall into any of the deep, black dusty holes.

'We can let the property out for you, or you may decide to sell it of course,' Mike smiled. 'Worth a lot, shops up here these days, because of the tourists.'

'What happened to the floor?'

'Oh, we ordered that. There was some question at the time that goods were missing. My uncle arranged a thorough search, but nothing was ever found.'

'What goods?'

'It was just a rumour. Apparently there was no stock-book. Ever. It took a lot of time to catalogue what was in here. Weeks in fact. There were three or four secretaries working full time, I understand. Fulham's on Charlotte Street handled the sale. We have catalogues I can show you.'

'But what was missing?' I pressed him.

'It was just a rumour,' he repeated. 'People said that items which had been in Mrs Savage's possession were missing but we never found them. We couldn't establish whether she'd ever owned anything like the items described. There were no photographs and no receipts. I'm sorry, I don't know any more than that.'

There was dust flying around in the light which flooded in from the open doorway but I turned away and began to creep up the curved stone staircase. In truth I found the place a bit eerie.

'Please, come with me,' I asked him.

So we climbed the stairs together, like little kids exploring, him in his old man's get-up and me in my respectable outfit.

'Good rents up here. You'd get quite a decent income from this,' he commented.

'I don't know what I'll do with it,' I said. 'It's going to take some time to sink in.'

Upstairs the walls were bare stone. I ran my hands along the cold, rough surface. When I was a kid they had been totally obscured by the rows and rows of Verney Martin cabinets with painted wooden insets which had housed Ma Polinski's stock. The gilded tips of the fretwork used to touch the low dark beams of the ceiling. I remember that. I remember staring upwards at them, the gilding glowing lowly in the dim light of the shop. I went over to the window and looked out over the city. It was chilly in there; I suppose it had been empty for years and, although they hadn't actually turned the electricity off, there wasn't any heating. Just a couple of open fireplaces which were probably blocked up after so long anyway. As we walked back down the stone staircase and down again into the basement I hugged my arms to try to warm myself up. It smelled of damp down there. Kind of fusty. And the filing cabinets, of course, were all gone. I walked right up to the back of the room, into the empty safe and I looked at the bare, gunmetal-grey shelves. Right at the back there was a piece of old mirror screwed into the wall. I could see Mike Williams behind me, waiting patiently at the door. I couldn't help but shudder in there. Not just because of the chill through the stone. The old safe gave me the spooks, as if someone was watching me. Other than Mike Williams, I mean. As if someone was waiting.

'There's nothing here,' I said absent-mindedly.

'No, everything was sold at auction,' Mike replied, as if he hadn't already told me that before.

Right then, I didn't want to go to see the house. It had been a long day already and I had been thrown off my stride by the whole thing so I decided to leave that for another time. Outside, back in the sunshine, I told Mike I'd be in touch the following week and I declined his offer of a lift.

'Can I keep the keys?' I asked him.

'They're all yours now. We have other sets in the office, so if there's anything you want me to do you just have to ring.'

'Thanks,' I smiled and I put on my sunglasses again and waited for him to get back into his car and drive off. I didn't want to speak to him any more. I suppose we never really clicked. Me and lawyers, well, I just don't really trust them. And Mike Williams, well, he was OK, I suppose, but I wasn't up for idle chat with him. It was as if he was on a different wavelength. I just wanted to be on my own and to think.

When he'd gone I turned westwards and began to walk up the High Street. It hadn't really sunk in, of course, though it was starting to. I was trying desperately to remember Ma Polinski. Every detail of the times I'd met her. Just how the shop had been. I was sifting through my mind for clues, trying to imagine why she might have done it. Just being inside the old place again had reminded me of things. I wandered along, staring at the old buildings. Ma Polinski had walked down that street every day on her way to work, I thought, and I wondered if she had ever noticed just how twee it is down there. But then, the Old Town must have seemed very different even twenty years ago, just before she died, never mind fifty or sixty years ago when she first got married and moved in. At that time the place hadn't undergone the huge development and restoration programme which has been around since she passed away, it hadn't thrown off the shadow of being the wrong side of town ever since James Craig designed the swish Georgian squares on the other side of the drained out loch which became the Gardens. I realised, as I tried to grasp what had just happened, that the spectre of the slums must have been very real to Ma Polinski. The stone of the buildings around her was blackened with pollution from centuries of smog only brought haltingly to an end by the Clean Air Act. The single-room households which were common, the outside toilets, the mud-covered cobblestones, the old second-day bakery in St Mary's Street for people who couldn't even afford fresh bread. The Old Town is so different now. A transformed place – it's so far away from the town she lived in. The medieval buildings just look like someone made them out of Lego and instead of a sense of danger, a feeling of something being masked, the thin cobbled streets have a sense of mystery as if you might turn down one of the narrow closes and step back through time and straight into an adventure. A lot of the tenements have been cleaned and the stone is honey-coloured and bright although every so often you do see a shadowy, dark monster of a building, which hasn't yet been touched by the restoration teams, or a dirty, purple-faced drunk wielding a plastic bottle of meths and mumbling to himself as he stumbles towards the Cowgate. Changed times. Even when I was a kid the Old Town was all like that and although I didn't remember too much of it from my childhood I do remember the general impression which was exciting, dangerous, threatening and shady. Down the dark, winding alleyways there are hidden gardens and secret courtyards and as you walk further up the Royal Mile away from Holyrood Palace and towards the Castle, if you turn and look behind you you can see all the way down to the sea at Leith. It looks as if it is only half a mile away. But it's further, I suppose. And the sea seems so blue. But then, when Ma Polinski lived there, it was a lot rougher and I thought that maybe she never saw the romance of it through the rubble of the old slums and the black-kneed poverty of the children playing down the closes. For those kids, the poor, underprivileged ones in the days before the NHS and before antibiotics, cod liver oil was the only medicine available and TB, polio and diphtheria were rife. They didn't have a great chance of survival. One child in twenty died before their first birthday in the bad old days when she'd been young and formed her opinions. And fifty years later, well, she'd left everything to me when I was only five. Eight million pounds. I looked around at the Scotland flags everywhere and coffee shops and kilted men busking and grinned at the huge buzz there was about the place because they were building the new Scottish Parliament right down the road. It didn't seem to make sense, really, to be honest. All that money from so long ago. I strolled along for a while, caught in a weird train of thought where our two periods of history were brought together by a geographical location. Where my present met her past and we could be close. Ma Polinski had been brought back into my life. She had seen to it herself that when I was twenty-five I'd be mysteriously, inexplicably provided for. And I could only wonder why. When the one o'clock gun went off I just about jumped out of my wits. I was miles away. They fire the cannon every day, but I'd been living in Glasgow and I'd forgotten. I laughed at the way my heart was pounding and then I kind of snapped out of it and decided that since I was in town anyway I might as well go home to visit Mum and Dad.

I suppose it was then, as I stood there by the Netherbow, that it hit me – I didn't want to tell them about the money. Actually, I was really uncomfortable about it. I knew that it was going to upset the balance of everything and I didn't want to do that. I suppose I just knew that it was going to turn out to be a huge deal for them. Because everything was. I hadn't figured it all out, of course, but I was sure anyway that one way or another it was going to be a big deal. All that money. And in my family, well, like I said before, money means a whole load of different things – power and security being the main ones – and my eight million was going to change the balance of all of that big time. Mum and Dad were still wary about me moving to Glasgow, for Christ's sake. I still felt as if they thought I'd betrayed them because of that. There was a strange note in their voices when they said the words 'since you moved', and they said those words a lot, come to think of it. Tacked on to any old sentence. I wondered if Mum and Dad knew that this money was coming, if that was why they had done all that stuff with the shop, if that was why they had cut me out, but when I went over it carefully in my mind, the exact way they had said things, the reasons that they'd given, the way that they were, I knew that they hadn't known and that this good fortune really had come entirely out of the blue. And what good fortune it was. Eight million quid. And I didn't want to tell them. I wasn't ready. I hadn't even taken it in myself.

I sat down on a wooden bench in the sunshine and I lay my head back and stretched out in the warmth and I let myself think about it. I contemplated being a multi-millionairess, a trust-fund babe, an heiress. I luxuriated in it. The glory of the unexpected. It wasn't as if I had never played the lottery and dreamed all Saturday afternoon about what I would do if I suddenly came into a lot of money, but believe you me, when it happens for real it's a whole different ball game even if you're basically well shoed and middle class and comfortable. Even if you've had money before. And this money had come from nowhere, so instead of the way that I would look on it if I'd earned it, it was surreal. I did have a bit of a grin, though, as I thought about Simon. There's part of me that still resents Simon being given so much by being given the business. I resent him being kept in the fold when I was cast out. And this made it even, I thought. This meant I could do whatever I wanted.

Mum and Dad have always been stringently unflash with their cash. Discreet in the extreme because their money is, for them, a security blanket. They just want it to be there for them if they need it to keep them warm and happy. To buy a little bit of quiet joy. They don't use their cash for all the things that you think you'd use money for if you had it. It's different, you see, once you've actually got your hands on the loot. It's different for me now. When they interview lottery winners they always say that they won't let it change their lives, but when it comes right down to it your life is pre-changed when something like that happens. It's strange. But that's the way it is. The whole thing is well out of your control, because your position changes and you change with it and that isn't always very comfortable. I didn't have to toe the line any more. I could do anything that took my fancy.

But that realisation was a long way away that sunny day I sat out on the High Street. Nothing had happened yet. It was all still very new and I just let go and I enjoyed it. 'Eight million quid,' I thought. 'I'll just keep it quiet for a while until I'm ready.'

Suddenly I realised that I was starving hungry. I hadn't had any breakfast or anything so I went back down the road and cut into the shady interior of Jenny McGraw's. The pub was pretty quiet and there was just the odd tourist and a few old men. I ordered myself some fish and chips and a glass of tonic with a shot of lime and I sat down on a velvet seat by the window to wait for it. I felt a lot better once I had eaten. Then I bought some cigarettes up at the bar and I smoked one and I felt better still. Whenever I smoke I always buy Silk Cut Blue because that's what Nina smokes. She's been giving up for years though. Since we met in fact. She had been away that week and I hadn't seen her. Nina's a bit of a high-flyer, I guess. She'd landed ten days' specialist work at the Tate. She'd rung me at work on Tuesday but a lot had happened since then. You go away for a week and boy, can things change. 'Nina will laugh her head off when I tell her about this,' I thought, as I stubbed the butt out in a Tennent's Special ashtray and planned the order that I would tell people in. The order that was only right. Mum and Dad and Simon first and then Nina, though of course it didn't turn out that way: I got bogged down and in the end it wasn't as easy as I thought. But at that moment in Jenny McGraw's any doubts I had fell away to nothing and I knew it was a dream come true. I'd deal with the difficult things as they came up, I decided, whatever they might be. I relaxed and, as I got up to leave, I had a big grin on my face suddenly and I just felt very, very happy and very, very free. And the rest of that day was a day of celebration. Really – I just enjoyed myself kind of quietly. Kind of privately. Total freedom. Eight million pounds.

Chapter Four

When I walked up the garden path at home it must have been around three that afternoon. I had gone for a run in the sunshine in the Queen's Park. Usually now you wouldn't catch me running, even for a bus and certainly not for pleasure, just to let off steam, but then that's how ecstatic I had been. Eventually, I hailed a cab to take me further down into Newington to the Grange, where Mum and Dad live. I used my key to get in and I stood in the doorway and shouted to see if there was anyone about. Voices came wafting towards me from the back of the house so I walked down the stairs and outside again into the buttery yellow light of the south-facing suntrap which is our garden at home. Mum was kneeling, weeding out the border of her herb plot which stretched all around one side of the lawn. Dad was sipping on a glass of red wine and reading a newspaper, the bottle half empty beside him. He was wearing a really stupid white hat to protect his bald patch from the sun.

'This is a lovely surprise,' Mum smiled at me as she got up.

And I froze for a second as what had happened flashed before me, but I didn't say anything about it. It just didn't seem right. It was instinct, I suppose, and in retrospect it was the right instinct, so I stuck with what I had decided. One thing at a time. I was too scared of what they might do.

'Can I stay tonight?' I asked, and Dad said, 'Course you can,' and that was fine, so we all went inside and I made a big pot of tea and we had Mr Kipling's fruit pies in the light, bright, pale green kitchen where big vases of soft-petalled mallows were spread out at intervals over the sideboard and table. I know, of course, that not telling my parents what had happened constituted a lie. It was a lie by omission, but it had been quite some day and I figured that I needed time to let the news settle in, I needed to come to terms with it myself before I told anyone else. That's what I thought the tightness in the pit of my stomach was, anyway. Still, I was fascinated at the thought of my benefactress and in that respect Mum and Dad were a valuable source of information for me. I mean, they actually knew Ma Polinski, both of them. So, on the spur of the moment I decided to ask them a few questions just to see what they might say. I concentrated on Dad really, because I figured that he must have known her best. I mean, he'd taken me there at least once a week that I can remember and he probably went to see her other times besides.

'I was down in the High Street today,' I started, leaning back in the old pine chair with saggy pillows which I'd pulled right up to the table. 'I saw Ma Polinski's old shop down Muir's Pend.'

Dad sipped on his mug and nodded. The kitchen looks right on to the garden so it faces south too and because the light was flooding in I had to screw my eyes up a bit to see him properly. His nose was coming up red from the sunshine and little specks of blackcurrant jam were spattered around his lips.

'I kind of remember her,' I tried to encourage him. 'What was she like, Dad?'

'Crazy old lady,' he said as he wiped his mouth and shook his head. 'Unpredictable. Whatever price we agreed on she always changed it. I'd sell her stuff and send around a bill and she'd always round it down and pay less than we had agreed. If I bought stuff, she'd round the figures up. Of course after a while I began to count for that, so I always overcharged her a bit when I was selling and I always went for the lowest price possible when I was buying from her, really pushed for it, because I knew she was going to add on a whack.'

'She was mean, d'you reckon?' I asked.

'Nah,' said Dad, 'she just wasn't used to dealing with dealers, you know. She bought most of her stuff from privates. And in the auction room sometimes. She travelled too. Bought things abroad. Difficult woman. Cantankerous. When she started none of the dealers would sell to her and then, later on, when she got established and they wanted to do business, well, she wouldn't have any of them. None of the older boys, anyway.'

'She built up her business, though,' I mused, moving my chair sideways to avoid the hot sun beaming through the window. It was just baking in there.

'Inherited it from her first husband,' Dad pointed out. 'Good business that was, it had been going for years. When he died everyone thought she'd sell up. I was just a kid then. It's years ago. I heard that the stock old man Savage had was worth a fortune though. But she didn't sell out at all. No intention of it. She dug in there. A lot of the boys went up and tried to buy her off, but she wouldn't budge. She wanted to keep it going and her old man had had a lot of private customers and they stuck with her. Old families. Good custom. The shop had been there for a long time. It was well established.'

I sipped on my tea. 'Didn't she have kids?' I asked. Well, I had to keep him going.

'No,' Dad shook his head. 'She didn't remarry until she was well into her forties. He was a bastard, eh?'

Mum had got up from the table and was pouring the milk from the bottle into an engraved glass jug. We never used a jug in the kitchen normally so I knew she was getting perturbed about something. She laid it down and looked at Dad with that retreat-to-the-castle-now look in her eyes. Dad was a bit drunk though, from the red wine and the sun, and he kept on going, his rosy cheeks robust in contrast with the now wilting, soft pink of the mallow flowers.

'When she died I tried to buy that business,' he reminisced, 'but the lawyer wouldn't have it. He decided to go to auction with the whole of her stock. The contents of the house and everything. It was crazy. Old man Dillon and the boys came up from London for the sale. It went on for three days solid over two salerooms. There were two auctioneers selling full pelt the whole time. There had never been anything like it in Scotland before – even the London boys were a bit bowled over. They stayed in the Caley and we split the lots between us every night. Mick Capaldi had the Knock Out in his room. Went on until after midnight. She had some stuff, I tell you, and I held on to a good part of it. But it didn't all go in the sale. I don't know what happened to the stuff from the safes, but none of it was catalogued. I asked the lawyer at the time and he just said that there was no record of it. I even thought about going to the police. I mean, someone had obviously nicked it. But then, what was the point? I mean, it all went to the government, didn't it? No kids. No husband. No will at all, I heard. What a waste.'

'What was missing, Dad?' I pressed him.

'Beautiful,' Dad waxed lyrical, his eyes now bright with enthusiasm, 'amazing pieces. I've never seen anything like it since. She showed me one day, down in the basement, you might even have been there, Rachel. It'd be worth a fortune nowadays. It was worth a fortune then. Stuff which came from her private customers and she'd put it aside for herself. Not to use, of course. Just to enjoy. Her own private collection. There was this one dressing table set. Tortoiseshell and silver. Austrian. Well, she said that an old lady had brought it to her. Came down on the train from Aberdeen for the day with it all trussed up in old newspapers. The family were old Jacobites. Jacobites since the Highland Clearances and on her husband's side of the family there was a direct forebear who had attended Bonnie Prince Charlie when he was in exile in France. They'd stayed on at the French court too. That dressing-table set had come out of France with them when the monarchy fell in the 1790s. It came from Versailles. Beautiful craftsmanship. The best. There was a jewel box as well, satinwood with ormolu mounts and flower-petal and butterfly-wing insets preserved in beeswax. It came from the same family. A lovely thing. I've seen a cabinet which matches it in the king's private rooms in Versailles. Recognised it straight away when I saw it. They pay a fortune to have all that stuff returned nowadays. The workmanship! But it was all gone. None of it was in the sale. Course I wasn't the only one who knew about it. There were lots of other pieces. Pieces from all over the world. Chinese jade and Dutch carvings. You wouldn't believe the quality of it. Old man Savage had bought some of it and other bits he probably inherited himself when he took over the business from his father. There were two big safes down there in that basement and they were pretty full. God, there was some speculation I can tell you. The police caught a couple of local guys in her garden, digging it up in the middle of the night. Rough types. No one ever found that stuff, not as far as I know, anyway. It's gone.'

'Wow,' I said, wondering what the hell could have happened to it all. I mean, Dad saw it. It was there. My hands felt weak and I laid them down on the kitchen table. I didn't want it to get too much. I didn't want to pass out again. 'Once a day is enough,' I thought, although things did seem to be happening mighty

56

quickly. Intrigue upon intrigue. Eight million pounds and stolen treasures. It was a lot to come out of the blue. I decided that I was going to have to go to see Mike Williams' uncle and I made a mental note to ring the lawyer's office on Monday morning and set something up. I was just on the point of asking more. Something about Ma Polinski's life. She had done really well for herself. I mean, she had all this amazing stuff. Why did she seem to be so on the edge of everything? Or put another way, 'Why had she had to leave everything to me?'

But I didn't have time to ask about it because then the front door slammed and I heard my brother's sure-footed step, walking past the hall table, throwing his car keys down into the huge shell where we kept the keys for everything, and striding on into the baking green brightness of the kitchen.

'Simon! In here, dear,' my mother shouted gratefully as she switched on the kettle again and fussed around at the windows with the curtains, trying to give us at least some shade. And there was no point in going on then so I left the whole thing aside for a while and didn't try to find out any more that afternoon, though I was surprised at myself when Simon said, 'Hi, sis,' and kissed my cheek, and there was just the tiniest frisson going through me because he didn't know and I wasn't going to tell him.

Chapter Five

That night I reckoned I was due a celebration so when Simon and his friend Scotty went to the movies, I tagged along. I know. I know. I should have flown off somewhere exotic and celebrated properly. You don't understand, though, just how surreal it is when it happens, and, well, I hadn't seen any of the money yet, and it was nearly the end of the month so I was pretty skint, as usual. I think, though, even if I'd been given a case of cash, I'd still have stuck with something pretty low-key. I wasn't exactly in denial, but I was close to it. That afternoon I'd lolled around in the garden sunning myself, dreaming dreams of cashmere cardigans and a pair of boots I'd seen in Russell & Bromley, but decided were too expensive. Sad, I know. Given the whole world, that was what I came up with in the first instance, but, well, it's the truth. It was a late-night show at the Cameo and I said I would drive so that they could drink beer because the Cameo would give you your pint in a plastic glass and let you drink it right through the film, which was considered pretty groovy. I'm not much of a drinker myself, you see. And well, I was just up for the outing. By the evening it was pissing down with rain, of course and you'd never have believed that the sun had shone hard on my face as I had done my lap of triumph around Arthur's Seat that afternoon. I borrowed one of Dad's old, khaki, stretched jumpers and a green hat which Mum had knitted for me when I was a kid and I spent ages adjusting the driver's seat and the steering wheel of Simon's car because my brother is very, very tall and likes to drive his dark blue TVR Cerbera virtually horizontal.

I've never been able to figure out Simon and Scotty. I mean, on the surface they seem so different. They went to school together, of course, but boy have they branched out in opposite directions or what? It's not just their natures either. Everything in their lives seems so different. I mean, Simon is the sharp but honest businessman who has taken over from his father, expanded what he inherited and kind of made good. Scotty on the other hand had squandered his trust fund by the time he got to his twenty-second birthday and ended up taking a job making violins by hand down in this workshop in Stockbridge. He started out just sweeping the floor because it was the only job he could find, and now, well, he's approaching thirty and he carves the wood himself, from the beginning when it arrives as a seasoned sheet, till the end, when he packs it up in a velvet-lined, black leather case and sends it off to its new proud owner. He has perfect pitch. Seriously. He can sing middle C in the most outrageous conditions. Once I saw him challenged to do it upside down, hanging off the climbing frame, swinging this way and that. And he managed no problem. Perfectly. Scotty takes home half nothing a week and he lives in this bedsit just off the back of the Grassmarket above an old garage. Simon has a whole townhouse to himself in the New Town. But their very different circumstances have never seemed to come between them. They are really good friends. Well, up until recently they were anyway. Up until recently when their differences hadn't come between them and the only apparent contrast in their lives was material.

Money, of course, in the last while, since I got some

of my own, has been on my mind. And it has occurred to me that people think that if you have a lot of money, like Simon, like my dad or for that matter, like me now, that you live this kind of luxurious lifestyle, like some kind of cross between Jilly Cooper and *Dallas*. It's like I said about my night of celebration seeming so tame. I suppose some people do go over the top when they get their hands on some loot, but well, Simon and Dad and Mum and me too now, we live really well with nice houses and nice cars and all of that. Nothing too over the top, nothing too flash, but still, well, nice stuff. And we go out to restaurants a lot and every now and again we throw a party and our parties are almost gothic in their proportions. Simon spends a bit of money on clothes and so do I and Dad goes through some killer wines, and of course, up until Ma Polinski took a hand in my finances, they kept bailing me out from time to time, and I'm a reasonably costly item, but basically, well, maybe it's because of Mum and what happened to her, but like I said before, most of their money is just like a security blanket. It's there just in case. I've never known my brother to take a holiday yet. Simon's inherited Mum's uneasiness about suitcases – he travels for work but not for pleasure. My father buys his clothes in this big discount warehouse on an industrial estate on the edge of town. My mother buys no-label goods at the supermarket. And you just get the feeling that all that money they are making beyond the amount of money that they actually need, well, it's proving something to them, it's making them safe. And Simon's friend Scotty, well, he must be just the opposite, because he blew everything that he had and it didn't even seem to faze him. He didn't need a security blanket, because he was really secure in himself. Not that I can condone Scotty's legendary drink, drugs and women binge of 1990, but just that his general attitude to money now, well, let's say it's a useful contrast, and me, I'm in between. I'm a hybrid. But when it comes right down to it I think I'd rather have Scotty's attitude to financial matters as it stands today (money as pleasure tokens), than my father's (money as an insurance for if and when they come to get you). It's healthier.

They were showing *Boogie Nights* at the late show and the place was completely packed out. People were arriving totally soaked and just heading straight into the overcrowded bar which smelled of cigarette smoke and wet woollen jumpers. Scotty was chain-smoking Marlboro Lights in the hallway when Simon and I showed up.

'You got the tickets?' Simon asked him.

'Nah, not yet,' said Scotty, because of course, he was broke as usual. Just like me.

Simon went off to stand in the queue for the box office and I began to take off my rain-speckled jumper and hat.

'How're you doing, Rachel?' Scotty asked me.

I smiled. He really is great and after the excesses of his youth he's kind of transpired into being my big brother's sensible friend for a while. I used to joke with Scotty that he was a superhero. I called him The Moderator because when Simon went out and got really drunk and was on the point of doing something really, really stupid, Scotty was the one who would always step in and make sure that he got home OK. A superhero with a brief against debauchery. A superhero for the nineties. He had this really great girlfriend for a while too. She was some titled chick, but she was pretty cool really. More his age than mine so when I was a teenager and she was in her early twenties, well, she always seemed very glam. Her name was Charlotte. When her dad found out about Scotty though, all hell broke loose because the family wanted Mr Right or bust, and poor Scotty, he just wouldn't cut the mustard.

Anyway, it couldn't have been true love because the next thing anyone knew Charlotte was holding down a big job on a glossy magazine in New York and hanging out with Matt Dillon, Donna Karan and most of the cast of *NYPD Blue*.

'I'm just dandy. It's a bit parky out there though,' I replied, tossing my head towards the doorway and then playing with the strands of my hair which had been pushed out of place on account of me wearing the green woolly hat.

'You cast your clout too soon,' Scotty smiled. 'It's six weeks until we'll be able to be justifiably pissed off when it turns cold after a spell of sunshine. How's your new job?'

I shrugged my shoulders. I'd spent most of the afternoon giving myself a hard time about how I ought to go back to Glasgow on Monday morning and pitch up for work despite the fact that I'd make more in interest just investing my millions wisely than I would working on the organisation of an exhibit I had planned about the indigenous people of the Russian plains from the ninth century until the early fourteenth. Don't get me wrong. I love my work. But well, like I said before, that much money can mess up your perception of everything and although I love archaeology, all of it, from the discovery of something new, to the restoration of exhibits which have been preserved for a couple of hundred years in a museum, well, the money had kind of thrown me. And that is kind of natural, given that anything was suddenly possible. The boundaries of my whole life had irreversibly moved. But then, I couldn't tell Scotty that. 'Things are great,' I said, copping out. And I let him talk on for a while about the musical instrument collection at the museum. Scotty is really passionate about all of that and I know a bit about it because there is a whole archive devoted to it in Glasgow. Everything from early medieval bagpipes to celtic bodhrán drums carved from bone. I know what he means, I know what he gets excited about. Sometimes you touch those old pieces, not just musical instruments but everyday artefacts, plates or combs or headdresses, and you feel the link between the generations and it stretches right back to the day the piece was made. It's a sense of history which gives you a perspective, because you have a plate and a comb and a hat as well.

Simon trudged back with the tickets and we got in some drinks and hit *Boogie Nights*. Scotty talked me into having a weak Irish coffee. To keep my strength up, he said. It tasted dead creamy and as we headed into the movie I felt the first glow of the whisky or maybe it was only from the sun. The place was hopping and we had a good time. Late night at the Cameo half the audience seem to know each other so we just chatted to lots of people until the film started. We were standing in the aisles and I was laughing and laughing at Scotty telling me and this girl, Fiona McCall, about trying to change a lightbulb the week before when he didn't have a ladder. I felt really smug. It was just where I wanted to be. After the film we headed out into the cold, pissing about for the block and a half to the car. I waltzed along with Simon, itching to tell him, but still holding back.

'You're rubbish at that,' Scotty shouted. 'Did no one ever teach you? One, two, three; one, two, three. Rubbish!' he shouted, and picked me up and tried to fling me into this skip which was lying illegally at the main Tollcross junction.

'One, two, three,' Simon was repeating, bemused as he hadn't noticed I wasn't there to dance with.

Later, we dropped Scotty off under the street light at the top of his close, watching him as he disappeared inside like a lean, black shadow. Then Simon told me to drive on and let him out at his place over on the other side of town and he'd lend me the car for the next day.

'If it's nice I'll go and look at Ma Polinski's house out at Morbrax,' I thought, as I used the rear-view mirror to watch him open up his huge, shiny, black front door and disappear into the safety of his warm and immaculate house. It took me all of ten minutes to make it back to Mum and Dad's. The traffic lights just turned green in my path. Mum and Dad were asleep, and as I crept up the stairs it was just like being a teenager again. I've never found a bed as comfortable as the bed in my room at home and I fell asleep thinking about sparkly emeralds and carved jade and Ma Polinski's millions and how they were now all mine. And later on in the morning, when I woke up again, the weather was beautiful. I could tell before I even opened the ruby-coloured, thick linen curtains. The light just seemed so pure that it had to be sunny out there. As I drew the material back I smiled to myself and pressed up against the window, taking in the view. Up above me there was a clear, cloudless blue sky and it looked absolutely set to be really warm all day, so I decided to shoulder my responsibilities and find out exactly what she'd left me. I went ahead and I took the drive out to Morbrax. I wanted to see Ma Polinski's house which, I smiled to myself, was now, after all, my pad in the country.

Chapter Six

Mum packed me a picnic and I set off with the soft top down. It took me ages to fold it back just right. I packed up a couple of jumpers and some gloves just in case the weather turned nasty and I said goodbye to the folks and left the house just after eleven with my sunglasses on as I drove into the light. I started to eat immediately – just as soon as I turned on to Cameron Toll in fact. I don't know why I do that. I wasn't hungry. But if someone gives me food then I always just start into it straight away. I never saved my sweeties as a kid. I never put snacks into my pocket for later. I don't even keep food in the fridge at my flat. If I do a weekly shop, like you're supposed to, it's all gone in a couple of days. I can't save food. So I ate the cheese and cucumber sandwiches and munched my way through a packet of crisps and an apple before it was eleven and then I sipped on the can of Coke and after all that, I was more or less there. I had driven south-west right past the Pentland Hills and along a winding B-road which took my full attention. The address on the keys just said 'Caitlyn House, Morbrax', and luckily for me, just as I had reckoned, the village turned out to be absolutely tiny, so the house was pretty easy to find.

God, that old lady had taste. I mean, the shop in the Old Town, well, she had inherited that. But she was right to stay on there and keep the business going. It's eerie all right. No question of that. But it's beautiful too. It has this amazing atmosphere about it. The old, curved stone stairs are uneven on the right-hand side, each step hand-carved and laid down in the sixteenth century so that if you had to fight to defend your place, you would have the advantage coming down the stairs as long as you held your sword in your right hand. She had preserved everything really well. She hadn't opened the windows fully to glass and she had kept the original oak panels at the bottom of the leaded panes which you'd open to chuck out your rubbish come ten o'clock at night right up until the time they built the New Town in the late 1700s. Nowadays people are educated to conservation. They tend not to go off and rip out original features without thinking hard about it. But she understood it early on, right through the period when most people were removing Adam fireplaces to make their houses look nice and modern, and hammering nails into their original oak floorboards or, worse still, laying down linoleum with that dreadful glue which you can never remove properly. She'd inherited that shop in the thirties after all.

The house at Morbrax was beautiful too. A small Georgian cottage, with a sweet little garden out the back replete with a sundial and a collection of rose bushes which had been pruned back ready for the summer growth. It had been well maintained of course. Mike Williams, or perhaps it was his uncle, seemed very good at that. It was warm last spring, and the pink and white clematis was already beginning to bud as it climbed up the stone walls. I circled the house once, peering through the windows into the empty rooms before I decided to open the front door. I wish I'd known what I was going to find. I wish someone had told me so I could have prepared myself, but then, well, it seems like I was the only one who'd ever seen it. Maybe she'd left it just for me. Maybe she knew I would be the kind of person who takes in the details. It was cold inside and shady. In the hallway there was a red plastic bucket full of cleaning materials, which someone had obviously left there for their annual or maybe biannual visits to make sure that the dust didn't take over the house completely. They'd sold everything. You could see on the wooden floors where the carpets had been pulled up, you could see on the walls the marks of pictures removed after years of hanging in the same place. The only fixtures left downstairs were a stone sink in the kitchen and an old, white, disconnected gas stove. I moved off up the creaky stairs to explore the upper floor, running one hand up the carved oak balustrade as I went, and pulling on the little gold chain she'd left with the other. I was marvelling, I suppose, at her good taste and my own good fortune. There were three bedrooms on the upper floor and they were all just full of light. It was almost midday by the time I got there and the sun was at its brightest. I sat down on the floor of the largest bedroom and I closed my eyes as the sun streamed in through the tiny panes of glass and when I looked down I realised that the lead beading cast a cagelike shadow all around me and I wondered again why I had been chosen by her, why I had been drawn in. It was so intriguing. The mystery of it. The infinite possibilities. It seemed fanciful and very romantic. It's funny now, I don't think the old lady would have had any truck with that in her life, but I really went for it.

I lay back on the stripped floorboards with my eyes closed, and I thought to myself 'I'm lying just where her bed must have been.' And I stretched out in the sunshine and relaxed for a few moments, baking myself in the warm yellow light. It seemed like such a comfortable place. It seemed so idyllic that I just totally relaxed and I began to daydream about taking over the house myself and furnishing it and living there. Nice dreams which welded the past to the present. It was, I told myself, what Ma Polinski would have wanted and that, of itself, made me feel safe, so it was what I wanted then too. But I suppose she wasn't really a cosy kind of lady and, well, I was about to find that out for sure. Right then in fact, just at that moment when I opened my eyes and I saw what was painted on the ceiling right above my head. And I knew then that she was a realist, as my whole body tightened and I jerked myself to my feet and the daydreams vanished and I ran, screaming, back down the stairs, tripping as I slammed the door behind me and ran down the driveway. It had given me a terrible shock. The first of many. And I blamed her for it as I sat shaking in the car for what seemed like for ever. It made me feel physically sick. All that panic. It was my first real clue, I suppose. The first thing that really touched me. My first glimpse into her world, her life and her reasons and it scared me half to death, coming straight from a romantic, silly stupor into reality.

In archaeology, symbol is everything. Cave paintings, the carvings on everyday objects, the rituals of birth and burial. The symbols define the way you live, your whole philosophy. If you have a cross on the wall and you look at it every day then that says something about you. Same goes for carrying a talisman with you, or burying a golden ornament to your chosen god. Symbols. Running deer. Carnival masks. Football colours. Every one an insight into an individual's beliefs. Ma Polinski had one on the ceiling above her bed, one that you didn't notice when you walked into the room because it was so vague it was almost cloudlike. A subtle mural in ghostly creams and greys that you could only see when you lay right beneath it. A skeleton with its arms stretched out, down towards you. An old bag of bones in need. And all I could think was what the fuck kind of twisted nightmares was the old lady having that she needed to wake up and see that every morning.

It took a lot for me to walk back up the driveway and make myself lock the door of her house properly. Then, with my heart still pounding away like a runaway pulse, and my head kind of light, I got back into the car and I drove into Edinburgh trying to dismiss the feeling that something was following me. Some old corpse, with her arms outstretched. Someone who'd left me eight million pounds because you'd need that kind of money to put up with her secrets. Because she wanted something. A ghost. A spirit. I dropped the car off at Simon's, walked up to Haymarket with my bag over my shoulder and resolutely took the train back to the west coast. I just wanted to get back to my own flat and my own life and I was fully resolved to ring Mike Williams the next day and have him put both the properties up for sale. It's the best thing, I told myself, I'll just bank all the cash, live off the interest from that and the other investments and forget where the hell it came from. All the gentle, flowery intrigue had disappeared from my mind and I was completely determined. As far as I was concerned I'd come to my senses and I was just going to get on with it. And I, the dedicated archaeologist, had no room in my mind or my life for messages from the dead or glimpses of the past. I wasn't going to dig anything up. I was resolved. No creepy old lady was going to fuck with my head and that was that. It had scared me way too much and I just bolted. But then, that straight-to-the-heart-of-it hardness, that no-messing-about, well, that was just like her and the reason it scared me, I suppose, was that it had touched me too. And I must have been quite like her really, because whatever I thought I was going to do, in the end I couldn't leave it alone.

Chapter Seven

I took Ma Polinski's jewellery into work with me the next day. I don't know why. I just didn't want to leave it at home so I packed it up in a grey felt jewellery roll and I popped it in at the bottom of my handbag. I really did mean to ring Mike Williams, but when I got into the office all hell had broken loose. We had two curatorial staff off work and a whole load of school groups booked in. Things get terribly busy around the summer term. It's our busiest time of the year in fact. On top of that, as soon as the good weather starts we get inundated by metal detector enthusiasts who haul Bronze Age stuff out of the ground over the weekend and then bring it into the museum on Monday morning to find out if they've got anything of value. I usually get the job of sitting there, sifting through the huge trawl of mediocre metal goods, though occasionally they do bring in something of real value in among the old axe-heads and broken pin-brooches. There was an amazing ring one time which some kid dug up on his dad's allotment, and another day an old man brought in a whole haul of silver coins which had been buried in a pisspot sometime around 1250. That Monday, though, there was nothing much of any real interest, nothing that we didn't already have more and better specimens of than we could ever possibly display. I thought I'd get a moment to myself later on in the morning, but it was well after five when I even managed to get my hands on a lunchtime sandwich and at six o'clock I realised that I'd missed my chance for the day. Not only that, but I was going to have to work late. I had a lot still to do for my planned exhibit on the plains people and I wouldn't have been happy going home on time. I had spent all day telling kids about the importance of preserving the relics of the past, and playing the *Antiques Roadshow* expert for a long line of disappointed metal detector heads. Not on the stuff that I love. Not on the nomads.

The culture of the plains fascinates me. Any of the many semi-nomadic tribes from anywhere around the world is fantastic to study and I'd been really lucky and bagged the Russian plains people as the first exhibit I ever got to direct. And their period, from the late tenth century onwards, is great as well – Vladimir was on the throne and the Russian Orthodox Church was founded. It was a crucial time for all the Slavic cultures. People think that archaeology is all about the Pharaohs and the Neanderthal Age and the Aztecs and stuff. Well, the ancients don't really interest me so much. My hobby-horse, after all, is the way the past impinges on the present. The way a people who seem to be gone, a culture which seems to have died, live on in the people living today. Plains people are the business for that. They are always ballsy people, people close to the basics and also, because they move around, they are people who knew how to change and develop to a certain degree. They had outside influences. They traded in silk and horses. They told campfire stories. Their women wore roughly-worked turquoise jewellery. They prayed to their gods in the towering mountains as they lay down to sleep under the wide, wide sky. Maybe that's what it is. That wide open sky thing. Gets me every time. But imagine living that close to the pulse of the whole world. Imagine the certainty of it. And the people of the region now still live like the plains people did then in many ways. It's a way of life that has gone on securely for so long. Imagine knowing all the stories of your past.

Anyhow, for the exhibit I had arranged to borrow some artefacts from the Victoria and Albert Museum Depository and they had arrived, so I stayed on late to unpack them down in the archives. There were big display boards with black-and-white photographs of some of the ice mummies which had been found, but of course they weren't my style and I didn't bother with them very much. Instead, I went straight for the artefact cases and started to remove the items one by one. A delicate headdress of felt and lapis which they had packed in a big box of styrofoam pieces. A wooden stool with its seat carved like a running deer and some pottery cups with their handles intact packed up together, swaddled in bubble wrap. And in the same package, a goatskin pouch containing a chipped, polished metal disc which they would have used as a mirror to ward off evil. Those tatty old remnants are the only physical things which are left and I began to think of the text I would write to piece an explanation together of how these people had lived and why they were so extraordinary. And then, of course, my eyes fell on my handbag and I remembered the jewellery I had been left myself and without thinking about it I reached down and opened it up, pouring the gemstones out on to the soft, thick blotting paper of the worktop so I could see them again. It seemed a million years since I'd been in Mike Williams' office, since I'd found out about Ma Polinski's things. The things she had chosen to leave me. They sparkled in the light of the anglepoise lamps fixed at each corner of the bare white work surface. The stones held the light, outshining by far the dowdy remnants dug up from the plains. The plains people wouldn't have been able to cut emeralds or diamonds, you see. Well beyond their capabilities in

72

fact – they would only have been able to use the softer, semi-precious stones. Lapis, turquoise, amber. Properties easy to mine and easy to fashion. Unlike the Colombian emeralds of Ma Polinski's necklace which shone like polished translucent pebbles in the harsh light of the archive table. Not as hard as diamonds, but still, they haul some pretty dense rocks out of the ground in South America. The plains people wouldn't even have known that America existed. In among the rough-cut lapis, Ma Polinski's jewellery shone out at me. Well-crafted, cultured jewellery. All the splendour of civilisation. And I knew that she knew her stuff. I put the ring on my finger, and struggled to close the clasp on the necklace so that it would lie flat under the collar of my shirt and cover up the chain which I'd been wearing. Then, at last, I laid the bracelet over my wrist and with the other hand I used the ancient bleary mirror to look at myself, peering at my reflection as if I was some ghost from the past. As if I was risen from the dead. I was only a blur of course. I was all out of focus, dressed in her finery, vaguely sparkling there in the harsh glare of the spotlight bulbs.

'Fuck it,' I thought. 'I have to find out.'

Well, I did. Didn't I? It was a bit of a U-turn but she was a crazy old lady, just trying to do her own thing. It would be sad, I thought, not to know. It seemed admirable of her not to sell up her husband's shop. To stay on and make it work. I liked her, the idea of her. The serious reverence which went with that game she used to play with the pink sugar biscuit in her cardigan pocket. The fondness of that memory. Her kindness to me. It's not that I forgot about the mural on her ceiling, though, with the darkness of the archive all around me, I did try to put it to the back of my mind. But the shock of it had worn off. And besides anything else, I think my professional instincts were kicking in. I mean, if you found a mural like that on a dig you'd be fascinated. It's a big find. It would fire you up so that you had to investigate more. Make new discoveries. You'd take on extra hands, try harder. You wouldn't run away screaming and just put it to the back of your mind. Can you imagine if the first Egyptologists had done that when they found mummies in the Valley of the Kings? 'Come on, lads, those Pharaohs were twisted. We're shipping out of Luxor tonight. Too damn hot here anyway.' I don't think so. And I suppose I thought, well, I've found it now. That's the scary bit over. I might as well go on and try to suss out the rest. It was my archaeological instinct really and that's what I fell back on once the shock had worn off and my interest had been rekindled in the fire of those amazing stones. So I was decided. Wary still, I think, but decided nonetheless to try to find out as much as I could about her.

When you are making a study of a long-extinct indigenous people, you always go to the region where they lived and you look for signs. Not just signs which you dig up out of the earth. No, like I said, in less developed cultures the people who are living there now probably have many of the same forces in their lives as their ancestors. You can learn a lot before you even pick up a shovel or an axe. Especially if there isn't a lot of communication or travel. People in those circumstances might look much the same as their forebears. They might have the same physical make-up, be subject to the same illnesses for example. Sometimes they have more or less the same myths and legends, and the derivation of the same gods. I carefully packed up the exhibits again, folded my own jewellery in the grey felt roll and decided to go back to Edinburgh as soon as I could to see what I could find. She'd died, after all, in my own lifetime so, I told myself, I should be able to find people who knew her. People, I thought, who could maybe help me to understand why she'd left me the money and what had been going on in her life that the only person she had was someone else's five-year-old daughter. It was kind of intriguing after all.

Chapter Eight

I worked all week of course. Well, I couldn't just let everything drop. They needed me at the museum and, pissing about aside, I knew that I'm the kind of person who has to be doing something. I'm not a lady of leisure, it doesn't suit me. I didn't want to give up my job and join the ranks of the Doing Fuck All Brigade no matter how much money I had in the bank, so I grafted away on the Russian thing for my full five-day week, which is a bit of a triumph for me. I was always getting into trouble at the museum because I did skive a bit. It's all the freedom of working the way you have to in an institution like that. I worked more or less on my own and that was my problem, or rather, it was often Bob Morris's problem, because he had a hard time tying me down. That week though, I was a model employee. I grafted hard. But Ma Polinski was on my mind the whole time. On the Wednesday Mike Williams rang me at my desk. His voice was just itching with tension.

'I wondered,' he started, 'because you hadn't rung me, if you realised that I can release some money to you. If you want me to set up a monthly or an annual payment, I can do it now.'

I thought for a second. That hadn't really occurred to me. After the mural had shocked me I almost felt like the money was mine, but only in trust. Like I could dream about using it for myself, but I shouldn't really touch it. Like it was somehow sacred, spiritual. It was, I suppose, those few days later, still quite surreal. Almost theoretical.

'I suppose that would be OK,' I mumbled. 'Yeah. It would be great.'

'Good,' he replied, with amazing relief in his voice. I think he would have called a shrink or something if I'd declined the offer. I suppose I wasn't reacting in the way he expected.

He said he'd transfer me two thousand pounds immediately, and on Thursday night I whooped it up, late-night shopping for clothes in the designer shops on Princes Square where, exercising tremendous I-can-have-anything constraint I only managed to spend half of the money in one go. Afterwards I treated myself and Nina to a champagne dinner up at the bar at Rogano's when the shops had finally closed. I was really glad that Nina was back in town. It had been a hell of a ten days since I'd seen her. She arrived all windswept by the spring gales on the evening train from London. First class, courtesy of the Tate.

'Yucky Scottish weather again,' she said as she ran her fingers through her hair and kissed me lightly on the cheek.

Nina's half Scottish, half Italian, but she only seems to consider herself Scottish at all during the fleeting summer months. When the weather is poor she metamorphoses into an Italian living abroad and complains like hell even though she's lived here since she was born.

'At least down south it isn't so cold,' she smiled as she eyed the shopping bags at my feet with dubiety.

'Mid-season sales,' I explained to her and she squinted at me sideways. 'Thank God you're back.'

We feasted ourselves on crayfish and bubbly, on thick, dark chocolate mousse and double espressos.

'What's all this in honour of?' she giggled, her dark

eyes dancing with delight.

'A celebration of life,' I told her and I ordered us double shots of Armagnac so that we could make a toast. Not that I told her then what had really happened. I didn't tell her that night. I didn't come clean till later. It was a great night, though, that Thursday. It was the first time that I felt real relief, I mean, it was the first time that I relaxed with the money and what it could buy me. I suppose because I'd never had money of my own before, not enough money for luxuries in any case, and well, because Dad cut me out, I've always worried that I'll end up as some kind of bag lady. I had never stood on my own two feet before, and I had no one but myself to blame for that. That Thursday night, I'm sure that I glowed with the pleasure of it. The prospect of independence. The prospect of security of my very own. I felt proud and I felt lucky. And I ate a lot and Nina and I talked and talked and I was very glad that she was back. Somehow just being around Nina always makes me feel that everything is possible. And in the end I was right about that.

Apart from Nina's great homecoming and sundry good buys on Princes Square, I had a pretty quiet week all in all. I made my arrangements for the weekend and planned to stay on in Edinburgh on the Monday. It was the long Glasgow weekend, which meant that the administrative section of the museum would be closed on Monday, although of course the exhibits were still open to the public. When I left Glasgow on Friday afternoon I got away early and I ran all the way to Queen Street and caught the four o'clock to Haymarket. Nina was going hillwalking that weekend, up near Loch Fyne, and I had been kind of glad that I had something else to do. I'm not really one to rough it. She's much more outdoorsy than I am despite her complaints about the weather. In fact, she sometimes gets quite evangelical about the west coast and its panoramic scenery and when I can't come up with a good enough excuse she often drags me along with this crowd of hillwalking types that I'm not really into.

Anyhow, on Friday at five I got out of the train in Edinburgh and I walked up to Simon's place at the West End where, as planned, he was waiting in his kitchen with two gin and tonics on ice in these huge, carved crystal beakers which were truly decadent.

'Thanks,' I said, and we clicked our glasses and I watched the slice of lemon waver up and down inside the liquid.

'Cheers,' he smiled right back at me and he drank deeply.

I sank down into one of the big mahogany carvers that he has around his table and I sipped delicately on my drink, as if I was acclimatising myself to being back on the east coast. Simon's place is really beautiful and I could just feel myself disappearing into the background there. When he bought it, it was a nice old Georgian house which had been lived in for years by some kooky old man who died there when he was well over a hundred. Simon spent three years and vast sums of money doing the place up with great style to be a pretty swish bachelor pad and he talked a lot about how it was a good investment. I think, though, it was more a labour of love. He started out just replacing the old lead piping, and having the place rewired so that death by electrocution wasn't imminent whenever you turned on an appliance, but he got carried away with the beautiful proportions of the house and ended up restoring everything. He has three public rooms downstairs, off the polished flagstone hallway. One of the rooms has a full-sized billiard table. Upstairs there are three bedrooms and a dressing room where Simon hangs his collection of well-cut, rather stunning clothes. He dresses beautifully, my brother. That night, though, he had gone for understated and he was wearing a pair of khakis and a big cream-coloured jumper so that he blended into the background in his kitchen which is done out in muted greens with pale fittings. Simon leaned on the work surface and played with his hair.

Simon's hair is a weird length. It's not really short, but it isn't long either. Like my hair, it has a slight curl to it and sometimes his curls form themselves into a lock of hair and that was what he was playing with – trying hard to make it stick behind his ear as he drank gulps of gin from his big, frosted glass. Sometimes it's kind of strange for me to be around Simon because he looks just like I'd look if I was a boy. I never used to notice it when we were kids and we lived in the same house. We were too familiar then. But since we both moved out it's something I now seem to notice every time we get together. We've the same blue eyes, exactly the same colouring, he's taller and broader, of course, but we're the same type – slightly taller than average and muscular. We're both quite strong. In the summer, when I wear shirts with no sleeves you can really see it. I'm a bit too taut and sometimes I worry that it's not entirely feminine, but then I figure my long locks make up for that, just like the curve of my waist, which in a tight-fitting summer dress can really make me new friends.

Anyhow, Simon knows me well and he figured that something was up. He just knew it. It's as if he has a sensor built in, like one of those earthquake predictors. Changes in power, shifts in influence. Family stuff. Simon didn't end up with all the money for nothing. He can sense those things and he can adapt, fit into anything. But Ma Polinski's bequest had caught him on the hop. It was a bit of a wild card, after all. He knew something had happened but he couldn't quite put his finger on what it was.

'Rachel,' he started slowly, 'are you OK?'

'Yeah,' I assured him. 'Why?'

'Well, you came home last weekend. And now you're home this weekend. And I just wondered if things were OK in Glasgow. I mean, did anything go wrong?'

'Nah,' I told him, pulling my legs up under me so that I was kneeling sideways comfortably on the chair. 'Things are fine, although I have been thinking about moving back to the east coast.'

'Great,' he grinned and now he was fiddling with the thick gold signet ring he always wears on the pinkie of his left hand, but at least he wasn't knocking his gin back at quite such an alarming pace. 'Going to move back in with Mum and Dad?' he asked.

'No. I was thinking of buying myself a flat through here,' I said absent-mindedly. I was really thinking about Ma Polinski of course. That's what my mind was focused on. This moving house stuff was far too far ahead for me to contemplate, but I had to say something to him. I had to reply.

'There are some nice flats up in Marchmont,' Simon started. 'Big ones. You could let out some rooms to help you pay your mortgage. I'll get you some furniture if you like.'

Marchmont is the area on the other side of the Meadows. It's mostly where students live. It kind of made me uneasy that Simon still thought of me like that. As if I was a student. I wasn't the one who was supposed to succeed, you see. That hadn't been part of the plan and Simon couldn't see me in any role other than the one the family had cast for me. I felt kind of pissed off about that.

'Actually, I was thinking of somewhere in town,' I said.

'Very expensive,' he retorted.

'I dunno,' I shrugged my shoulders, letting it go. 'It's just something I'm half considering. We'll see. Maybe something small in the Old Town,' I said and I kind of left it at that.

We dumped my stuff in his spare bedroom and then walked over the Dean Bridge and down into Stockbridge for dinner at Maison Hector, but it was just so busy that we shipped out to Pizza Express instead after only one drink. I really didn't want to tell him about the money however tempting it was, so I kept pretty stumm and just asked him about how the shop was doing and what he was up to. We chatted on just fine. Simon's started really hitting the big time. He flies off two or three times a year now to bid at Christie's in Beverly Hills or Phillips in New York for the really big sales and he has been developing a great upmarket clientele for big-time pieces of jewellery. Politicians, pop stars and rich businessmen. In fact, he was about to go off to Geneva for some big jewellery auction at Sotheby's the following week, so we talked about that for a while.

There is a big difference between the kind of stock jewellery shops normally keep with middle-class engagement rings and pretty Victorian brooches and earrings, and the kind of shop which has that stuff out in the front and sells bags of it because that's what most people want, but when you get into the back office you can ask the guy in charge to try to find you special items. Unusual items. Upmarket rarities and collector's pieces. There are things now which are so scarce that only the really professional guys can find them and they tend to buy them on commission for a wealthy client. Simon's restructured everything totally since the days when we worked Saturdays, when Dad had the shop. He can deal with bankers in a way that Dad never could and he's organised overdrafts and mortgages that Dad never would have organised in a thousand years, despite my father's apparent willingness to do anything he could about the Tax Situation.

Simon has a grasp of notional money, money which only exists in computers, which my father would have found too risky and too insubstantial. Granted he's been handed a lot on a plate, but he's making the best of it really and it doesn't seem to have spoilt him. Not personally. Not in anything except his attitude to me. His need to pick up the reins of power where he feels Mum and Dad left off. I always kind of admired the fact that he works really hard. In at eight in the morning, out at six at night. A millionaire by twenty-one by inheritance, true, but all set to be a multi multi-millionaire at thirty by hard graft. And yeah, sure, he likes his luxuries, but he's kind of sensible with it too, kind of restrained like I said before, because of Mum. I think it's always at the back of their minds, you know, and I suppose my mind too, that money might have helped her family to get out of Munich, where they lived before they were sent to the death camp. It's always there that somehow money might have fixed things and so, for all of us, there is that urge to have your money by you, just in case. It wouldn't have helped at all, of course. It couldn't have and it's an historical fact that it didn't. Multimillionaires died alongside their broke neighbours. The Germans killed millions of people from every gradation of the social scale who had one thing in common – they had fallen foul of the Nazis for one reason or another. Their genes, their friends, their beliefs. But well, it's only human nature to want to believe that something you could do, something you could have made, might have saved you. Simon's driven by it. And my father too. Definitely. Like I said, they draw their money around them, like a discreet black cashmere coat on a biting cold day. Like father like son. And Simon is a good businessman and I don't think he's ever put a foot wrong, actually. Whatever he buys seems to have appreciated – all his flats, all his cars and most certainly, all of the jewellery and silver. That night, I didn't resent his money one bit. I hadn't really realised that I'd resented it before just as much as I obviously had. But now I had my own fortune I recognised the difference in my tone when I spoke to him, and it was as if an accustomed tightness had been removed from my chest and I silently thanked Ma Polinski for that, safe as I was in a cashmere stole of my own. His attitude to me, his patronising asides, well, that was a different matter. But the money issue was at least resolved. In my mind anyway.

At ten o'clock we hailed a cab and nipped up town for last orders at the Arts Club on Rutland Square where we sat ensconsed in leather armchairs by the open fires and nursed a double Drambuie each. When we got back home to his place I left Simon to watch the late-night boxing on TV and I gave him a big hug – he's my brother after all – and went straight to bed because I wanted to be up pretty early.

It was Scotty who woke me at nine. He arrived at the front door with coffee and croissants in hand and just stood there with his finger on the bell until I stumbled out into the hallway and then fumbled my way down the stairs to open the front door. Simon had drawn the heavy, velvet burgundy curtains at the top of the stairs so I wasn't prepared for how bright it was outside and I had to shield my eyes. Those gins which had seemed so innocuous in the earlier part of the evening must have been triple measures because I didn't drink all that much over dinner and as long as I take it reasonably easy I usually have no problems in getting up early after a night on the tiles.

'Rachel. Fuck,' Scotty grinned from behind really dark sunglasses. There are times when Scotty is just pop-star cool. 'That was easy. It usually takes ten minutes on the bell before Simon gets up.'

'Hi,' I said weakly, worried momentarily that I looked as rat-arsed shite as I felt.

Scotty took pity and he gave me his own coffee, which was really sweet of him though I had to concentrate hard on not spilling it as I wobbled back up the stairs. I declined his kind offer of a croissant and crawled back into the spare bedroom, while he made for Simon's room. After I'd splashed my face and combed my hair I began to feel a lot better and I could hear them laughing on the other side of the house, so I pulled on some clothes, gulped down the caffeine, and wandered along the hallway to sit on the end of Simon's bed. They were going up to Mortonhall to play golf, in which I habitually have no interest, so it was easy to get away by saying that I'd rather go into town to do some shopping. I arranged to meet them later on for dinner and so, duly dispatched, I left them arguing about whether two sets of golf clubs would fit in any way comfortably into Simon's slick sports car and I grabbed my handbag and set off for a day of investigation.

The atmosphere changes from the New Town, with its austere, well-planned four-storey houses of a uniform pale-grey stone, when you cross over Princes Street Gardens and hit the Old Town with its ramshackle, crowded buildings with multicoloured paintwork and its crazy mixture of dark and light façades. The New Town is far too grand for me, really. The Old Town, now that's a little village in the centre of the city. It suits me better and I like it a lot. I walked down the hill, eyeing the tourists suspiciously. It was only the start of the season but there seemed to be just so many of them about. My first port of call had to be Ma Polinski's shop, of course.

I figured that I had to check the old place again in case there was a clue which I had missed. My hands were clammy as I gave the shop the once over. I was nervous, I suppose, that I might find something like that mural out at Morbrax. It didn't take long to satisfy myself that there really wasn't anything, though, so I locked the place up again and caught my bearings as I sat on the little flight of worn stone steps which led up to the front door. I knew what I was looking for. Basics. Where she got her food, her medicine and her clothes. And then, not so basic, the City Chambers further up from the Canongate, opposite St Giles High Kirk, on the Royal Mile. Mike Williams had said that she sat on the City Council so, I figured, there would be records of her there. I started to walk back up the High Street looking past the souvenir shops, which certainly weren't there when Ma Polinski was alive, or at least not in quite such force. That day there was again a veritable festival of tartan flags hanging out on to the street and the smell of freshly made fudge wafted my way gently on the breeze as I wandered up past John Knox's house. I was getting used to that, though, and I hardly took it in. I stopped off at the old waterhead cistern and had a little drink from the fountain and then I wandered straight into the pharmacy on the other side of the road. It was, I figured, a shop which might well have been there when Ma Polinski was alive and might well have been somewhere that she used.

Inside, it was cool away from the sun and I felt kind of awkward. I mean usually, when you're investigating something, you're in Africa or India or somewhere. Somewhere else. Somewhere completely alien, where you aren't known and you can't fit in. In that situation, when you go into a shop to ask questions, well, I don't know, it's just different.

'What am I doing?' I thought to myself. 'What the hell am I looking for?'

I bought some sugarfree sweets and scrutinised the staff behind the counter, but they were all about the same age as I am, which was far too young to know anything about her anyway. So I chickened out and I walked back out on to the street, feeling like a failure, feeling that it was hopeless and deciding to myself, in consolation, that the City Chambers was the only place to start. I wished Nina was with me. I wished for her great sense of purpose and that inspired me a bit as I tramped up to the City Chambers opposite St Giles.

Edinburgh City Chambers was built on the site of Mary King's Close. There are said to be ghosts there from the time of the plague. Well, it is a matter of historical record that the close was bricked up with plague victims left inside to die. There is no historical proof for the ghosts, of course – they are a matter for speculation – but after they opened the old close up and removed the bodies, there were so many supernatural sightings that no one would move into the old houses which had stood on the site even though the rent was a pittance. After a while, the City Corporation of the time pulled the whole close down and built again from scratch for their own offices. Five storeys on the High Street dropping to ten storeys behind because of the steepness of the hill. You still hear ghost stories about the Chambers and, at night, they run guided tours for the visitors who flock to Edinburgh in their droves, and men dressed in black capes, with their faces whited out, jump nightly from the dark recesses to scare the paying guests. Rumours abound about how dogs won't go into the sub-basement of the building because *something* is still lurking about, and even the guidebooks tell the tale of the psychic who saw the spectre of a little girl crying because she had been bricked up in her home without her favourite doll. The woman immediately ran out to a toyshop and came back with a replacement to appease the unhappy little spirit. The doll is still down there, and people bring other gifts for the apparitions. It's become a bit of a tradition for tourists to leave stuff down there whether they see the ghosts or not. But I reckon it's all window dressing these days – I don't think any self-respecting ghost would hang around too long in that atmosphere, and there haven't been any real sightings of paranormal phenomena for quite a while. *Real* sightings! Listen to me. But I do believe in ghosts, no doubt about it. The unsettled spirits of the dead. Well, you know, I've seen one, maybe more, and in my mind I try to allow for as many possibilities as I can – in fact, I think all archaeologists are like that. We're the last people to go to if you want a definite answer about anything. So I don't discount the spirits even though it's only hearsay. I just take it that absence of evidence isn't evidence of absence, and constitutionally, myself, I'm inclined to believe that they *are* there and they do exist. Just take Ma Polinski. She was with me all along. I think she's with me still.

I strolled in across the courtyard in front of the Chambers and got a security pass at reception to allow me down into the archive. It was three floors below street level although, like I said, because of the hill there were big windows which opened out on to Cockburn Street at the back. I have to admit, walking down the yellow tiled staircase, deeper and deeper into the lower floors, I did get a little frisson of nervousness. The corridors were deserted and my footsteps echoed, but once I got down to the archive I forgot all about the ghost stories because there was too much else to take up my attention. It's in the empty moments, the silences and the dreams that the dead intrude and question. Not the bustle of activity. Somehow then they can't quite get through. Anyway, I ended up getting some good information at the council. Public records are always a good place to start and, well, I had my museum identification card, so I suppose they were predisposed to be amenable. I chatted for a bit with the archivist who set me off on the right track and I did find out a lot about Ma Polinski. She really was growing on me. The more I found out the more I liked her. She was an interesting woman and she had an amazing story.

It looked like it had all started when her first husband died. He had sat on the council himself, and after his death the seat, which was in one of the two Canongate wards, came up for re-election. There were only six or seven other women councillors at that time and they were mostly old ladies, mostly county types, so I can imagine that Ma Polinski, well, she was only twenty-three or so, and she must have seemed very young and foolish. Edinburgh had had female bailiffs all through medieval times, almost since the City Corporation began to sit, but they usually weren't young, and usually weren't quite so fiery. Ma Polinski fought the seat, and she won it against two men, Michael McLean, who I have never heard of, and Iain Yallop, who I figure must have been part of the family who owned an antiques shop in the Grassmarket which I often visited with my father. It's still there, though these days it's run by Johnny Yallop who is probably in his late forties now. Anyhow, I wouldn't be the least surprised if Iain Yallop hadn't led the party of antiques dealers who tried to buy her out of her business at the same time. She dug her heels in though on both accounts and she sat on the City Corporation as an independent for over twenty-five years. Right through the time they were clearing out the slums. She was for restoration of course. She was dead set against razing the buildings like they did and moving families who had lived in the city centre for generations out of town. When I looked through the minutes carefully she just kept arguing for people to be kept together in an integrated city centre community and for the money set aside to build the housing estates to be used to restore the old buildings. But she was outvoted every step of the way and they ripped down the slums all around her. They had a point, I suppose. There were several thousand people too many living in too small a space. There was terrible poverty and rife disease. But some of those buildings dated from the sixteenth century. They shouldn't have demolished them, even if they did have to move out the people who lived there. The Canongate would now be a very different place if they hadn't. The buildings were lower than those at the top end of the High Street and originally they were the homes of the aristocracy and the clergy who wanted to be near the court at Holyrood Palace. Ma Polinski did her best. She brought up the most fascinating stories about some of the old buildings. She recounted the historic things that had happened there, the court intrigue and the folklore. But it was no use. They were slums now and they had just sunk too low, in the opinion of most people, to be worthy of restoration. When I read the minutes of the meetings she seemed so passionate, so clued in to it all.

She was quoted on other topics as well, of course. Licencing laws, street lighting initiatives, social welfare projects. She was congratulated on her second marriage to Tomasz Polinski – they even held a reception for the newly-weds. But looking at the records, the restoration of medieval Edinburgh was obviously the thing which she cared about the most. It was her burning issue. The only subject she talked on consistently over the whole of the twenty-five years that she kept her seat, although once or twice she got into a scrap with some of the Protestant Action councillors who preached streams of abuse, rivers of blood, against the Catholics every Sunday on soapboxes on the Mound more or less right up to the time Ma Polinski died.

I stared at the photographs of her in the record books and I tried to imagine what it would have been like to see her in action, all fired up and excited, but in the early photos she seemed too pretty, somehow too delicate. And in the later ones she just looked like a crotchety old lady. I had read a lot that day, but I knew that although I did kind of like her, I still didn't have her sussed. She wasn't alive in my mind and I couldn't anticipate what she would have done in certain situations. I couldn't see any clues as to why she might have left her fortune to me, no rousing speeches about the penniless daughters of antiques dealers or women's lib for that matter. Nothing. The only clue was that she seemed so unpredictable. In the minutes of one of the earlier meetings she attended there was another councillor who was getting really pompous and he was talking about the wisdom of age and how there was nothing romantic about the slums, nothing worth preserving, and his speech just seemed to be going on and on and at one point he stopped to blow his nose. Ma Polinski reached out and pulled the handkerchief out of his fingers just as he was blowing and well, everything went into the palm of his hand. It completely deflated him and she was a heroine in the local papers that evening and the old guy, well, he was just a standing joke. It didn't seem exactly consistent though, did it? I mean, there was nothing else anywhere to suggest such an impish sense of humour, such a fondness for schoolgirl pranks, but then she was very young.

Once I'd read nearly everything that they had, I signed the visitors' book and climbed the three flights back up to reception where I handed in my security pass and left. Back out on the main street there were still flocks of tourists everywhere and the sun had come out. A barechested man was playing a pair of tartan bagpipes beside the Mercat Cross. He was wearing a kilt and a crowd was forming around him. I began to wander down to the Canongate again where I knew it would be a bit quieter and I went to sit outside the old Canongate Kirk by the People's Museum. It was only a short walk. Maybe ten minutes or so, but it makes a world of difference when you move away from the main tourist drag and even though you are so close to Holyrood Palace, and I suppose every tourist has to want to go there, well, it just seems quieter, that's all. And, of course, it was nearer to Ma Polinski's old shop too. I sat down on one of the public benches and it was there, back on her own territory, that I had the stroke of luck.

Opposite me, under the spring trees which hung over the railings from the graveyard, there was an old man sitting on another one of the benches in a cloud of fallen blossoms. He was feeding the pigeons. There must have been a hundred of them swarming around his feet as he ripped up slices of bread into tiny pieces and scattered them in handfuls over the pavement. I settled down on the slatted wood and watched him for a while, drawing my feet up on to the top of the bench to keep away from the birds and letting the information from the archive sink in. I still didn't really see why she would want to leave all her money to me and I was, rather shamefully, running out of inspiration. I lay my head back on the wooden headrest behind me, and closed my eyes in the sunshine. As I looked up again I jumped because there were two pigeons right next to me. They must have flown up while I had my eyes closed. The old guy noticed me starting and kicking out slightly to scare the birds away.

'Don't you like pigeons?' he called over.

'Don't mind them. Not on my feet, though,' I said. 'Not too close.'

'I love pigeons. People think they're vermin, but they're not. You can eat pigeons. Can't eat a rat now, can you? Or a mouse?' he said.

I laughed. I mean, he was so nuts. Completely crazy. He looked eccentric too, kind of grubby and dishevelled except that he had a hat perched tidily on his head. It was dusted with the fragile petals which were falling from the trees above him. He seemed part of the place somehow. Maybe it was because I'd just read all that stuff, but I let my mind wander and it wandered right over to him. I imagined him living in some small, top-floor, one-bedroom studio with dead pigeons airing, hung up from the laundry pulley which I had, in my mind, placed right in front of the open fireplace on which I imagined him cooking all of his food. There would be a gamey smell about the place, despite the odd open window. And piles of feathers for stuffing his cushions which, of course, he never got round to. Pigeon pie. Pigeon dumplings. Pigeon stew. Roasted whole bird. He looked crazy enough for it so I just conjured it all up. Years of training in historical accuracy that takes. Pure supposition. Maybe the old guy sensed it but, well, he decided he wanted to talk to me. He leaned forward conspiratorially.

'Nice around here, isn't it? Sunny.' he said.

I just nodded. It felt kind of calming to listen to him. Soothing.

'I've lived here all my life,' he stated finally, and well, when you're handed it on a plate, you have to ask, don't you? So of course, I did.

'Did you ever know a woman called Molly Savage?' I said.

The old man threw the last of his bread to the ground.

'Oh yes,' he smiled. 'I knew her all right. Old Ma Polinski.'

He took me down Dunbar's Close into this little public garden behind black iron gates at the end of the cobblestoned recess and we walked together down to the orchard where there were bleached stone benches. One or two of the pigeons followed him hopefully and they perched themselves at his feet and pecked at the lavender and rosemary bushes which grew between the apple trees. I had a sudden vision of him reaching out and picking one up, twisting its neck and putting it in his pocket for later. There was something about him. And of course, people around the Old Town used to eat any bird – sparrows, thrushes, pigeons, whatever they could catch. Like the working class anywhere before the days of supermarkets, they considered everything a possible source of food. This old man, there was something crazy about him, like he came from the past. Something almost primal. Dangerous. Like he carried history with him. Like he was a ghost. I sat at the opposite end of the seat and put my handbag down in between us.

'You got the keys to the shop,' he commented, pointing at the keyring which was protruding from the side of the bag. His hands were very dry and there were wrinkles, deep grooves in his skin.

I pulled the keys out and showed him and he stretched out his fingers and touched the worn leather ring.

'Those are her keys,' he said wistfully.

For a moment, just a moment, I entertained the thought that this old man could have been her lover. His eyes were rheumy, but they were a soft brown colour still. And I could see that though his skin was worn and red he might have been handsome in his day. Perhaps he had been driven to his obvious eccentricity by despair. Talking to young girls in the street. Feeding crumbs to the pigeons.

'What was she like?' I asked him gently.

'Old cow,' he smiled. 'Real old cow. I hated her. What do you want to know about her for anyway?' And then, well, I knew he wasn't a ghost. Then I wasn't scared at all.

'When I was little, really small,' I started, because I wanted to explain to him, 'my dad used to take me to visit her but I can't remember her very well.'

'Vain old bitch,' he laughed. 'Tick tock, tick tock, trying to turn the clock back. Loved her clocks more than anything. Tinkered away all day with those clocks. She smelled of aniseed too. Used to buy aniseed balls and munch on them, working late. Made her breath smell. Her husband, old Tom, used to shout at her. Wouldn't kiss her for the aniseed. They were always having fights about that.'

'Tom?' I encouraged him.

'Very dapper gent,' the old guy smiled. 'Foreigner. A war hero. He fought at Sebastopol. Got a medal and everything.'

'And they argued? Weren't they happy?'

'Happy? You don't know about people, do you? You never can tell, but he had a temper, that much I do know and he hated those aniseed balls. Only married her to stay in the country. That's what everyone said. Younger than she was and good-looking too. A gent. Not like old Molly. She drove him to the drink. My mother used to do for her. Cleaned that filthy old shop of hers for years. Used to scrub the steps no matter how cold it was. Till the old cow fired her. Years she'd worked there, and Ma Polinski just threw her out one day. On her ear. Mum had never broken anything before. Wasn't even broken properly. Just chipped. It wasn't fair.'

'What was it?' I asked.

'I don't know. Some old plate or something. Stupid old bitch used to stack them far too precariously. You'd walk past and the piles would creak. Bloody thing would have toppled over anyway. Shaky. I never liked her. That old cow just gave my mum a couple of quid and told her not to come back again ever. Twenty years she'd worked there. Three times a week.' And he grinned at me, crazy old guy. 'November 1968,' he smiled as if he was proud of his long memory. 'It was a Friday.'

We chatted for a bit, but really he didn't have anything else he could tell me and after a while we

95

walked out again on to the High Street and he shook my hand.

'Very pleased to meet you,' he said, 'very pleased indeed.'

And I grinned at him and nodded.

'Goodbye,' I said and as I walked off I realised that researching modern history isn't as easy as ancient. Maybe that imagination of mine was just constantly being undermined so that things couldn't be consistent for me, not the way I would have liked. Time hadn't smoothed out the inconsistencies. One way or another, things definitely weren't falling into place nicely and I felt really frustrated because I still had no idea at all why she had left me the money. Not even an inkling. I wasn't for giving up though. She was just so interesting, so quirky. Firing her cleaning lady for smashing a plate, or pulling away a councillor's hanky so he got his hand all snotty. After all those years that old tramp still had fire in his voice when he talked about her. He still hated her, whereas I, from the records, could only dig up good things – her crusade to save the Old Town most of all.

I was beginning to think that Ma Polinski went down better for posterity than she ever had done in person. It can't have been easy for her. She'd had to fight every step of the way to keep her shop, even just to stock it, in fact. She'd fought for her seat on the council and she'd fought the majority view the whole of the time she was there. And, looking back on it, she was right. She really was. But no one seemed to actually like her. She might have been right, but she wasn't amenable. And that day as I walked up the road I felt quite hopeless really, quite lost. I thought I hadn't made any progress at all but looking back on it, I suppose that as I wandered away from the Canongate Kirk that Saturday I had already completely discounted the idea that perhaps she had left me the money just to be nice. She wasn't a nice kind of person. She didn't do nice things. Everything I could find out about her had a stern kind of purpose to it. A reason. I suppose I had been harbouring the suspicion that I had been a dalliance for her, a frippery, a whim. But she just wasn't like that – she was deadly practical, and not at all romantic. And at least that was some kind of progress, even if I had only arrived at it by elimination. Anyway, I realised that I couldn't go any further without meeting someone who actually knew her well. Someone sane and relatively uninvolved. And I figured that my best bet at that was probably Mike Williams' uncle and there wasn't really anything I could do about that until Monday. So I abandoned the Royal Mile and wandered back down to Princes Street, staring in the shop windows as I passed. Putting things in boxes in my head. Tidying up. Ma Polinski – Monday. Tell the family after that and then a glorious celebration with Nina. A cocktail party. A weekend somewhere glamorous. A round of pints in our local pub. It was getting cold so I nipped into Jenners on the corner and bought myself a cardigan in the ladies' department on the second floor, just because I could. It was soft red chenille and I paid for it with my credit card, safe in the knowledge that there was still about half of the money which Mike Williams had sent languishing in my account. I felt very free. Kind of confident. Everything was planned in my head.

'I'll wear it,' I told the sales lady and she helped me put it on in front of a long hinged mirror. I pulled it around me, and rubbed my arms through the velvety wool.

'That really suits you,' she commented and handed me my jacket and my bag. I stared at my reflection for a second or two, swaddled in luxury, pleased with myself that the rich red of the cardigan suited the deep brown colour of my hair. I took the back stairs down to the ground floor, came out through the men's department on to St David's Street and caught a cab back to Simon's place where I went upstairs to have a shower. The boys had left me a message on the kitchen table with instructions, so that night I met Simon and Scotty at eight thirty and we ate Chinese food at the Kweilin on Dundas Street and I just enjoyed myself and set Ma Polinski aside. I might have worn the cardigan I'd bought with her money but for the rest of the weekend I didn't think about her or what she'd left me any more.

Chapter Nine

That Sunday I went over to Mum and Dad's for the whole afternoon and played gin rummy for matchsticks sitting in the big bay window of their vast living room where they had sat to play cards and stare out at the wind in the green-yellow leaves of the beech trees in their front garden since I was a child. I stuck to my resolution and I didn't ask them any more about Ma Polinski because apart from anything else, I didn't want to arouse any suspicions and also, well, I knew that when I did decide to tell them that if I'd spent weeks asking questions about her, well, they'd feel really resentful, as if I'd played them for fools. It was almost a relief, actually, to just concentrate hard on winning as many matchsticks as I could and then building them into delicate towers on the green felt surface of the card table. It was like being a kid again, all safe. Afterwards I sat on the phone for ages to Nina and we laughed like drains. She'd hurt her toe hiking right across some peninsula where the views had been great. I made a couple of other calls. Old friends in Edinburgh. Just gossip. Nothing special. And after that there was chicken and salad for supper and we all watched the news together before Mum ran me back into town in her car. It was a pedestrian sort of Sunday afternoon, and it felt completely normal. I hugged her as she dropped me off and she had a comforting, familiar smell. Honey and lavender. I breathed in deeply.

'Night-night, dear,' she smiled.

And as I wandered down to Stockbridge to play pool for an hour or two, just like I used to on Sundays when I lived at home, I assured myself that Mum and Dad didn't suspect a thing. I'd pick the right time to tell them what had happened, I told myself, and they would be glad. It was a lot of money, after all. It was a massive piece of good luck and I looked back on the day we'd spent together and convinced myself that money didn't really matter to them, that they were more concerned with chicken and salad and games of cards. I potted more balls than ever before. I was, after all, on form, and I slept well that Sunday night and I was sure that the next day would bring me some answers. And it did, though unlike pool or cards it wasn't easy and the answers only raised questions of their own.

On Monday morning, Simon went to the airport early to catch the Geneva flight so he could view that sale he'd been talking about the week before. He left me a croissant and a cooling cup of coffee on the kitchen table before he went and knocked on my bedroom door to whisper a hushed goodbye. I got up slowly, and then I walked downstairs, luxuriating in the atmosphere of his authentically dark-walled hallway and watching the sunlight fall on to the floor of each of his rooms as I wandered barefoot around the beautiful house, trying to make things clear in my mind. I observed myself in the huge gilded mirrors in the living room as I sipped my coffee and curled up on Simon's red velvet *chaise-longue* contemplating the new and sudden possibility of my own plush *chaise-longue*, in my own spacious living room. And as I stared at myself I remember realising with surprise that, even in a pair of Simon's blue cotton pyjamas, I looked like an expensively kept woman these days. Maybe it was because Simon chose his pyjamas to match the colour of his (and my) eyes. But then maybe it was just because I was feeling kind of smug. The reality of what had happened was just about sinking in around then, a whole ten days after I first found out about Ma Polinski's bequest. There was the thrill, of course, that money brings with it. The shopping list which I was working through bit by bit in my mind. The little items I wanted to buy, and the big ones too. That wasn't all though. It seems weird to say it, but I realised that this money was my first ever secret. Of course, there were things I hadn't told my family before. The occasional unsuitable boyfriend. The time at college when I blew the whole of my allowance for the term on a wild, lost weekend and had to get a job waiting tables so that I could eat until the next payment came in. They weren't secrets, though. Not real secrets. They were indiscretions. Secrets are much more powerful than that – they give you the ability to hurt people. To shock them. They give you the ability to bestow confidences, to choose favourites. To change the balance of power. And for once I was on the inside. I was in the driver's seat and I decided that it didn't suit me – it didn't really feel comfortable. It was my parents' job to be the keepers of great secrets, not mine. And I think I realised then that it was a lonely occupation and, well, I'm not really one to go things absolutely alone. 'I'll find out all I can today,' I told myself, reverting to my plan as if it was a mantra, 'and then I'll tell them everything. Next weekend I'll come through from Glasgow and Mum and Dad and Simon and I will sit in the kitchen at the Grange and I'll just tell them the story. This old lady left me her money because she was trying to get back at her husband. This old lady left me her money because she had no children of her own and she was lonely. This old lady left me her money for some old reason or other that I haven't figured out yet. She was quite, quite mad. And it's not going to change my life. I'm keeping my job. But I am going to buy myself a great big house and a car. And some presents for you.' Now all I needed to find was the reason and then, I told myself, I'd be comfortable at last. Then I'd have no problem about coming clean. Then I'd manage to keep my family round me. Then, well, I'd understand everything. I was terrified. Of course I was. I'd have come up with any reason not to tell them because when you speak up, speak out, stand up, in my family, well, it's a betrayal, that's all. And I was afraid they might say, 'You can't be part of us any more. You reneged on our plan for you. We don't love you. We never loved you all along.' It's crazy, I know. But looking back on it that was what I was thinking. That's exactly why I was so scared. Why it took me so long, though I'd never have admitted it even to myself.

I left my empty mug in the kitchen sink and I went upstairs to get changed. In his absence, I borrowed a great shirt from Simon's wardrobe. An Issey Miyake, white cotton, men's shirt and I pulled on my own jeans and then spent ages staring at myself in the bathroom mirror fiddling with my hair and flossing my teeth. Trying to make myself look like I'd earned it.

When I was finally ready I walked through town to Heriot Row again, to call in to the lawyer's office. It was ten o'clock when I arrived there ready to do battle with Ma Polinski's memory. Ready to sort out some facts. I didn't have an appointment. I sat down in the hallway to wait, but Mike came trotting obediently down the stairs too quickly, before I could even really settle in my seat, and he ushered me eagerly into one of the interview rooms. It had taken him about thirty seconds from the time the receptionist had used the intercom to tell him that I was there which is certainly faster than I have ever been seen by a professional in my life.

'Miss White,' he grinned. 'Did you get the money all right?'

'Yes,' I smiled right back. 'I spent it all too,' I lied because I knew it would put him at his ease.

'So,' he indicated for me to take a seat opposite him. 'You want a weekly allowance?'

'No,' I shook my head. 'No. I wondered if it might be possible to meet with your uncle. I want to ask him some questions about my benefactor.'

Mike dropped his head. 'My uncle is retired, Miss White. He doesn't work here any more. If you have any questions I'd be glad to relay them to him and let you know what he says.'

'I have a million questions,' I mumbled. 'At least. All relating to why she might have left me such a huge sum of money.'

'It happens,' Mike smiled at me. 'People leave bequests all the time.'

'If I could speak to your uncle,' I pushed him, 'it would really put my mind to rest.'

Mike got up and ran his fingers through his hair. He stared out of the window for a moment before deciding to come clean and be frank with me.

'My uncle won't remember anything in any kind of detail. He doesn't exactly make much sense any more, I'm afraid. He's eighty-nine and he has Alzheimer's.'

'I'm sorry,' I said. 'I didn't think. It didn't occur to me.'

'That's all right,' Mike smiled. 'He's my great-uncle really. He founded the company, you know. Worked every day right up to his eighty-fifth birthday. But he is very ill. Rapid deterioration. He can't remember anything much, nowadays. He can't even eat on his own or anything. He's in a home in Juniper Green. They can look after him properly there. I'm sorry. He won't be able to help you. He doesn't even know who any of us are most of the time, and we're family.'

'I just hoped that he might know why she'd done it,' I said quietly. 'That's all. It doesn't matter.'

It felt like history was shutting down on me. Retreating from the memories of people who had been alive at the same time as Ma Polinski. The vital elements of first-hand accounts. The information which I needed from people who I'd hoped would be more sane than the man with the pigeons. Mike Williams stayed silent. I don't think he really knew quite what to say.

'Well,' I carried on eventually, because by this stage I was getting quite determined, 'maybe you could show me the catalogues, the papers, all your files about her. Maybe I'll find something in there.'

And he just nodded and left the room to go and organise it.

It took half an hour to fetch everything from the basement and when the boxes did come up they covered the whole of the table. Mike looked kind of smug. I don't think he realised that I'm used to sifting my way through lots of information. It's part of my job. Something like that would faze most people because when you start, it just seems like the most enormous task imaginable. All those papers, all that detail.

'Coffee?' Mike offered me.

'Yes,' I mumbled. 'Coffee.'

And I began to systematically work my way through everything. Thirteen boxes. Lucky for some.

The papers relating to the auction sale were interesting but didn't really tell me anything that I didn't know already. However, they did kind of hammer home the fact that she had the most amazing stock, 34,853 items of which went into the sale at Fulham's of Charlotte Street. There were a 180 silver snuffboxes alone. And 562 clocks and watches including four original carriage clocks by Le Roy of Paris and even a pair of bracket clocks by Tompion which went for an absolute fortune. There were also seven old Swiss pocket watches by Breuget. It was a hell of a collection. The documentation took up eight of the thirteen boxes and I looked at every page, studied every photograph in the catalogues. The pieces which had come out of her house were lovely – there were wall-mounted shell cameos of mermaids and princesses, which are the eighteenth-century cameos carved by Italian apprentices before they became master carvers. She had Elspeth Buchanan watercolours in Georgian, Parisian, gilded pine frames and box-mounted painted fans with carved mother-of-pearl and ivory handles. It all seemed strangely at odds with the painting on her bedroom ceiling. I moved on. There was a box containing information about the money I had inherited. Details of where investments had been made for me – shares bought in blue-chip companies, money kept in off shore accounts, fees deducted annually for the services of Mike's great uncle, and in the last four years or so, for the services of Mike himself.

At twelve thirty, Mike Williams dutifully delivered a sandwich and a mineral water. I think he had expected me to give up by then and I got the feeling that he was taking me more seriously because I was just getting on with the job.

'I won't disturb you,' he said and closed the door behind him gently.

The next box I opened contained deeds for her properties. The provenance of the shop on Muir's Pend stretched back through her first husband's family for over 150 years. Before that it had been a bootmakers. The house out at Morbrax she had bought in 1945. For herself it would seem, because her first husband was long dead by then and she hadn't met Tomasz Polinski yet. He didn't even enter the country until the following year. I don't know where she lived before she moved to Morbrax. There was no indication – on the deeds her address was given as 5 Muir's Pend, but I can't imagine that she'd have lived in the shop although that isn't impossible. Maybe things had been tight for her early on. Maybe those antiques dealers had given her a run for her money. After I'd finished my lunch I decided to clear up a bit. So, one by one I hauled the boxes I'd finished with off the table and stacked them up at the door ready to go back to the basement. It gave me more room to spread things out.

The other documents ranged right through her life. She was extraordinarily litigious and had sued people left, right and centre for about ten years solid after her first husband had died. Perhaps it was the grief or maybe, like Dad had said, she was just incredibly cantankerous. But then she had stopped suddenly at the end of the Second World War, and there were no more notices of lawyers' consultation fees until the mid 1950s when she took up the case of Tomasz Polinski, the Romanian Pole whose parents had moved north from Bucharest towards the Volga Basin and had settled, on the way, in Lvov, where he had been raised. Before she married Tomasz Polinski, Molly Savage had engaged her lawyers on his behalf to defend him when he was under investigation by the Foreign Office who questioned the post-war entry visa which he had used to come and live in the UK after fighting under General Anders in North Africa. He had also, it seemed, served in Italy, helping to capture Monte Cassino from the Nazis. There had been great losses in taking the monastery fortress and by the time the Poles had taken on the job many other regiments had been decimated in the attempt. Those who survived the war were awarded British citizenship as a reward. But in the fifties, the Foreign Office had questioned Tomasz Polinski's credentials and he had had to fight once more, this time for his right to stay in the country. He had married old Molly Savage in December 1957 and that put an end to the debate. I wondered perhaps if the crazy pigeon man had been right about their marriage. Tomasz Polinski was ten years younger than his new wife. And, judging from the photographs which I found in among the papers, he was beautiful in a kind of smooth, 1950s lounge bar kind of way. They seemed an odd couple – she with her baggy cardigans and he in his wide-cut, pale-grey trouser suits and little thin moustache. After 1957, they had travelled a lot together and whenever they went away Ma Polinski would deposit a set of keys with her lawyer for safe keeping in case of trouble at her shop. And because of this there was an accurate record of when and where they had gone. It read like a list of the great antiques auctions of the period. The contact numbers a string of five-star hotels all over the world. And then, in the final box, the records of their deaths. In a hired car, while in Brazil attending a sale of jewellery, they had driven up into the Brazilian Highlands, staying quite near the coast, exploring the mountains right along the Serra da Mantiqueira. Tomasz was at the wheel, Ma Polinski right beside him. They had died instantaneously on impact, plunging off a difficult bend in the low mountain road and falling down into a steep valley below. It had been raining heavily and the verdant summertime countryside had been covered in mud but when the car burst into flames it had burned for a long time until the petrol in the engine had run out and the bodies were charred and almost unrecognisable. Mike's great-uncle had gone to São Paulo himself to arrange for their safe return. It had taken some weeks to ship them home and all the export papers in Portuguese were filed away carefully. They didn't tell me too much. After that Mr and Mrs Polinski were buried in separate graves, side by side, at the cemetery at Morbrax. I cursed myself that I hadn't checked in the church while I was there. I would have liked to have seen the gravestones which had been erected eighteen months after their interment. The receipts for those were, rather fittingly, the last thing in the last box. *Here lies Molly Savage. Born 25 April 1909. Died 18 June 1978*. She had been sixty-nine years old. I had been only five.

At four thirty, Mike knocked respectfully on the door and came into the room. The place was awash with papers.

'Any luck?' he asked.

'Well,' I grinned. 'My main question is this second husband of hers. Was it a love match?'

'Let me see,' Mike asked, and I passed him one of the newspaper clippings.

'Couldn't have been, could it?' he smiled.

And I had to wonder. They were such an odd-looking couple. And she hadn't used his name. She had left me the money in the name Molly Savage, not Molly Polinski, although that had been what everyone else seemed to call her. Married names – a social minefield. But, I thought to myself, I bet there weren't many women in the fifties and sixties who didn't take their husband's name as a matter of course.

'Fancy a drink?' Mike asked me.

'Yeah,' I said. 'Yeah. I do.'

We left the room for some poor trainee clerk to deal with and we blew the office and walked down the hill to the Cumberland, which wasn't busy yet, because it was still so early. Mike had a whisky and soda and I ordered a pint of stout. I felt that I needed something substantial. Reading all those files had really taken it out of me. Mike paid for the drinks and chose us a table and I padded around after him, walking in his footsteps, allowing myself to be looked after. He carried both the drinks from the bar, set them down on a table, took off his jacket and rolled up his sleeves as if he was limbering up for something rather energetic, some kind of hard work. He took a deep breath.

'I hope you don't mind me saying this,' he started slowly, 'but why don't you just live off the money? Why aren't you enjoying this?'

I didn't know quite what to say. I mean, I didn't really know the answer to his question, and besides, he was my lawyer and I have a natural wariness about lawyers. It was rather candid of him to ask anything like that at all and I shifted uncomfortably in my seat. He had chosen us one of the hard oak benches in the front section of the pub.

'I'm suspicious,' I admitted and I started to sip from my glass. 'Some old lady leaves me a fortune for no apparent reason. It just doesn't tie up for me. I'm suspicious. And I suppose that I won't feel right about accepting it until I know why on earth she did it. What she expected.'

'You think she's got some plan for you? From beyond the grave? From twenty odd years ago?' he teased.

'I know. I'm crazy. I'm nuts. Anyone else I know would just throw their hat in the air and buy lots of new clothes.'

Mike eyed Simon's Issey Miyake shirt. 'New?' he enquired.

'Kinda.'

'Looks nice.'

I ignored that. I just didn't think Mike Williams' sartorial approval counted for much, I guess.

'Well,' I said, 'I don't know. I'd just like a reason. I mean, she doesn't give any reason in her will. And it seems to me, well, if it was me, I would want to leave the child a letter. A letter of good wishes. A card to go with the present. Don't you think?'

Mike took a swig of his whisky.

'My wife,' he said, 'had a bequest last year. An old uncle. It wasn't eight million pounds of course. But it was a nice tidy sum nonetheless. Unexpected. Entirely without reason.'

'An old uncle doesn't need a reason. A stranger does,' I pointed out.

'What do your friends say?' he asked me.

I pushed my forefinger through the thick, creamy foam of the beer and brought it up to my lips.

'I didn't tell anyone yet,' I admitted.

'What?'

I shrugged my shoulders. 'It just didn't feel right,' I said by way of an explanation.

Mike laughed. It was an unexpected laugh. An incredulous, boyish giggle. 'No one at all?' he asked. 'Don't you have a boyfriend or something? Isn't there anyone special you want to tell?'

'No, no one,' I said cagily because, well, I was understandably defensive. I mean, I wanted to tell people, but I just couldn't.

He stared at me for a second and I couldn't even hold his gaze. He had a five-o'clock shadow which made him look a lot less like a little boy than he had the week before, or even when I had arrived that morning. And well, when a lawyer talks to you directly it's kind of disarming, never mind a lawyer who you don't really like much. Someone who comes from such a different kind of world and asks the right questions. The ones that cut straight to the heart of the thing.

'Take my advice. Take it easy, Rachel. You should enjoy it,' he said smugly.

And I realised that if I was going to dig into this, if I was really going to find out why she left me all that money, I'd have to contend with the Mike Williamses of the world. That I'd have to want that knowledge with a real sense of purpose. And, I suppose, I realised that I did want it that way. The whole thing zoomed into focus. I needed a reason to bring home. I needed to know why so that I could tell my family. So it wouldn't be my fault. So I could explain. There are some things you know without thinking too hard. There are some things which are just gut instinct and make absolute sense when you realise them. Like when you're testing pearls by running them across your teeth and you just know from the gritty feel whether they are natural pearls or whether they are cultured. There isn't a way to measure it. But you know that the cultured pearls are too smooth. And Mike Williams' just lie-back-and-enjoy-it attitude was way too smooth for me and I just wanted to get rid of him.

'OK. I'll try to have fun,' I smiled. And just at that moment I hoped that it wouldn't be too long before I'd be able to tell Nina, before the whole thing was, as I saw it, out of the way. I desperately wanted her take on what had happened. Mike Williams was sitting back in his seat. I think he thought that we'd just bonded, that him telling me how I ought to feel was a form of communication. I lifted my glass to him as if I was toasting and I drank as much of the beer as I could.

'Thanks for the drink,' I said, smiling, and it was clear that I wanted to leave.

We walked back up Dundas Street just as everyone else seemed to be walking down. It was nearly five thirty and the offices were emptying out. Four number 23 buses passed us, all of them full, crawling up the hill in the heavy traffic.

'So? Any instructions?' Mike asked me just before he was about to turn off along Heriot Row again to go back to the office.

'Another two thousand, please,' I said. But it was only to put his mind at rest really. It was only to get rid of him. Though later on it did come in handy, I suppose. I shook his hand firmly and waved him off and then I walked up towards Queen Street and bravely turned right towards Simon's, feeling that I'd done the right thing. At least by then I was determined. At least I'd begun to see why I wanted it so badly. From time to time, walking through the city, I could have sworn she was with me. All that day and many days after. A ghost of my very own. A spirit. An angel. So much happened last year it seems breathtaking. And not just Ma Polinski either. All sorts of things happened. But if it hadn't been for Ma Polinski I wouldn't have been in Edinburgh that Monday. And that Monday, that April holiday Monday, well, even Ma Polinski aside, I had a bit of a seminal evening.

Chapter Ten

When I got back to Simon's flat I had intended to pack up my bag and catch one of the evening trains through to Glasgow. Simon had left a list with alarm codes and instructions because he wasn't due back from Geneva till the following day, so I walked back there all set to pick up my stuff and set the locks on Simon's fortress. I figured I'd have to give up on Ma Polinski for another week or so and I toyed with the idea of running some newspaper ads to try to find people who knew her and I was calm by the time I turned the corner into the street and saw that Scotty was sitting on the stone doorstep waiting for me. He was wearing some of Simon's old clothes: a stretched cable-knit jumper and a pair of long-discarded chinos. He had a Tesco bag full of what he claimed to be the ingredients of dinner sitting in between his legs, and I realised that I wouldn't be going back to the west coast that evening as planned. I was surprised at how glad I was to see him. We went inside and when we emptied the bag out on the kitchen table it turned out to contain three bars of chocolate, some frozen raspberries, a packet of pink and white marsh-mallows and a pot of double cream. Together we hit Simon's wine closet and put a bottle of his Baumes de Venise into the freezer to chill and then I ferreted around the cupboards until I found a fondue set. Chocolate fondue with marshmallows and raspberries.

'Scotty,' I grinned. 'You really are brilliant.'

'Ready, steady, cook,' he beamed back at me with one eye on the clock to see if we might manage to do it in twenty minutes, just like they do on TV.

And while we were waiting for the chocolate to melt so that we could beat it into a pool of cherry brandy, and while we were waiting for the wine to get all cold and delicious, Scotty played Simon's baby grand piano for me in one of the downstairs rooms. 'Highland Cathedral' over and over. I kicked off my sandals and stood by the sash windows watching the light fade out of the spring sky and thinking about Ma Polinski and about Fate – how some things are just meant to happen – and when Scotty finished playing and quietly closed the lid over the keys I realised that the music had made my heart flutter.

He came over and leaned against the other side of the window frame and we stood there for a moment in silence, fringed by the heavy gold brocade of the green velvet curtains. His eyes were steady.

'I've something to tell you,' he smiled. 'I should have told you before.' And he brushed his hair behind his ear and, for a second, he moved just like my brother.

I wished really hard for something to burn in the kitchen, for the phone to ring or the doorbell to go. Anything. Anything but more secrets which I'd have to keep. But there was another moment's silence and then he moved in front of the glass panes across the window towards me and he kissed me full on the lips. And, to be honest, I kissed him back. I couldn't help myself.

Popular psychology has it that you never do anything without a reason. That all your actions are for some kind of purpose even if you're not aware of it. And whether they're Freudian or Jungian or whatever, psychiatrists and counsellors all seem to agree these days that that is probably true. It's an interesting theory. I mean, what reasons could I possibly have had for kissing Scotty right back? Apart from the obvious ones. His deep green eyes and his shy familiar grin. The way I could hear his heart pounding as he pushed himself against me, sandwiching me tight up against the open shutters, catching my head on the edge of the velvet curtains. The way I was so excited I could hardly breathe. Maybe I wanted to hurt Simon. Maybe I was beginning to get off on the power of the secrets thing. Maybe I was ready to move further away from my family than I ever had before. Maybe I'd always wanted to kiss him, because it felt so right. After he'd kissed me for a bit he stood back and we smiled at each other, grinning ridiculously. I really didn't know what to say. He reached out and took my hand.

'Wanted to do that for a long time,' he admitted. 'Ten years at least.'

And I laughed. We went into the kitchen together and we feasted ourselves on the melted chocolate and we talked about nothing in particular for a while, kissing in between. The fondue tasted amazing – sweet and fresh at the same time. And then, as we finished the last of the wine, Scotty leaned forward. He put out his hand and ran his finger along my cheek, around my ear and down my neck, stopping at the little hollow at my shoulder.

'I'm serious about this, you know,' he said. 'I've thought about it for a long time, Rachel. I know there'll be a fuss. I don't think they treat you right. They never have. You're amazing.'

And when he said that my lip began to quiver.

'Do you think?' I whispered as big tears rolled down my cheeks and I let go completely.

'Yeah,' Scotty said, 'I really do.'

And it felt amazing for someone to have faith in me like that. To feel appreciated. Who'd have thought it of Scotty? Perfect timing really.

You see what I mean, though, don't you? 1998 – the

year I got haunted, the year I got rich and the year I hooked up with my brother's best friend. So much seemed to be happening so fast and I was blissfully, blissfully happy along with my nervousness. So many changes, you see. A lot of things to take in.

Scotty downed the last of his glass and then he took my hand and pulled me out into the hallway and around the base of the banister with a fluid, childlike enthusiasm.

'Don't cry,' he said and he tugged at my arm. He wanted to go up the stairs.

'No,' I said, far too firmly to mean it, as if I was trying to teach a naughty puppy that its behaviour wasn't acceptable. 'No.'

'Don't be silly. We're not going to bed,' he replied. 'Come on. I want to show you something up here. You'll like it.'

He held me for a moment there at the bottom of the stairs and I brushed my tears away and swayed slightly on the thick, deep red carpet. I don't think I've ever felt so safe. Then I followed him kind of unwillingly upstairs into the hallway where he opened the door of the laundry cupboard.

'Come on,' he smiled and he climbed like a green-eyed cat up the slatted shelves, pushing open a trapdoor in the ceiling which I had never even noticed before. And then he hauled himself up into the dirty, brick-walled attic where he opened a skylight window and climbed up again, though this time out on to the roof. I followed him like a disciple and he dutifully pulled me out each time behind him and led me along carefully to a dip in the slatework where he crouched down. He is very strong, Scotty. He has very strong arms. As I sat down on the smooth tar, I could see right over the Forth estuary. Right over to Fife. In the other direction I could just make out the top of the black stone of Castle Rock, lit up by the spotlights from

Princes Street Gardens. Scotty put his arms around me to keep me warm and I nestled into him. And again it felt like I belonged there. I wasn't excited any more. I wasn't exultant or crazy. It just felt absolutely natural. I think I was totally calm. That's the way I remember it. I couldn't understand why I hadn't realised before that it was the perfect thing, and we sat there for ages the two of us, sealed together in the silence feeling perfectly together until I said, 'It's beautiful.'

'The best bit of Simon's house,' Scotty nodded laying his head back and breathing in the cool evening air. The sky was clear and there were lots and lots of stars and when he kissed me again he still tasted of the melted chocolate.

'I didn't even know this was here. I didn't know we could get up on to the roof,' I said.

'Neither does Simon,' Scotty grinned.

And at that moment for some reason I knew that whatever else happened, whatever came up, that I could deal with it. I was absolutely certain that everything was going to be all right. I was in love.

Chapter Eleven

Between the Ma Polinski conundrum and Scotty's chocolate kisses, well, the west didn't seem to have quite so much to offer. But I caught the seven o'clock train back to work nonetheless. I was being a good girl, you see. I wasn't ready yet to make too many breaks. It had been quite a weekend. When I woke up (and for the record, I woke up alone) I spent a long time trying to figure out if I'd dreamed about the chocolate fondue and the kiss in front of the window and the view from the top of the house, never mind the eight million pounds I'd inherited out of nowhere.

'Fate,' I thought, 'is dealing me rather a lot of cards all at once.'

Scotty had said good night around midnight. He had helped me down from the roof, trailing me back to the downstairs hallway where we had kissed for a long time in the huge dark arc of the open door, my heart pounding nearly as much as I had felt his hammering away too. After he left I had stood in the window of the front room and I watched him as he made his way down the street, turning southwards finally, up the hill towards his own home. When he had gone I had sunk down on to the thick, pale carpet with an inane grin on my face and I had stared at the full moon for nearly an hour. I had an awful lot to take in, but it didn't disturb me at all. 'I'm blessed,' I thought to myself. 'It's destiny.' Then I pictured sitting Simon and Mum and Dad down and saying 'Well, I've two things to tell you' and I wasn't sure which of the things would shock them more. I wasn't perturbed any more, though. Not at all. I was blissful. I felt like I was in the grip of warm, safe arms and I didn't have to take responsibility for anything on my own any more. Scotty is a very calming influence even though he'd kind of hit me like a ton of bricks.

After that, I had as good as floated upstairs and into my bed where I slept for five hours solid, going to sleep and waking up with the same tingling excitement in the base of my spine. In the morning, once I had come to the inevitable conclusion that I hadn't dreamed the whole thing, I just shrugged my shoulders, tidied up my things hurriedly and ran to make the train. I was in my office at the museum at half past eight and I turned on my computer screen and started to write the text for the exhibit. The founding of the Russian Orthodox Church and the trade routes to the Baltic Sea took up all my concentration. I wasn't even thinking about anything else really. It was as if I was on automatic pilot and everything was suddenly, miraculously settled, as if I had nothing at all to figure out, only things to be getting on with. I got a lot done. At lunchtime I tried to ring Nina but they said she wouldn't be back till after two thirty, so instead I walked into town and sat in Bar Ten like some kind of observer from a higher plane. I just stared at what was going on around me, people having their lunch, couples talking, guys in second-hand jeans up at the bar drinking beer from the bottle. I felt so far away from that, so separate that it made me laugh, but I suppose I knew then I would be going back to Edinburgh for sure. Even if I wasn't entirely compos mentis, and even if it all moved very quickly, I honestly knew then that, whatever happened, I belonged with Scotty. Those strong, guiding arms still had a grip of me and well, it took Ma Polinski to knock me out of them. To instill, strangely enough, some responsibility into me. To ground me. Comforting arms aren't for real girls after all – real girls have arms of their own and stand steady on their own two feet. I moved back to Edinburgh all right, to be with him. But when I moved back I had my own life there. In the end I made my own decisions, which is the important thing.

That Monday, though, I was out of it and with Nina away from her desk at the Burrell I had no one but Ma Polinski to haul me back down to earth. After lunch I walked the twenty minutes back to work still dazed as ever and when I got there, there was a message from my father which someone had scrawled on a Post-it note and stuck to my desk. *Ring home*, it said. For a second I was nervous. My pulse rate went up. Dad never rings me at work. It was a bolt from the blue really. A jolt to my system. I panicked for a moment or two that I'd been rumbled. That Dad knew about one or other of my secrets. 'What have I been doing all day?' I thought and I realised that once you've been kissed like Scotty kissed me, well, it doesn't half distract you. But then I assured myself that Dad couldn't really have found out about anything and I made myself settle down, got myself an outside line and rang him back to see what he wanted. The phone rang three or four times before he picked it up.

'It's me, Dad,' I said.

'Hi, doll,' he replied joyfully. He is always very bluff on the telephone. 'Just spoke to Simon and I thought I'd ring you. You know you were asking about Ma Polinski the other day – that stuff that went missing – well, Simon bought a piece yesterday at the sale and I saw it this morning. It was one of her things.'

My heart skipped a beat at that and I was right back in there, right back on track.

'God, Dad, are you sure?' I asked, kind of breathless,

because this was very important. This was real. Just before I left home I remember walking in on my mum in the kitchen. She was cooking and the house smelled of frying onions and that, I suppose, was what had brought me downstairs. I stood in the doorway between the kitchen and the hall and I remember just watching Mum while she was having a conversation with someone who wasn't there. She was talking in German, so I couldn't understand what she was saying into the thin air, but when I say that she was having a conversation I mean it. She was listening to almost silent answers, disagreeing with what whoever-it-was was saying. I could hear a whispering too. A reply. She was, quite simply, talking to a ghost. It spooked me a bit at the time and I hung back. I sneaked off. Now, with Dad on the phone, telling me that out of the blue one of the lost treasures from Ma Polinski's safe had surfaced, well, I had the same spooky feeling. The old woman was talking to me. Indirectly perhaps, but well, she was making her point nonetheless.

'Are you sure, Dad?' I repeated.

'Yeah,' Dad laughed. 'Just thought it was strange. You mentioning it and then something turning up. Don't feel like mentioning a big pair of Sèvres vases going cheap, do you?' he joked. But I was intent. The contents of Ma Polinski's safes were certainly the key to something.

'What did Simon buy?' I asked him. 'Do you know what it is?'

Dad ignored the second question. He knows what everything is. 'It's a gold and amethyst necklet,' he replied. 'She bought it at the King Farouk sale in the fifties. Carved amethysts. A real collector's piece. Simon's got a buyer for it already. Some rich Persian family who have settled in Dundee. They got the provenance all wrong in the catalogue. You know what the salerooms are like. He got it very cheaply in my opinion. Anyhow, I just thought you'd like to know.'

'Dad, we should ring the police,' I gushed. 'I mean, this has to mean that it was stolen. It belonged to her and it was stolen. Whoever put it into the auction, well, they could be the thief.'

'Nah,' Dad replied. 'No point. I mean, it would be more trouble than it's worth. Besides, if it is stolen goods, dolly face, they'll take it off Simon. And we definitely don't want that.'

I was stunned. I didn't know quite how to say it, but I did want the necklace taken off Simon because, well, I knew that it meant something and I wanted to fucking know what it was. No question of it. I held it in though. When I hung up I buried my head in my hands and blinked very, very hard trying to take it all in. Trying to figure out why I felt so strongly. It wasn't that the necklace was mine, although technically that was true. If anything was recovered it, by rights, belonged to me. It wasn't exactly that, though. I mean, I had my eight million, which is more than any sane person can spend in any normal life, so it definitely wasn't that. It was a justice thing. I mean, it was like someone robbing a grave. Someone getting away with a murder. Someone lying for their own advantage. It was wrong and there was a little spark inside of me which wanted to right that wrong, and besides that, if I'm honest, it kind of got my goat that Simon had bought himself cheap something which really belonged to me. There was part of me which just screamed inside that he had quite enough of what really belonged to me already.

It was tricky, though, so instead of my anger about that I focused on finding out who had put the necklace up for sale, because whoever they were, they were part of a chain of hands, long or short, which had to lead right back to Ma Polinski. In short, the necklace was a clue. At the museum we had a long list of contacts in the police, in the National Trust, in every conservation and restoration agency in the country. All the people who can help in finding the provenance of unusual items. With this necklace, though, I was on shaky ground. I wasn't sure what the hell to tell them when they picked up the phone. I wasn't sure how on earth I could explain. I didn't even have a list of what I thought had been in the safes, which certainly would be one of the questions anyone who was any good would have asked. All I had was some hearsay and I knew that wasn't enough. Eventually, I lifted my head up out of my hands, and I picked up the phone and, on automatic pilot, I called Simon at work realising that I'd have to follow it up all on my own, try to establish something myself before I could get anyone else involved. He faxed me some pages from the catalogue of the auction which arrived all grainy at my desk ten minutes later. There was a photograph of the necklace and beside that a description and then at the bottom of the paragraph it just said 'Property of the Contessa di Gilberti', and well, it was my only lead so I had to go for that and to my mind going for it meant only one thing. Nina.

My Italian is shocking – there's no two ways about it. All archaeologists speak bits of just about every language going. It's a kind of archaeological joke. You learn to say 'Be careful with that' and 'Dig deeper' and 'Call me a helicopter immediately' in any dialect you care to mention, but unless you really, really specialise and you end up digging in one place and you're there for years and years, you can't carry on any kind of a normal conversation in a foreign language at all. That didn't matter, though, because Nina was due back at work any moment, and well, she's half Italian, like I said. And though I hadn't wanted to involve her at all until I was ready to tell her about Ma Polinski and my incredible good fortune – well, I needed her just then and I knew she'd understand the ins and outs of catalogued lots in the saleroom so I wouldn't have to spend ages explaining what I needed to know. It flickered through my mind at my desk that afternoon that I didn't have to tell her yet, that I could elicit her help and somehow still manage to tell my parents about Ma Polinski before I told anyone else. I decided that it was possible without really thinking it through. But well, I suppose I knew then I was beginning to accept that I needed people around me to help. I knew that I wasn't going to be able to figure it out all on my own and that maybe I'd been on my own too long. And who else but Nina? Like I said, she is my best friend and, well, in the end, you have to trust your best friend, don't you? That's what it's all about and we two have a long history together. It stretches back to Neanderthal Man. You could say that with justification.

Nina is so cool. Sometimes I wonder, because I see other girls with their best friends and they seem to care about a whole mess of different stuff from us. There's something light and frivolous about their friendships. Nina and I – we go deep. She's my best friend, because we have about a million things in common. Apart from the museum thing, on the surface you wouldn't think that Nina and I were that similar. She comes from a huge, close Italian family who emigrated to Scotland in the 1960s and at first in college, well, the only similar trait that we shared was that we were so different from most people who were on our course – people who were very middle class and very settled. There were perhaps fifty or so archaeology students in the college then and there might have been ten of us who were female. If that. But our differences weren't enough to immediately bring us together and I didn't really speak to her all that much in our first year, not till the summer when she was there too on the Tower of Babel dig at Shan Yat and that was where we first really got to be friends. Nina had the camp bed next to mine and we'd sit and talk, whispering after lights out. She'd fall asleep well before I did, of course, and although I never told her about the nightmares I had about the woman we were digging out of the sand, I think that she knew. She seemed to try to stay awake with me for as long as she could. One way or another, that was when we became firm friends, and that was when I realised we had both grown up in families which had a kind of difficult past. Nina's family talked about what happened to them. They talked kind of endlessly, in fact. Why they'd decided to emigrate out of the poverty and political tensions of southern Italy in the early sixties. My parents, of course, didn't talk about their past at all. But without even really discussing it, Nina and I had a bond between us. We felt it. We decided to stay on in Israel for two weeks after the dig had wound up, and we went everywhere – sightseeing, hanging out – together. It was the first time we got really close.

After Shan Yat we were inseparable and in lots of ways we still are. Sometimes I know exactly what she's thinking, and we don't even have to speak. I'll never forget that fortnight we spent together in Israel and the last day of the dig when we were pulling out of the camp in an old grey bus for the last time. We climbed Massada in the blistering heat (which we hardly even noticed after all the time we'd spent digging in the desert). We visited the Holocaust memorial at Yad Vashem and we both cried. We trekked up to the Dome of the Rock in Jerusalem and then we both went to pray at the Wailing Wall. In our last week we hitch-hiked down to Eilat and did some deep-sea diving. Back at home the following term we decided to share a flat together and we got this great Victorian two-bedroom place where we spent some of our happiest times. Nina got a job waitressing in the evenings at the local fish-and-chip shop just off the Meadows. I used to go down really late at night to pick her up and we'd walk home together each with a free poke of chips and a selection of whatever was left over after the sit-in section of the café closed up. We ate little else for the six months that she worked there, frantically saving our money to pay for our summertime excursions around the world, hitch-hiking or flying stand-by from dig to dig.

In our last two years at college we had to specialise and while I chose to go into the jewellery side of artefacts, Nina got big time into textiles and, after college, the first job she got was in Madrid as an assistant in this research lab they have which is the biggest one in the world for the analysis of ancient fabrics. It's amazing what you can find out from the kind of needles that have been used or the way cloth is woven and the way it is dyed. I went to the airport to see her off. There was a big line of us. Her mother was crying into a black handkerchief and her granny was in a wheelchair and I'd turned up with a big bunch of flowers just to say goodbye. I know that her mother thought that she would hardly see Nina again. Nina's three brothers and two sisters, it has to be said, have for the main part been conspicuously disinterested in leaving home. There are six of them and, excepting Nina, all but one still live with their parents. The other evacuee, Nina's elder brother, moved out of home and into a flat around the corner. So when Nina left the country, you can imagine, it was a huge, big deal. Her mother needn't have worried though, because deep down Nina is a home girl (not entirely unlike me) and she lasted all of eighteen months in Madrid away from the bosom of her family. She spent a lot of her time there conducting a crazy love affair with this complete dickhead that she fell for. But eighteen months was enough of all that and when a job in textile conservation came up at the Burrell Collection it really had her name on it.

Anyhow, when I needed to chase up that carved amethyst necklace, the first person I rang was Nina because I was fairly sure that she was the best person to find out about the Contessa di Gilberti although, like I said, I hadn't really figured out what I was going to say to her and how I was going to get away without explaining why I was interested. Nina and I have always somehow just known what was up with each other. We've mostly never had to really spell things out, which always suited me. I mean, I'm used to that. It's how we do it at home. We tend to talk to each other after dark. It's something I've noticed over the years. We talk about our serious things at night and when we talk like that we almost always drink, so stone-cold sober, and in daylight, well, I'm not a good liar and I floundered a bit over what to say because I hadn't planned it. I'd just rung without really thinking it through. I mean, I hardly made it sound casual. I didn't embed it in 'Hope your foot's feeling better, you idiot hiker' or 'Whatchya have for lunch, then?' I just babbled on in there.

'Nina, I need you to make a phone call for me. In Italian,' I started when she answered her extension.

And true to form Nina was up for it. 'Sure,' she laughed. 'What's up?'

I couldn't tell her that so I panicked a little bit. I was sure, absolutely positive that I couldn't tell anyone, you see, until Mum and Dad knew. In a moment of clarity, which came too late, I decided that I should have rung Mike Williams even if I didn't like him, and got him to deal with the whole thing as a disinterested party. But well, Nina was on the phone now and I had to think of something to say to her. There was a pause, which I know she must have thought was kind of strange, then I started in at a hundred miles an hour. I was babbling. This was the first time I'd told a soul anything about what had happened. I was breaking my duck.

'There is a necklace which was sold two days ago in a sale in Geneva which came originally from the King Farouk sale,' I started. 'The provenance of it wasn't picked up properly in the auction house, so the vendor may not even know it was once used by the Egyptian royal family. The woman is Italian and I want to know where she got the necklace, because I'm wondering if she has other stuff from the same sale, or if the person she got it from has any more items.'

I remember Nina pausing too. A momentary pause. It was something which someone who wasn't used to the way we usually spoke to each other might hardly have noticed. And then she spoke.

'Sure,' she said. 'No problem.'

'Thanks. I'll fax you over everything.' I wondered if the relief I felt showed in my voice.

I told myself that it wasn't exactly a lie. That it wasn't really as easy as that. Not as cut and dried. It was expedient, though. And Nina doesn't only speak Italian but is charming with it, so I figured some kind of explanation from the Contessa was probably in the bag.

'Why don't we go to Vittorio's tonight?' I suggested. Vittorio's is this great Italian café just around the corner from the Variety pub where we go once a week or so to eat cheap pasta and nurse capuccinos and big red wines into the wee small hours and discuss absolutely everything. 'My treat.'

'Eight thirty,' Nina agreed. 'I'll do my best to come up with something by then. See you there.'

Chapter Twelve

Since she got her job at the Burrell, Nina wears a lot of black. I don't quite know if that's because lace shows up particularly well against it, and in her capacity as textile conservator extraordinaire she spends a lot of time with lace, or if they did something to her sense of colour in Madrid, or what. But she has this one black trouser suit and it's never off her back. She bought the material for it in a flea market in Paris when we were (rather glamorously) passing through one Sunday. It was our last summer at college and we were on our way back to the UK and had landed ourselves stand-by tickets as far as Charles de Gaulle. We were tired after a whole summer of digging and, as I remember it, we were pretty broke. I guess we must have looked a bit of a sight as well – grit under our nails no doubt, workmen's hands and a dark, dark tan on uncared-for skin. We were probably wearing our least dirty clothes by then and we were marooned. We couldn't get a cheap flight out of Paris for twenty-four hours so we wandered around, ending up at La Pousse where Nina found this bolt of fabric laid out on the ground on one of the grubby, downmarket stalls away from the antiques section. She bought the whole bolt for twenty pounds and when she got home she had it made up into straight-legged trousers and an immaculately tailored jacket. It really suits her. In the winter she wears black leather Chelsea boots under it. In the summer she wears high-heeled mules. Whatever the season, though, she looks stunning because she wears her black hair in a really short bob and she has this great knack of putting on absolutely perfect make-up and, well, she just looks very, very groomed. She has a natural kind of grace, Nina. People turn around when she walks into a room. It's amazing. I don't know if that happens in varying degrees to everyone in their mid twenties, and perhaps, if so, that was why I had started to look like a rich woman, but we were dressed far too upmarket to be in Vittorio's and that was the truth. That evening I was gracing the place in a whisper of a navy mohair minidress which I had picked up in the January sales at Whistles and I had a huge beret pulled down over my hair. Very Woody Allen heroine. Anyhow, we both looked pretty well together and if the cappuccinos weren't so brilliant I'm sure we'd have blown the place years ago. When I arrived Nina had bagged a booth seat and she was sipping a Campari and smoking a sly cigarette to herself. She was supposed to have given up smoking ages ago but had gone down from about twenty a day to maybe three or four instead because she just can't kick the habit completely. She's been trying ever since I first met her and that has to be eight years ago now.

'Down to low tar,' she pointed out as I slid along the plastic seat and nestled in the corner next to the formica clad wall.

I reached over and took a cigarette out of the packet and lit up with her Zippo.

'Wow,' she said. I never smoke normally. Only in times of stress. Like in the pub that first day in Edinburgh after Mike Williams told me about the money.

'Are you OK?' Nina asked.

I smiled. I smiled a big smile. It's one thing not telling your best friend that you have inherited a small fortune.

I mean, money doesn't matter all that much, not when it comes right down to it. Funny that. I mean, it was the richest I'd ever been and there were ways which that got to me, like the clothes I'd bought, like that stupid overpriced cardigan I'd picked up in Jenners. But even then, when the money was at its most important to me really, when I first realised that it made me feel equal to my businessman brother and that I could be independent, really independent from my family, well, even then it didn't mean all that much. Not in itself. Not even for its qualities as a luxurious, soft blanket to hide in. It just changed some circumstances, that's all. So I didn't intend to spill the beans to Nina that evening. Not about Ma Polinski. But well, I couldn't hold out on her about Scotty. She'd never have forgiven me.

We ordered two plates of spaghetti with meatballs and a good bottle of Barolo (I have never quite figured out how Vittorio's has all this pasta on the menu for three or four quid a plate, but then the wine list goes from really crappy house wine which no one could possibly order more than once up to stuff at forty or fifty quid a bottle). Anyway, we ordered and we settled down, and as I took a deep breath I caught a whiff of bergamot oil, which Nina always uses on her skin. It focused me completely on what I had to say. I love the smell of Nina — it's very subtle that bergamot stuff, unlike most over-engineered, commercial perfumes. It doesn't hit you in between the eyes. And when she wears it, it's woody which probably comes from the tobacco and the fact she's been using the stuff for years so it's kind of ingrained into her skin. It reassured me and I went ahead and I spilled the beans about Scotty although I wasn't entirely sure how that was going to go down with Nina because since what happened to her in Madrid she has had a bit of a twisted attitude towards men. But I still wanted to tell her. Jesus, more than anything, I just wanted to tell someone because when you tingle the way that I tingled when Scotty kissed me, well, you just can't keep that sort of thing all to yourself. Ma Polinski or not.

Nina and I are pretty frank with each other about guys I guess. Of course, there were one or two at college. Boys we kissed in Potter Row. Late nights and loud music. Med students and philosophers and, for some reason, guys studying Russian. Nina was the first of the two of us to really fall in love, though. It happened to her in Spain and, like I said, she chose very badly. For most of the eighteen months she was away from home, Nina dated an international business tycoon. His company had endowed some new wing of the museum in Madrid because it counted as a tax loss and that was how she met him. His name was José Ignatius and, although I have never seen him myself, by all accounts he was lean and mean and dark. Everything you look for in a latin lover and it worked for Nina and she fell in love with José big time. Actually, he is the only guy that she's ever really fallen in love with. So far. There's been no one since. He took her for weekends in Venice and she moved into his penthouse apartment in the heart of Madrid and they went for holidays together on his yacht. The letters she sent home were ecstatic. She had never been so happy. Yeah, and I know what you're thinking, but it definitely wasn't the money. Nina is kind of surreal about money. Kind of like me. It doesn't sink in with her. Maybe that's one reason why we feel so comfortable together. Maybe that's one reason why we're friends. In fact, when I think about it, Nina is the least acquisitive person I've ever met. Like I said, she just has the one black trouser suit and that's about it. Her flat is really minimal too. She doesn't wear jewellery. She has what she needs, and that is just enough and as a result she has an incredibly self-sufficient air about her. It's almost as if possessions don't really stick to her, don't really mean anything. So it wasn't José's money that she got into. It was him she loved and if she did have a thing about possessions, it was possession of his soul which really turned her on. At the time I remember being jealous because she just seemed so passionate, so completely in love, and I was stuck back at home doing my PhD with a lot of alarmingly unattractive post-graduate archaeologists. Anyway, José went away on business a lot and one time she decided that she would surprise him and take some time off from work and turn up in Paris when he was supposed to be there. She flew up to Roissy ready for a night of passion and instead she caught him in his hotel room at the Georges Cinq with two black prostitutes. And that was it. All over. Not her decision you understand, but his. Nina tried to talk to him about why he'd done it. She spent weeks trying to work it out, but he wouldn't have any of it and he kind of took the line that he was the man, he wore the trousers and if he wanted to fuck a bit of old tart in a hotel room in Paris, well, she deserved everything that she got if she was stupid enough to turn up there. I was infuriated. She was being a total wimp. I mean, she even apologised to him. Can you imagine it? But well, when people are in love like that they are just so desperate about things. José took her back to Madrid and then down to the coast for a few days. Nina cried a lot and she lost the plot a bit. One day when she was at the beach with him, he ordered two scoops of chocolate ice cream and it was all too much for her. By the end of that week she had cried so much that she got dehydrated and the doctor had to be called in. He gave her salt tablets on prescription and everything. It was awful and she just couldn't stop it. I was at home in Edinburgh and Nina called me every night so I got the whole story through a series of long-distance phone calls which she made while José wasn't there. She

133

would go on and on for hours in a dreadful, repetitive loop, and then one evening there was no call, and then the next evening there was no call either. And after four days of silence, when I was just thinking maybe I ought to phone her, Nina turned up back in Scotland with her one white leather suitcase and her bloodshot, tear-stained eyes masked behind dark sunglasses. And like I said, she hasn't gone out with anyone since.

So anyhow, I was kind of nervous of telling her about Scotty, because since all of that she's become a bit cynical about love. I shouldn't have worried though. I mean Nina, she's cool.

'I'm not surprised, you know,' she said sagely when I had spilled the lot in agonising detail and told her everything. She took a slow drag on her last cigarette of the day and tossed her hair back from her face so that a little cloud of the bergamot smell wafted over at me again. 'I've seen him looking at you before,' she said.

'Really?' I think I must have sounded just so eager.

'Yeah. Once when your mum and dad had that garden party and you came walking up the lawn in that muslin dress. It was very Early Princess Di. Almost completely see-through in the light. Scotty definitely looked at you then.'

I shrugged my shoulders. 'Well, he hasn't rung,' I said.

Nina consulted her watch. 'It's not even twenty-four hours since he left you. If he'd been in touch today it would be too keen. Much too keen. He'll ring you tomorrow. You mark my words.'

'Oh, I dunno. But he is nice, isn't he? I mean, it's difficult when you've known someone for ever and you've never really thought about them that way.'

'Good kisser?' she enquired.

I blushed. Blushed. God, I thought, I'm turning into a kid again. Just the mention of kissing raises my colour. I felt ridiculous.

'Yes,' I mumbled. But it wasn't adequate to do justice to the softness of his lips or the way he'd run his rough, violin-maker's hand down my back.

'Will Simon be upset?' she asked.

And well, there was the real issue and it brought things right back down to Ma Polinski's bequest as well. The secrets. I had a hefty gulp of the wine and I waited for a moment or two, trying to make my thoughts clear, but in the end the only thing the wine could do for me was make my tongue feel kind of dry. There were no two ways about it – Simon definitely wasn't going to be pleased about Scotty. He might be his best friend but he still looked on him as some kind of dosser. And Simon has always been very possessive about people. We are so close in age that we've sometimes had friends in common before, but in the end I've always deferred to Simon when it came right down to it. If he wanted to get close to someone I've always backed off. Maybe we were never taught to share properly when we were kids, maybe it's the way he got all of Dad's money and a job for life. Who knows? It's been a thing before, though in a small way – that little competition over mutual friends. And I suppose, anyhow, that I was kind of gearing up to back down to him over Scotty even though I didn't really want to. I knew he wasn't going to be pleased and if anyone was going to have to stand up to him it was going to be Scotty. Not me. Nina reached over the table and tousled my hair.

'Hey, wake up, sleepyhead,' she teased me. 'Don't worry about it. Maybe by the time you've decided that you like him, he'll have spoken to Simon himself. He'll see him before you do, after all. But one of you has to tell him. And soon. It'll fester if you don't.'

'Yeah,' I smiled, 'maybe. I just want to be sure that it's the right time. I mean, there is no point in telling him about it and then Scotty and I go off each other really quickly and we've caused all that upset over nothing.'

'You can't keep it a secret. That's worse than any-thing,' Nina said as she stubbed out her cigarette with a kind of finality. 'You ought to speak to Scotty about the best way for you two to do it, and then come clean. It'd be really crap for Simon if he wasn't one of the first people to be told. I mean, imagine if you go out for a few weeks and all your other friends know. You know what Edinburgh is like. It's tiny. Imagine if Simon found out from someone else.'

I nodded. I mean, she was right. It would be awful. She was totally right. And not just about Scotty and me either.

I must have looked very distant. I mean, I was definitely a million miles away but I must have looked it, because Nina reached out and took my hand and squeezed my fingers quite tightly.

'This man is obviously quite something. Do you need an espresso?' she asked.

I shook my head. An espresso was the last thing I needed. My mind was spinning. I'd had half a bottle of Barolo, which is enough all on its own, but I'd also drunk three or four of Vittorio's cappuccinos and they have double shots of strong coffee in them too. Nina always seems to be able to take any amount of booze and as many coffees as you can brew, but not me. My heart rate was way up and I felt kind of warm. She was so sensible about it that it was really comforting.

'Nina,' I started. 'There is something else.'

'Hmm?' she asked inquisitively but kind of gently at the same time.

I took a deep breath and despite everything I'd tried to convince myself before, I decided to take the plunge and tell her about the money. It wasn't an easy decision. But after what she'd said I couldn't really keep it to myself any longer. It wouldn't have been right. It was a difficult thing to say, partly, I suppose, because I couldn't really express what it was all about and why I felt so uneasy about it. Anyway, it took me ages to get the whole story out. I was almost surprised at how much I had to tell her about what had been going on. About Mike Williams and the jewellery and all the money and how I just knew there was something else there, something I couldn't quite grasp. I told her everything, all the stuff I'd found out up to then about old Ma Polinski out at Morbrax and in the Old Town and in the files at Mike Williams' office. Nina stared wide-eyed and silent. I don't know what I'd been expecting. Shrieking. Shock. Accusations. But Nina just listened. Even when I talked about the old lady, about how I could feel her sometimes. About how she was just there. Nina just listened away. She gave up on fag quota rules, though. Nina smokes quite slowly. The story took up six cigarettes. I went on for a long time, I suppose. It was the biggest thing that had ever happened to me. Six cigarettes worth was probably pretty good going. At the end, when I'd finished, and said finally, breathlessly, 'So there's eight million pounds and I don't know why the old lady gave it to me,' Nina just smiled quietly.

I was scared, I suppose, of what she might say. I was afraid she might accuse me of lying. Of that ultimate betrayal in friendship, of holding out. There was a moment's unbearable silence when I held my breath and listened to Nina, waiting for the world to explode. It didn't of course. Nina just began to laugh.

'Well, if anyone's qualified to find out why someone might have done something like that, it's us,' she said. 'That's not going to be a problem.'

And the relief must have shown in my eyes. Nina slapped my arm and stubbed her cigarette out in the now overflowing Peroni ashtray.

'I wondered what was going on,' she said. 'So, dinner is on you then?'

I don't think I've ever felt so relieved about anything. A problem shared and all that. A problem halved and Nina on my side, in my corner. No one has ever done that before, no one who has ever mattered. When it comes down to it my family always overreact. It's house rules. But not Nina. She was dead pragmatic.

'What do you reckon about this mural, then?' she asked me and we got down to it.

For the rest of the night after that we huddled low over our drinks. Nina had a double shot of amaretto di Sarrono with big blocks of ice floating in it and I quaffed down a mineral water as we talked. Nina had tracked down the Contessa that afternoon. She was an elderly lady in her late sixties and she lived in Florence, but she wasn't going to be at home for the whole of the month – not until the beginning of May in fact. She was on holiday about an hour away from Florence down on the coast at Forte dei Marmi where she had a villa. Nina had tried to get a number for the villa but it was unlisted and the staff at the Contessa's house in town were under strict instructions not to give it out. The auction house had been unhelpful too, though that was par for the course – they always are.

'She'll be back in a couple of weeks,' Nina smiled. 'You need to be careful, though. I mean, you really ought to decide when you're going to tell your parents. You ought to set a date or something and then stick to it. If it drags on for months it'll be awful.'

I shrugged into my glassful. 'You don't think I'm crazy, do you?' I asked her. 'Does it make any sense?'

Nina sipped slowly. I knew I was talking to the right person. I mean, if anyone understands messages from beyond the grave, then it's someone with a background in archaeology, right? Someone who understands history. I knew I could rely on Nina for an honest appraisal of my mental health with regard to it. Nina paused. She was applying all her best sleuthing skills to the problem. She was taking it seriously. I held my breath again and I was kind of glad when she necked back the last of her amaretto and agreed with me that it was a problem. That there might be something there to find out. If she'd taken the Mike Williams it-just-happens-line, then I might well have given up at that point because I would have been afraid that I was kind of paranoid or something. But she agreed with me. There was something going on.

'It's weird,' she said slowly. 'Definitely weird. And I don't get this lawyer guy at all. Why won't he let you see his uncle? I mean, people with Alzheimer's do remember the past. It's the present they aren't so good at. Unless it's extreme, really extreme. I mean, as time goes on their memory will get progressively worse, but still, they have good days and bad days too. Maybe if you got him on a good day . . .'

I shook my head. 'No. The way Mike Williams told me. I don't think he's messing around. I think the old guy is really ill. He's staying in a home out in Juniper Green.'

'Well, in that case, if the old lawyer is out, then we need to go back to her house in the country,' Nina said very definitely. 'The graves are there and you might have missed something at the house, running out like you did. It's the only lead left that we can follow up straight away.'

'We?'

'You.'

'No,' I begged. 'Come with me. Please.'

And we agreed to try at the weekend.

It was after one when we finally left Vittorio's and I felt about a hundred times better than when I had walked in. We wandered together arm in arm up Sauchiehall Street, homeward bound. It was freezing cold. I could feel my ears burning in the vicious, dense, west coast chill and I knew that my nose would be getting red too. I thought, thank God there isn't any wind tonight, and Nina and I pulled each other on, picking up the pace as the heat of Vittorio's subsided in our bodies and we got colder and colder. As we made it to Charing Cross, though, it started to rain lightly and we began to walk even faster, knowing that at that time of night during the week we would have been damn lucky to hail a cab on the street.

'We should have rung from the restaurant,' Nina said, and I just nodded.

Her place was closer than mine and I couldn't face another ten minutes walking alone through the biting, freezing air so we climbed the stone tenement stairs together up to her flat on the second floor. Nina drew all the curtains and lit up the fire in her living room and we sat on the floor huddled in front of it. Her flat is really plain, you know. We painted it white like I said, and Nina has this old, comfortable furniture which is kind of shabby. On the walls she's hung textile printing blocks and fabric design sheets which are quite colourful. Her curtains, though, are sailcloth. We huddled up together in front of the fire.

'I can't believe it's nearly summer,' I moaned, just like everyone moans every year, because for some reason there is this common belief that it gets warm in May and then stays warm until September even though that never happens. Last summer though, well, the weather was truly crap. The worst summer for a long, long time. But then it was only the end of April and we still had some hope that the good weather was coming.

Nina smiled 'Cast ne'er a clout,' she said, just like Scotty had.

'I suppose you're right,' I admitted. 'It's Scotland, after all.'

And Nina lay on her back and made bad bagpipe noises which I think was supposed to be a rendition of 'Flower of Scotland', but just wasn't. It didn't take long until we were both rolling around in fits.

'Why don't you stay?' she asked, and I said that I would and then I remembered the grey felt jewellery roll in my handbag. I brought out the diamonds and emeralds and we sat in front of the fire staring at the way the flames made the stones sparkle, mesmerised by it, and I held up the thin, gold chain as if I was dowsing.

'Weird,' Nina pronounced. 'An odd combination.'

But by two we couldn't think about it any more, so she lent me some pyjamas, tucked me up on the sofa with some old tartan rugs and I slept really well because I wasn't on my own any more. Because I had my best friend on my side.

Chapter Thirteen

The rest of that week went along just fine. Scotty rang me the next day, just like Nina had predicted, and we sat on the phone for nearly an hour like expectant teenagers and, well, he was the one who brought up the subject of Simon.

'I suppose we have to decide what we want to do,' he said, 'but I think we ought to tell him together.'

'Isn't it early for that?' I asked, because after all, well, we had only kissed that one evening. That was all.

'No,' Scotty replied. 'I don't think so.' And my heart just soared and I twisted the phone cord all up my arm in my excitement.

That was the high point of the week for me, no question about it. Looking back on it, in the dark corners, in the edges of my life, though, I still felt like there was something waiting for me. As if there was someone there in the shadows as I walked out of the staff exit at work and into the dim, dusky evening atmosphere, as if there was a dream that I couldn't quite remember as I woke up in the morning, things that were there, but intangible, just out of my reach like I was a baby grasping for something which I couldn't quite focus on yet, my fingers pawing the air. I dreamed about her too. Ma Polinski. Not scary, disturbing dreams, not nightmares. Nothing like the mural. Just following her down into the labyrinthine basement of her shop on Muir's Pend, or watching her sip her tea out of an old jam jar as she pored over a faded, dusty book laid out on her cedarwood desk as her clocks ticked all around her. I suppose she was becoming real to me, I was beginning to know her a bit more. On the Thursday night I went swimming. Long lengths up and down the restored Victorian swimming baths at the bottom of my road. Up and down I went, and I couldn't help noticing that as I swam towards the end of the pool I was reaching out to a reflection in the water which receded from me the closer I got to it, until it disappeared entirely as I finally reached the greeny-blue tiling at the edge of the pool. It occurred to me that I had felt like that all week and that I might have found it frightening if I hadn't had Scotty to look forward to, or if I hadn't confided in Nina.

At the weekend Nina borrowed her mum's car, an old, brown-leather-seated, silver Alfa Romeo which her dad had driven back from Italy twenty years ago and which had really stood the test of time. On the Saturday morning we got a bus over to her mum's place to pick the old banger up from the big, red stone, ground-floor and basement flat where Nina had been brought up. Nina's mum, Rosita, made us frothy hot chocolate as we sat around the heavy, wooden kitchen table.

'Terrible Scottish weather,' she complained even though it was quite sunny.

She handed us a plate of biscuits which we both tucked in to.

'The clutch,' Rosita began to explain, 'needs extra. Stephano will show you.'

Nina's brother got up dutifully from the sofa on the other side of the room and began to explain with expansive hand movements the intricacies of the clutch. Rosita wouldn't leave him to it, though. She kept butting in with her RAC number and how we would be covered if we broke down because she had family cover. Then Nina's sister came in. She was only just up and she started into a long speech on her opinion of the clutch and how it needed substantial renovation. It's always like that at Nina's and in the end we fled the house and the clutch, of course, when it came down to it, was fine.

'Wow,' Nina said as we headed out of town. 'I didn't think we were going to get out of there alive.'

I laughed. 'Your family,' I said, 'are so different from mine. Everyone talks about everything.'

'Yeah. A bit of peace and quiet would go down all right,' Nina replied. I don't think she'd quite picked up the tone of awed admiration in my voice.

We decided to make for Morbrax and then head on into Edinburgh to go and see an exhibition we both fancied at the Scottish Portrait Gallery. After that we'd planned that Nina would drive back to Glasgow while I was going to go out for dinner with Scotty and just catch the midnight train home again.

We cut off the motorway quite early on and made our way eastwards cross-country on the B-roads. It was a pretty dull kind of day in that part of the country, though the sun did come out later, as we drove away from Glasgow. I suppose it took us just over an hour to get there because you can't make any speed at all on those windy, tiny back roads and as you cut off towards Morbrax you hit the Lang Wynd, which is notorious for the high-speed crashes on its hairpin bends. We made it to Morbrax in one piece, though, and parked a little way along the main road. I showed Nina the house and this time we climbed up into the attic, which was empty as well, of course, apart from the wispy cobwebs threaded between its dark beams. It looked as if we had come to a dead end. Back downstairs, on the first floor, in the old lady's bedroom, Nina stared at the mural on the ceiling from lots of different angles, and then she shuddered, but there wasn't really anything to say. We weren't getting any answers out of the old place. We made our way back down to the ground floor and I locked the door behind us and we wandered around the garden slowly, admiring the flowers. Neither of us wanted to get back into the car so soon, so we settled down on an oak bench near the back door.

'It's a beautiful spot. You fancy moving in here?' Nina asked me dreamily, tossing her dark hair and taking in the wonderful view from our vantage point at the back of the house.

'No. I'd just think about that mural all the time. Even if I painted it out,' I replied.

Then the sun came out and we both laid back and turned our faces up to the warmth automatically as if we were sunflowers. After a minute or two Nina got up and wandered over to the worn, stone sundial beside the French windows.

'Funny,' she commented. 'It tells the wrong time.'

I checked my watch. Nina was right. The sundial was set an hour ahead of GMT and it shouldn't have been.

'Can't see why she would have had it set to summertime,' Nina mumbled and wandered off to smell the roses, which were just budding up. She took long strides across the grass, breathing in deeply as she went. I moved over towards the sundial to have a closer look.

'I don't get it,' I said, examining the face of the clock.

From a distance I could see that Nina shrugged her shoulders and then disappeared down a little grassy path between the flowerbeds. I checked the sundial over carefully, trying to see if it had been moved recently, but there weren't any signs of that, the lichens on its base all matched each other, the stone was worn evenly according to the forces of the weather, the west side of the base more so than the east side because that is the direction the wind most commonly comes from.

There was no sign of movement on the granite paving stones beneath it either and I concluded that no one had moved that sundial in many years. It was an old one, of course. Consistent with the period of the house, not a reproduction. There was a faded engraving which I think read 1735 and a maker's signature which was also almost worn away but seemed to read Thomas Wright. Beside that there was a figure which had faded out completely but was probably the latitude which the dial was made for. It might well have been there since the place was built, before time became standardised with the coming of the railways. An hour out, though. Too much to be explained away by that and also too exact by far to be a coincidence. It was strange, I thought to myself, with Ma Polinski's interest in clocks. She'd tinkered away with them for hours, the pigeon man had said. She knew how they worked. She'd had an impressive collection of accurate timepieces – there had been a whole catalogue dedicated to them in the auction of her things. It wasn't right.

'She must have moved it before she died,' I shouted over to Nina who emerged around the perimeter of the flowerbed farthest away from the house.

'How do you know?' she asked, strolling across the lawn back towards me.

'She must have. Look, she knew about clocks. They were a hobby of hers. A speciality. She was a perfectionist too. The dial is set ahead of time because she wanted it set ahead of time. An hour. What's an hour ahead?'

Nina brought her diary out of her handbag and consulted the information on the flimsy front pages. She held out the map towards me.

'Amsterdam, Brussels, Budapest, Copenhagen, Frankfurt, Lagos, Lisbon, Malta, Oslo, Paris, Rome, Stockholm, Vienna, Warsaw, Zurich,' she reeled off obligingly, reading the names upside down.

'Her husband was from the Lvov, the necklace turned up in Italy,' I pondered, 'they're both on the right time line.'

'Along with most of Europe. It's hardly conclusive,' Nina started. 'Maybe she just moved it around a bit so that if it was noticed, if it was moved back, well, maybe there's something underneath it, hidden.'

We set ourselves the task of moving it to see, but we couldn't shift it. The base was solid granite and the dial itself was made of brass. It was heavy and it was bolted very securely in place. We tried all sorts of things, but we had no luck with it until eventually Nina went to investigate the toolbox in the boot of the car and came back with a kind of a crowbar.

'We might damage it if we use this,' she commented.

'Doesn't matter,' I replied though it was against the grain. 'It's mine, we can do what we want to it.'

It took the full weight of both of our bodies, but in the end we prised the brass plate away from the stone but there was nothing underneath it.

'Anything perishable would be long gone after more than twenty years,' Nina pointed out.

But I felt that there had never been anything hidden in there. It hadn't been removed from its plinth since the day it was made. Somehow I could just tell. We lay the brass plate back on the stone disconsolately and propped the crowbar against it. Nina tossed her hair back from her face again, sighed and sat down on the bench.

'It was just a thought,' she said. 'She might have left a message.'

And something, then, moved me. I don't know exactly what it was, but I took the crowbar and I prised the flat top stone away from the plinth and I squealed when I saw what was underneath it.

'Look, Nina,' I said. 'Look.'

And we pulled out the little black bag which had

been concealed in a shallow pocket carved into the stone. My fingers were shaking as I opened it and caught the contents in the palm of my hand. It was a small, cheap, red-gold locket. An absolutely plain, oval shape. I was on my knees and Nina crouched down next to me as I scrambled to open it, prising it carefully with the long nail on my thumb. It only took a second or two, although I fumbled a bit in my excitement. Inside there was a picture of her. A black-and-white photo and a lock of hair. A tiny brown ringlet. One of my own, I realised. Cut secretly perhaps. I don't remember.

'Oh my God,' I said, and I pulled the chain she'd left me from round my neck. It matched exactly. Of course it did.

'It's her,' I said. 'And it's me,' and I held out the locket so Nina could see properly.

'What does it mean?' she asked.

And I just shrugged my shoulders. 'It means that we're on the right track,' I said. 'It means that I've not spent the last fortnight going mad.'

Once we'd recovered from our find and reckoned we weren't quite so wide eyed, Nina and I walked around the house one last time and over into the old churchyard to see what we could find over there. After all, now we'd started maybe we were on a roll. It was the kind of graveyard that you see in films, all ivy-covered and mossy and ancient. We found a grave there from 1729 and a few others which were probably older because the writing had worn right off. Molly Savage and Tomasz Polinski were buried side by side to the south of the church, around to the left of the building under a big old sycamore tree.

'She wanted to be brought back here,' I told Nina. 'She specified that she wanted to be buried in Morbrax.'

Nina stood on Tomasz's grave. She brushed her hand

over the black marble of the headstone.

'Maybe we're concentrating too much on *her* for clues,' Nina mused. 'Did *he* leave a will?' she asked, pointing at the the ground where he was buried.

I couldn't stop bringing my hand up to the locket which I'd strung around its chain and fastened back round my neck.

'I don't know,' I said. 'That's a good idea. I'll check it out on Monday.'

We figured that there wasn't much more we could do in East Lothian, so after we left the cemetery we hopped back into the car and drove up to Edinburgh, mostly in silence because we were both really thinking hard. The old lady had left a very specific signal. Something which would last a long time. As long as it had to. Something that only the right person could possibly understand. A message from beyond the grave with an address on it, or as good as. We were absorbed. It didn't seem to take very long for us to get up to town and we parked on York Place right at the east end of Queen Street just after two o'clock. It was only then we realised that we were starving so we walked over to Valvona and Crolla on Elm Row and had a couple of ham and tomato sandwiches in the café at the back of the shop.

'Maybe it's a cry for help,' Nina said.

'Maybe it's a marker,' I replied.

'Or both,' we compromised. 'It could be both at once.'

But the truth is we didn't know. We didn't realise then just how confused and desperate the old lady must have been. We were guessing, just like archaeologists always do, but we didn't have the full facts so we were guessing in the dark. After lunch we traipsed out of the restaurant slowly, scanning the shelves in the delicatessen for culinary treasures and meandering up past the Playhouse. When we got back up to the

Scottish Portrait Gallery it was after three and it had just started to rain again. We darted inside the huge double doors to avoid the downpour. The gallery building is a very ornate, Gothic, red stone affair which to me always really looks as if it belongs in Glasgow because that's where that terracotta stonework usually comes from. How we reckoned we were going to be able to take in anything else that afternoon, I don't know. But we were dead set on that exhibition for some reason. I can't even remember what it was about now. Nina's probably just as vague.

'There is something going on, isn't there?' she observed as we crossed the tiled hallway and stared up at the ceiling which is painted with stars. I stopped in my tracks. It was the first thing either of us had really said since we hit the road in Morbrax.

'Yeah,' I said. 'There is. The missing treasure, the mural, the sundial and me.'

'No, it's him. That's what really bothers me,' Nina said. 'The more I think about it – cutting her husband out like that. It's something to do with him. She couldn't have known they were going to die together. And she was older than he was. She left you messages expecting him to live on beyond her.'

I asked Nina if I could look at that page in her diary again, the one with the map of European time zones and when she handed it over I traced with my fingernail more or less where I thought Lvov was – just over the Polish–Ukrainian border, slightly to the west of Warsaw.

'That's where he was from. An hour ahead,' I said to her.

'Yeah, like I said, so is half of the rest of Europe. It's too dubious, Rachel,' she said sensibly. That was why I was glad to have her along. 'You need to look at his will,' she continued. 'And any other records – army service information, doctor's files, police reports.'

'Jesus, yes, I hadn't thought of that. They tried to deport him, didn't they?'

'Got your work cut out for you next week, then,' Nina smirked as she made her way towards the lush, claret-coloured carpeted staircase which leads up to the viewing gallery.

'*Our* work,' I replied, as I followed her and she just grinned because I knew that, kind of like me, now we were definitely on to something she was beginning to really enjoy it.

Chapter Fourteen

That night, once Nina had headed off back to Glasgow
I went, well, I suppose I went on my first date with
Scotty. He ended up cooking me dinner and this time it
wasn't just an extended dessert course, he really
cooked a whole meal. We met up for a drink at the
Ceilidh House behind the Tron Kirk on Hunter Square
where between us we must have bumped into at least
half a dozen people we knew. Afterwards, we
wandered along the Cowgate to his place. I have to say,
I hadn't quite anticipated Scotty's flat. I mean, I didn't
really have him down as someone who was house-
proud at all, but it was a lovely place even if it was kind
of untidy. As we cut down the alleyway I could feel
him kind of tense up. 'It's quite small,' he said
nervously and I just took his hand as he led me over to
the wooden door in the side of the old garage and up
the stairs. Scotty lived in the coombs. As we came to
the top of the staircase, I gasped. It was dark all right
and it was untidy. But it was something else. I mean, it
was a great place. Amazing. It had been the old hayloft
and, I suppose, the garage downstairs had originally
been a stables. It was kind of basic of course, there was
a wooden floor which had a couple of old rugs cast over
it, the walls were unplastered stone and the ceiling had
its dark beams open to the room. I kind of recognised
some of the furniture there from Scotty's father's place.

He must have inherited the stuff – old, heavy, good quality furniture which I suppose he held on to somehow after the débâcle with his trust fund. My memory of the huge house in Inverleith where Scotty grew up is very hazy, but let's just say he's definitely come down in the world by moving to his place in the Grassmarket, although the flat wasn't unpleasant by any means. It was one quite large room and there was a red, chintzy screen in one corner behind which there was a big, old, white enamel bath with brass taps, a toilet and a wash-hand basin. The decommissioned gas lamps still hung useless from the ceiling. Propped up against one of the walls there was a beautiful Georgian oil painting, but it was kind of hidden behind a pile of rags. It was a great place though, kind of scruffy but kind of posh too and, like I somehow would have expected from Scotty, there was an absolute absence of technology – no phone, no television or video, no radio. The only things which made you realise that you were actually in the late twentieth century were an immaculate Linn LP 12 turntable with Armageddon and a pair of Troac Studio One speakers which were placed perfectly so that the sound would reverberate around the contours of the room. Well, reverberate as perfectly as possible, given that the place had coombs, like I said. I breathed in deeply and realised that it smelled musky, like a mixture of brewing coffee and old wood. A boy's smell.

'It is so cool here,' I breathed out, as Scotty turned on an old glass lamp on one of the sidetables and I had a chance to take in the dark colours of the paintings and the carpets which had all seemed to be shades of brown in the half light but, once the lamp was on, turned out to be burgundy and forest green and midnight blue.

'A bit untidy,' he replied. 'Sorry.'

He was right there, the bed was unmade, the washing up undone, there were books piled up the wall, newspapers open over the table, and wood shavings scattered about from a workbench in the corner. I wandered over to the workbench and picked up a couple of wooden tubes he seemed to be turning out.

'What is this?' I asked.

'Bagpipes,' Scotty said, quite solemnly. 'Well, they will be when I've finished them.'

'Hang on,' I laughed, 'you work all day making violins and when you get home you make bagpipes for recreational purposes?'

'Yep. Completely different set of tools. Absolutely different kind of thing,' Scotty said with such seriousness that I decided not to pursue it further. He was clearing the table, piling all the dirty plates up in the sink.

'Can I help at all?' I asked.

'Nah,' he grinned. 'You sit down and I'll make you a drink in a minute.'

He found a clean glass with a thick twisted stem and poured me some wine from a bottle in the fridge and then he opened up one of the cupboards which seemed to hold hundreds of old vinyl records.

'You're a bit of a purist, aren't you, Scotty?' I teased him.

'Far better sound quality. Wait till you hear it,' he predicted, as he set some old Bob Dylan LP on to the turntable. He was right about the quality. Bob was sounding pretty good. I cast my eyes upwards. You could see stars through the skylights – the brown reflection of the city at night didn't quite cancel them out. I sipped on my drink and then I got up and whirled around the carpet, half dancing, half walking in time to the music. I felt very happy there straight away, I felt almost at home. Things between us were so easy. We'd known each other for ever, I suppose.

Scotty can cook. That is to say, Scotty can cook two sauces for pasta, one kind of vegetable broth and a stew. And I don't mean to be sexist or anything but, in my experience, for a guy that is pretty good going. That evening, if I remember rightly, he made one of the pasta dishes. A creamy sauce with prawns and garlic spread over perfectly cooked tagliatelle. We laughed as we ate, telling each other the stories of our week. The tiny details of what we had been up to, and I thought to myself, I remember thinking, that it was strange how if you want to grow, to change, to develop, you can find people around you who'll help. There's always a cure. And Scotty was kind of a panacea all right. He knew exactly where I'd come from and how hard it had been when I was growing up. Just like I knew exactly what he'd done, the stuff which had happened to him. It made it all seem very easy, though I can't say there's never been the odd misunderstanding.

'Tomorrow, I thought we could go over to Simon's and take him for brunch down on the Shore,' Scotty said after the meal, as he made the coffee.

'Oh,' I replied, kind of surprised, 'I was going to catch the midnight train.'

Scotty turned back towards me at the table and he reached out and touched my cheek and then he blinked very, very slowly. I bit my lip and as he moved towards me away from the kettle he knocked me right off my seat and we kissed for a long time on the floor, rolling around lazily. I could have sworn we did that in slow motion. All those kisses. There must have been a thousand. They engulfed me like some kind of all consuming dream where I became very alive and very relaxed at the same time. I melted. So did he. I know it. It was after midnight when we surfaced again, so there really wasn't any way that I could get back to Glasgow that evening. Even if I had wanted to, which I didn't, of course. Scotty brought over some old patchwork pillows and put them under my head and then he lay himself down next to me and stroked my hair and it felt eternal. It felt like love. Now, I can't say I didn't want to jump him. I can't say that I'd have objected had he jumped. But somehow we just lay there, contented, and I don't even remember falling asleep. He must have carried me over to the bed because I don't remember walking over there either. When I woke up I could just make out his outline, lying on top of the covers next to me, still in his jeans and old T-shirt. I was under the covers and although he'd taken my shoes off, I was wearing my clothes too. It was beginning to look like Scotty was a gentleman. I smiled to myself, enjoying the situation. Enjoying the fact that he didn't want to rush me. Enjoying the fact that I wasn't perturbed that I hadn't been rushed. I breathed in deeply, stretching myself out like a contented cat, sinking down further into the deep, soft mattress, a quiver of excitement running through me because we had all the time in the world, half asleep and in bed together.

'You OK?' Scotty whispered.

'Yeah,' I said. 'I'm fine,' and I reached out for his hand before closing my eyes again and drifting off.

'Sleep tight,' I heard him mumble last of all.

We were lying so close I could feel the warmth of him. I could feel him move as he breathed. Things were perfect. Don't they always feel perfect when you're in the throes of something like that? I was so blissful that things seemed to just fall into place. I figured to myself that I had Scotty, I had the money, and Nina was helping me out with the Ma Polinski conundrum. I was warm and I was comfortable and things were going to be fine. After all, what could possibly go wrong? It was all so under control that nothing felt important or pressing and I didn't have anything on my mind.

'When we're ready,' I thought. And I settled for that. I didn't realise that I'd only just started. I didn't anticipate what a long way there was to go.

Chapter Fifteen

It was between seven and eight the next morning when we were woken up by the hammering on the door. I opened my eyes kind of suddenly and it took me a while to realise exactly where I was and who I was with. Scotty just sat up next to me in the bed and looked dazed as well. I stared at him quizzically and he smiled and then shrugged his shoulders.

'You stay here,' he said and he gave me a little squeeze.

Scotty hauled himself out of the bed, scratched his head a bit and set off to answer the door, disappearing down the wooden stairs towards the noise. Then the knocking got louder and more violent as the moments passed and I could hear the vague noise of someone frantically shouting as well, although I couldn't really make out any individual words. The walls of the old garage were too thick for that. I was a bit scared, I suppose. I pushed my hair about a bit and scanned the room for evidence of a mirror. It was, at least, something I could do. Something to keep me occupied. There didn't seem to be one, though, so I just tried to smooth my hair down as much as possible and hoped that it looked all right. 'It's OK. It's OK. I'm coming,' Scotty was shouting, although the angry voice outside didn't seem to be taking any notice of him. I heard the creaking of the old iron lock and then as Scotty opened the door to the street I heard Simon's voice more clearly. 'Simon,' I thought, 'what the hell is he here for?' and then there was a rumpus as Scotty scrambled up the stairs ahead of Simon's advance, obviously trying to get away. It was exactly what I hadn't wanted to happen. My fingers were weak with the shock. Edinburgh's too small, you see, to leave the Tron Ceilidh House with someone, to walk all along the Cowgate on a Saturday night hand in hand and expect not to be seen. And Simon, of course, was furious. He'd heard about it in some New Town basement bar, drinking after hours. It didn't take long for the jungle drums to work. *'Saw your sister tonight. How long's she been seeing Scotty for, Simon?'* And I wasn't even supposed to be in town. Simon couldn't even look at me. I'm not sure who he thought had betrayed him more, but he took it out on Scotty first. As he caught up with him at the top of the stairs he just pushed him up against the wall there and shouted.

'You bastard. Bastard,' he shrieked like some kind of medieval madman. I don't think I've ever seen him as angry about anything. His colour was heightened, his cheeks seemed to actually glow and his eyes were all wild.

'Bastard. Say something,' he shouted straight into Scotty's face as he pinned him securely against the stonework.

'What is it?' Scotty asked him. 'Calm down, man.'

And then when Simon hit him, I squealed of course and that only made it far, far worse. Simon wheeled around, letting Scotty go. Poor Scotty just bent over double and tried to catch his breath. Simon had caught him a full punch in the chest and he was wheezing, although that passed quite quickly. It must have really hurt and later on he had a bruise, a kidney-shaped, red one where Simon's knuckles had made contact with the thin skin over his ribs. Simon now turned his attention to me over in the bed and I was terrified. I could hardly move, let alone speak normally.

'Get out of there,' Simon said, his voice low and dangerous as he advanced towards me across the room. 'Come on, get out. I'm taking you home.'

And I knew I'd have to make a stand. 'I'm not going anywhere,' I stuttered very slowly even though my heart was beating very fast and I couldn't feel my fingertips properly. 'I'm certainly not going anywhere with you in that state. I'm staying here.'

Simon stopped for a moment at the bottom of the bed as if he was taking in this information and processing it somehow. Then he started to pull the covers off the mattress kind of frantically and when at last they were piled up on the floor, he reached forward and grabbed hold of me and pulled my arm really hard towards him. He's bigger than I am and he's very, very strong even when he isn't angry. He dragged me across the mattress and then held me upright with an arm on either side, as if I was some kind of large toddler who was having a bit of a tantrum.

'You're coming home and we're going to sort this out if I have to drag you by the hair,' he snarled.

'We can sort it out here,' I spat back at him. 'Why don't you just let me go? Why don't you sit down and we can talk to each other?' I was trying to sound calm but it didn't quite come across like that and he started to pull me towards the stairwell. In fact, he got me about halfway across the room when he came face to face with Scotty who, I have to say, proved that he just doesn't have any kind of a temper. I think if it had been me in that position I would have hit Simon hard with something very heavy. It was just that I couldn't quite get hold of anything myself because he had both my arms clasped tightly together by my side. I don't think

I've ever hated anyone quite so hard in all of my life. Just that moment I was seething with it because he made me feel absolutely powerless as he dragged me towards the door. 'Let me go,' I shrieked. 'Let me go.' And then, of course, we came up to where Scotty was still standing with his eyes narrowed and his head slightly to one side because, I suppose, he couldn't quite believe it.

Scotty put a hand firmly on each of Simon's shoulders and just held him still really, really definitely but also with a strong sense of calm. He took a deep breath and he spoke very slowly.

'I made Rachel dinner, I kissed her, I'm going to take her out and get to know her more.'

Simon looked like a cornered animal and I felt a tremendous relief. Scotty was standing up for me and it felt really good. No one had ever done that before. Ever, in the whole of my life. Simon, of course, didn't take it at all well. As far as he was concerned I was his little sister, not anyone in my own right.

'No,' he shouted. 'It's my sister. She's my, my, mine,' he stuttered and then his grip loosened slightly and he looked down. For a moment I thought that he was actually going to cry. It really looked that way. I pulled my arms back and rubbed the pink marks where his fingers had pressed into my flesh.

'I want to see Scotty. I want to,' I said quietly, made brave myself by Scotty's bravery.

'How long?' Simon half whispered.

'Last night. Just last night,' Scotty replied. 'We were going to tell you today.'

And then Simon seemed to give up, to realise that he was overreacting completely and that it just looked ridiculous. That he was wrong and this time no one was going to back him up. He cradled his head in his hands and Scotty reached out and gave him a big hug and I realised in a blinding flash just why I was finding it difficult to tell my family about Ma Polinski's bequest when this was the kind of reaction I instinctively expected to any kind of bid for independence. When this wounded violence was normal. Because as far as they were concerned I belonged to them and any deviation from what they expected from me was a betrayal of trust.

'It's OK, Simon. It's going to be OK,' Scotty said very quietly and Simon just crumpled on to the floor and banged hard with his fist several times with a dull thud on the carpet. I backed towards the kitchen area and put the kettle on the stove while Scotty squatted down on his haunches and tried to comfort my brother. And five minutes later we all looked quite civilised really, sitting around Scotty's old oak table nursing mugs of milky coffee together and talking. Though Simon never said that he was sorry. Not that day or any of the days after. And later on, when he walked Scotty over to the Italian delicatessen on the other side of the marketplace to buy some rolls for breakfast it occurred to me, left alone in the flat, trying in five minutes, for some reason to clear up years and years' worth of Scotty's junk, that Simon couldn't bear to share anything. Not the money, not me, not anything. And I felt very sorry for him and very, very glad that I wouldn't have to rely on him for furniture for my flat or any of the other kind offers which he'd made over the years which suddenly, in the light of his violent temper, didn't seem quite so kind any more and I wondered to myself if that was why Ma Polinski had done what she did. If somehow the old lady had seen it coming. If maybe she'd come from something similar herself and had somehow known. I looked around nervously, wondering why she always seemed to be there. Wondering what was happening. And I was glad when Simon and Scotty came back with a big bag of bread and the Sunday papers, and I

didn't think about that any more. I just opened
Scotty's big window to air the place a bit, swept my
hair back and settled down to a leisurely breakfast.

Chapter Sixteen

After Simon's arrival at the flat in the Grassmarket that day my first reaction was to expect some kind of crazy scene with Mum and Dad when they found out about Scotty and me. Once Simon had left after breakfast I got really scared about telling them, in fact, but I knew that if I didn't grasp the bull by the horns on that Sunday, then Simon would probably tell them before I could, and I didn't want his peculiar slant on things being the first that they heard about it all, so I just had to take a deep breath and get on with the job. I had a bath, borrowed a cleanish shirt from Scotty and hailed a cab in the street to go over to the Grange. Mum and Dad were eating in the back garden when I arrived. Yeah, I know, all they ever seem to do is hang out in the house and eat. Well, actually, apart from work, that's what they really enjoy – being safe and sound at home. It's how they spend most of their time. I was so nervous that I hardly even said hello, let alone sat down, before I blurted out that I'd decided to start seeing Scotty. Of course I'd thought about it a lot on the way over. I'd anticipated their reactions. And well, once I had considered it, I reckoned that Mum wouldn't challenge anything. That would be her way. And I figured that Dad would get kind of cross, which would be his. But whatever they said I knew that underneath it there would be an unnamed anger. A pulse of dissent and disappointment. But I figured that in the end as long as I stood firm, they'd have to accept what I'd decided. It wouldn't be worth losing me over, you see. The stakes were too high. My pulse, though, was thumping as I stood on the grass in front of them. My heart was in my mouth and I felt sick. But I did it all the same and when I'd finished there was a moment's pause and Mum smiled.

'That's nice, dear,' she grinned, just as I'd thought she would. As if she didn't care. 'Scotty is a good boy, isn't he?' And her eyes didn't move at all as she said it.

Dad looked a bit gruff for a moment. 'Hasn't a penny, mind,' he commented.

That was always Dad's first thought, of course. Whenever anyone paired off, got engaged or married, his first reaction always depended heavily on the groom's bank balance. 'It could work,' he would say, 'the family are very wealthy.' Even when this old schoolfriend of mine got engaged to this crazy, off the rails, American guy she met at a wedding and it was apparent to everyone else that they wouldn't last more than a year or two at the most, Dad shook his head and dispensed his words of wisdom because the guy's father owned some big conglomerate, so he was sure that everything was going to be OK. 'The rich and the famous get divorced too, you know, Dad,' I remember trying to reason with him. But, as usual, Dad stood firm in his opinions and really believed that money made everything OK. In this case I kind of knew that the only way to deal with him was to be firm like I'd said. There was certainly no point in trying to reason with him.

'I like Scotty,' I said, 'I've known him for a long time and I'm going to give it a try.'

Dad went a bit quiet after that. He just mumbled, 'Well, you know what's best for you,' without really meaning it. Thirty years earlier, with less experience, who knows – he might have knocked the door down at

Scotty's place that morning himself and tried to drag me home. That stuff doesn't come out of nowhere in a family and well, I knew they were finding it weird and I also knew that was only the half of it. They didn't know about Ma Polinski's money yet. But it wasn't the time to tell them about that. I didn't know enough to be sure of my ground. Mum still hadn't blinked and I knew once I'd left there'd be one of those conversations on the subject of what they could do. Things were beating away between them like jungle drums. Secret messages. Classified alert codes. I could feel them, although on the surface we were all pretending it was fine.

I shared Mum's sandwich and crouched down next to her in the sun for a bit because I didn't want to leave and let them get on with it. I wanted things to feel normal between us before I went away. It was the only thing I'd ever wanted. Since I was very small. It's the thing I'd tried for most of all. I don't think I've ever felt that they really liked me. Not really. I've certainly never been a patch on Simon, that's for sure. So I sat for a while, waiting and hoping, realising bit by bit that I had to let them get on with it. That I couldn't make them be something they weren't any more than they could make me. Wishing that the desperate feeling in the pit of my stomach would somehow subside.

It took me half an hour to get back to the Grassmarket after I left them and when I finally made it Scotty was out, so I bought myself a coffee and a pastry and decided to lounge about in the sun. I sat down on one of the benches right in the middle of the marketplace and nibbled on the dainty as an endless stream of pigeons fluttered down to peck up my crumbs. It reminded me of the old man I'd met in the Canongate.

'I have to sort this out,' I thought, and I wondered nervously what Mum and Dad were saying to each other and whether I should have left them at all.

Whether maybe I should have sat it out for as long as it took. For ever. I was relieved when Scotty turned up and we walked down to Holyrood together and played frisbee in the park against the backdrop of Arthur's Seat until the chill came on and the sky darkened and it was time for me to leave. We talked about Simon, and Scotty promised to smooth things out while I was away that week.

'I'll take him for a couple of pints, nine holes and a game of poker,' he said. 'I might even let him win a bit more than usual. He'll settle down, you'll see.'

That afternoon he was an angel, Scotty, really great. He just listened for ages, and all my worries, all my concerns came tumbling out one by one. He was so patient and later on, towards seven o'clock or so, I told him all about Mum and Dad and some things I thought I had forgotten about from when Simon and I were little. Things which had been hidden inside my mind and had only just surfaced into coherence. The small wheels which ran the machine.

'I was always bad and he was always good,' I said.

'And your parents went for that?' he asked.

We were walking hand in hand up the High Street on our way to Waverley Station by then.

'Yeah,' I shrugged my shoulders. 'I asked too many questions.'

Scotty stopped in the street. He pulled me close into him and kissed me in that gentle way of his. Then he held me and, well, my family didn't seem so important any more.

'We can take this as slowly as you like,' he said. 'You make the pace. They've never treated you right, Rachel. But it's going to be OK. I told you – you're amazing. And soon it will end. It'll have to.'

'Thanks,' I grinned and I felt all tearful because Scotty is so cool.

He saw me right down to the station. We drank Costa

coffees out of paper cups and shared a tuna sandwich while we waited for the Glasgow train to arrive. We laughed as we watched a couple of ruddy-faced drunks stumble towards the station bar and then stumble back out again as they were turned away. When the show was over I sat up, cross-legged on the hard, green metal station bench and watched Scotty instead as he sipped on the last of his tea. It was a far better view.

'Next weekend,' he said, 'maybe we could hang out together some more.'

'If you put a padlock on your door, sure,' I grinned.

'OK,' he said, 'a padlock. To hold off your crazed male relations.'

It was just like *Brief Encounter* on the platform as he saw me on to the train and we kissed for ages before I finally climbed aboard and hung out of the window waving as it set off for the west along the tracks through Princes Street Gardens. I touched my lips like some lovesick teenager, and ran my hand down my cheek, just the way he had done after he'd kissed me. I realised that I was grinning inanely, for no other reason than I had been kissed and I let out a low, girlish giggle. Then, as I settled back into a scratchy, velvet seat I thought to myself that I was one secret down, and the big one was still to go, but with Nina on my side I figured that it should only take me half the time to get my head around the Ma Polinski conundrum. I tried not to think of what it might be like telling Mum and Dad about that. Kissing some guy was one thing, but financial matters of that magnitude would, I was sure, evoke quite a different response from them. They weren't going to be just quietly pissed off about it anyway. There would, no doubt, be fireworks.

'It'll end soon,' I said to myself, echoing Scotty. 'It'll have to.'

I got into Glasgow at nine and settled myself down to get on with the job in hand. I suppose there were some ways I'd abdicated all responsibility by then. Scotty was dealing with Simon and making me feel good. Nina was on to the Ma Polinski thing. I allowed myself to be guided by others. Defined by them. It was easier that way. I let everyone else take the lead even though it wasn't right, and Nina sensed it, I think. Nina got on to my case. That's what best friends are for. Making you face up to things.

The weather wasn't too bad, all in all, that first week in May of last year. Nina and I planned some working picnic lunches sitting out in the park. I'd bring fizzy mineral water, some French bread and a carton of the first of the summer's strawberries, and she'd bring some cheese from Iain Mellis and we'd sit out and sun ourselves on the grass and make open cheese sandwiches while we gently got brown. The daffodils had come and gone, but there were tulips in the park and still some of the spring's late blossom on the trees. It was really beautiful. I think our lunch in the park plan only went awry on the Thursday when it chucked it down from ten in the morning until seven at night and we had to remove to the local greasy spoon café for chips and mayonnaise and cups of hot tea instead. Over the course of the week Nina got me organised, she kicked me right up the arse because really, up until then, I hadn't even written anything down. It's funny how, when you write things down, actually make your mark on the paper, you settle them and somehow it's easier to see what is really going on. On the first day we made lists of the information that we had, and lists of possible leads too. Nina smiled a lazy smile as she finished up the last of her sandwich and pressed a strawberry between her teeth, grinding it up slowly.

'Delicious,' she grinned and then she cocked her head to one side and rolled over on to her back, basking in the heat. It got measurably hotter when the sun peeped out from behind the clouds from time to time. You had to take advantage of it. 'There'll be even more cloud coming this afternoon,' she said, 'but for now it's just dandy.'

I sat up and watched two guys in short sleeved T-shirts and baseball caps who were rollerblading on a collision course with each other further up the path on the other side of the grass. They were playing chicken, swooping this way and that at speed, missing each other by inches and then turning around and starting again.

'Have you thought about what you're going to do with the money?' Nina asked with her eyes closed.

I settled back down next to her to consider it for a moment and stopped watching the near crashes which were taking place only a few yards away.

'Not really,' I shrugged. 'Buy a house, I suppose. I might move back to Edinburgh. It's only been two weeks since I found out about it. I haven't really had enough time to figure it out.'

'You going to keep on working?'

'Sure. Yes. Of course.' I must have sounded shocked. It hadn't really occurred to me that I would give up my job. Not after the first, heady realisation that it was possible. It had never entered my mind as a real possibility. I turned over on to my tummy and leaned on my arm, watching Nina's face for any hint of what she was getting at. 'Why? Do you think that I should?' I asked.

'No,' said Nina. 'Just asking. I mean, you haven't spent any of it yet. It's like you can't believe that it's really yours.'

'I spent a thousand pounds on clothes at Princes Square,' I pointed out. 'I paid for dinner.'

Nina's eyebrows raised almost imperceptibly, so I knew that this required further explanation and a few designer clothes and some food wasn't going to get me off the hook. She didn't say anything, only stretched the edges of her mouth and touched up her already perfect red lipstick.

'I suppose I feel that the money isn't mine. Not really,' I started. 'It was hers and I want to know why she left it to me before I lay into the shopping. I mean, I want to know if there was a reason for it. I guess I'm not sure what I ought to do because eight million quid is such a huge amount. I kind of think that if I know why she left it to me then I'll somehow just know what I want to do. I'll know what'll feel right.'

'That's bogging,' said Nina and she opened her eyes. 'Ma Polinski is dead, Rachel. She's gone. She was a crazy old lady and now she's kicked the bucket. I mean, of course we should try to find out why she left you all her earthly possessions. It's intriguing. It's a message from beyond the grave which she certainly meant for you. I do think that she wanted you to know something all right. And that's important. But as for the money, well, it's happened. It's real. And I get the feeling that you'd like to ignore it. You just want to throw yourself into a puzzle. A crisis. A drama. You shouldn't let that stop you enjoying what she left you – Jesus Christ, sweetheart, you've got to do what you want to do. And no dead old lady is going to get you off that. I don't think it works that way. You've spent years fucked up about money, Rachel. As long as I've known you. That whole Simon thing has been a millstone. Well, here's your chance and you're fucking ignoring it.'

'Shit,' I said, and I lay back in the sun. 'It just doesn't feel right to spend any of it yet.'

'Well, one thing's for sure,' said Nina, 'that old lady was savvy with her money. She wouldn't have wanted you to just sit on it.'

And then we lay there for a while and I spent ages thinking about what it is that you ought to do when you've got that much money, because Nina after all (as always) was pretty well right. At two o'clock we headed our separate ways and Nina had had her go at me and didn't say any more about it. We hugged at the park gates and then I virtually jogged back to work. Nina gets great lunch breaks out at the Burrell because she works so hard that they let her take the odd liberty here and there and don't seem to really mind how late she gets back after lunch. I went back knowing that I was on a shorter leash, but determined to sort out the Ma Polinski conundrum, so much so that I didn't really care if I was half an hour late back at my desk. I was half pissed off with Nina for not humouring me about the money too. At least, though, it hotted me up and I wanted to really get on with it and maybe that was her point. Not that I hadn't spent enough cash, but that I hadn't got on and taken responsibility for myself. I hadn't thought about what I really wanted to do. I had got lazy in my obligations. So later that afternoon while Nina was swanning around the light, glass-walled hallways of the Burrell, I took my side of the list in hand in my small, dark office and I rang Mike Williams and enquired into Tomasz Polinski's will, and I also made calls to the Home Office and of course to the police. It took a long time to turn anything up and, with the officials at any rate, I reckon it was only my credentials at the museum which meant that I got hold of any information at all. I spun them a line about a planned wartime exhibit and left only my work number for their return calls.

Two days it took. And while I waited for them to ring back I doodled. A house and a car and a big pile of books and Scotty and I in a sea of candles. And Nina with a big pile of money in her hand, smiling. And for some reason there was a little puppy at her heels, and beside all that a list of the information I turned up. Pages of it as it came in bit by bit, about Molly Savage's second husband. Tomasz Polinski was an extraordinarily nasty piece of work, as it turned out. A drinker. A liar. A cheat. A violent man. I'm convinced now that Molly, when she first met him, didn't know what he was really like. She couldn't have. She'd never have married him. And as the information came in I began to build up a picture. A profile. First off, well, the guy hadn't made a will at all. When we looked into it, that was because he didn't have anything to leave anyone. Tomasz Polinski was penniless and always had been, so, I suppose, it was just as well that he had bagged himself a very wealthy wife. His suits and his shoes had been handmade in London and he had smoked Henry Clay cigars. He drove a chocolate-brown Rolls-Royce Phantom, you know. None of these things ever came cheap. They still don't today and he was the talk of the Edinburgh gossip columns on account of his expensive tastes. Considered flamboyant and exotic because of his foreign background and his rather heroic years during the Second World War, he seemed to be a bit of a dandy. Nina did some sterling work pulling information out of the newspaper archive where she found it easier to gain access than I did. She didn't cover the political columns, which I'd already worked over in the City Chambers archive. She hit gossip columns and the local news. Gossip columns in those days, well, society columns as they were known, were nothing like *Hello!* or *OK!* or anything else with an exclamation mark after the title. But Molly and Tomasz attended their fair share of public-spirited events and so were duly snapped all over the place. The columns were useful. They provided more detail and way more colour – there were the photos of the couple attending openings and launches, there were those society column reports of parties they had attended together and a couple of references to the travels they had undertaken abroad which were particularly note-worthy at a time when foreign holidays weren't at all common. They were, as it turned out, considered rather flash. All that information was especially useful because it was there, on the library microfiches, that we found out Tomasz Polinski had a police record.

He'd been taken to court twice for brawling and drunken outbursts and one night, as he arrived home from an evening of vodka with whisky chasers at the Polish Ex-Serviceman's Club in the New Town, his wife had called the police because she was afraid of his violent temper. It was riveting stuff. It brought them alive, I suppose. There were rumours he'd assaulted a British ex-serviceman in a dockside bar at the Shore, but no charges were brought. He was, if nothing else, a lucky bastard. Nina had printed the lot out and we pored over it at Vittorio's on Wednesday night. The next day I tried to get hold of the police records relating to the incidents but once someone's dead all their criminal records are wiped and well, besides that, I suppose that the police probably wouldn't have released the information anyway because of the Data Protection Act. It was worth a try though. There were eight probable drunk and disorderlies and three assaults that we could find.

On the Thursday night Nina and I wandered all around town. It was weird. We just couldn't settle anywhere. We went into a couple of pubs now and again to try to sit down and just have a drink, but in the end we weren't really in much of a mood for it. I felt really sorry for old Molly Savage. I mean, her first husband was an old man and he died within eighteen months of their marriage. Then everyone tried to stop her from doing what she wanted to do, keeping on the business she had inherited and her husband's place on the council. Then she met this guy who probably seemed like a real gentleman and she did him a huge favour by marrying him, because otherwise he might have been deported. But then he turned out to be a real nightmare. A drinker with a violent temper to boot. A petty criminal. I just kept thinking about that stupid game she used to play with the pink sugar biscuits, hiding them away in her pockets and making me guess where they were, and it seemed to me kind of touching that she bothered to play with me like that, when she must have been so miserable for so much of the time.

'Well, there you are,' said Nina after dinner as she sipped half-heartedly on a pint of Director's up at the bar in the Variety. We'd eaten fish and chips in the end and then moved around the corner to the pub for a quick one. 'Her husband was a bastard. She didn't want to leave her millions to him to be frittered away on fast cars and slick outfits. She wanted to leave her money to someone she liked. So she chose you, sugar. You lucky thing.'

'Mmm,' I murmured, holding on tight to the locket round my neck. I wasn't entirely convinced. 'I know why she didn't leave it to him all right. I just can't see why she left it to me, if you see what I mean. There's more to it. What about the mural? It seems to me that an unhappy marriage just isn't enough.'

Nina deliberated. She leaned slowly over the bar and motioned towards the barman to fetch her a packet of smoky bacon crisps and then she paid him slowly out of the change which was lying out on the bar top in front of her. Then she shrugged.

'I don't know about that but I do know it's possible she didn't have anyone else to leave her money to,' she pointed out. 'Maybe you were the best of a bad lot of possible heirs. Maybe she was just fond of you. Confused. Maybe she'd no one else to reach out to.'

I grinned and watched Nina toying with the crisps and then, in seconds, giving up and getting out her cigarettes because, of course, it was a cigarette that she really wanted. She lit up slowly, savouring her first fag of the day. It was nine or so in the evening and she'd held out really well. She gave a little gasp as she exhaled for the first time and then she turned to me, waiting to see if I agreed with her.

'Well, I don't go for that. For one thing,' I pointed out, 'why, for example, didn't she leave it to those kids?'

The kids in question had been the children who lived in the slums all around her. Tomasz Polinski wasn't the only one who'd had some colour added to his story by Nina's forays into the newspaper archive on the Monday and Tuesday of that week. She'd also found out the reason why Molly Savage had gone down in history as Ma Polinski even though she didn't seem to actually use her married name herself. At the time it happened she must have come across as really kooky, absolutely barmy in fact. The National Health Service had just opened its doors and it was a big hit. There were queues of people every day for the first few months, prolonging doctors' surgeries for hours on end as the nation caught up on the huge backlog of untreated illnesses brought about by doctors' fees which most people couldn't afford. Suddenly all treatment was free, so there was this huge rush not just for doctors of course, but for opticians and dentists too. They prescribed an amazing number of spectacles during those first few months of the health service. It was like the nation could suddenly see properly. The same went for fillings. All at once, people could eat without pain. Anyway, just, in fact, like the doctors themselves, initially, Ma Polinski was dubious about the National Health Service and she was quoted in the papers warning about the enormous immunisation programme which was underway and talking about natural, homeopathic cures and herbal remedies and local, personal care. It turns out that she had run a bit of a dispensary herself, prescribing the odd pill for her neighbours. It turns out that well, in that respect anyway, she was a bit of a hippy before her time. There was one photograph of her in the *Edinburgh Evening News*, just surrounded by children whom she had treated over the years and the strapline read 'Old Ma Polinski'. It seems like it really stuck, but then I do kind of understand why. It was a great photo. She looked like some kind of grey-haired white witch doling out herbal cures and the kids around her looked really eager and just covered in smiles. Beside that, the other photos in the society columns just paled into insignificance. Once you'd seen it, she was Ma Polinski and that was that.

'Why didn't she leave it to the kids then?' I asked Nina.

But she only shrugged. 'How do you leave something like that to whole bunch of young kids? Slum kids to boot. In the fucking seventies. Look, Rachel, maybe she just liked you. Maybe she could see that your dad was going to cut you out. Just like she had been expected to disappear after her first husband died. Maybe she wanted to give it to you because of that.'

'I suppose,' I conceded. 'I suppose you're right. I just wish we could speak to someone who knew her. Really knew her. And I still don't get the mural thing, too,' I said, pulling on the locket, 'the way it was hidden and everything. It's specific. It's a specific thing.'

Nina nodded and then she pulled her notebook from her pocket as if it was a last resort. 'Well, I have done a little extra background research,' she said, almost involuntarily, as she flicked through the pages, 'and I know you didn't want to, but I came up with this.' She pushed the notepad over to me open at the right page where she had printed carefully *Hamish Williams, Cherry Gates Care Hotel, Juniper Green,* a phone number and a couple of other names.

'I know your lawyer said that his great-uncle was impossible to communicate with, but well, I spoke to them at the home and although they say he's pretty incoherent and everything, they did say that he's better on the past than the present just now,' she said. 'Maybe he knows something. Maybe he can explain.'

I laid my head in my hands.

'It's relatives only,' Nina continued, 'so I said I was a great-niece of his. From Turin.'

'What?' I asked her in disbelief.

'Well, it's the only way we were going to get in.'

'You made an appointment?'

'Not exactly,' she admitted. 'I just said that I was in the country for a couple of weeks and would be interested in coming to visit him. We can go after midday any day that you like. It's our only outstanding lead. It's all we've got if you want to go on.'

I thought about it for a moment. I mean, it did kind of make sense. He was our only direct link with Ma Polinski and, well, he might remember something, anything. She had to be easily his most eccentric and interesting client, after all. He'd known her for years. And I figured we didn't have a lot to lose. Nina was right. There was nowhere else to go and there were still things which needed to be explained.

'Oh, fuck it. Why not?' I said, raising my pint glass and thinking to myself that it was the last thing we'd do – our last lead. That it would round the whole thing off nicely. Nina grinned and lifted her own drink up to click brims with me.

'Cheers,' she said. 'To Hamish Williams.'

'Yeah, to Hamish Williams. Here's hoping the old guy remembers whatever it is that he knows.'

Chapter Seventeen

We pulled into the drive at the Cherry Gates Care Hotel at about half twelve. It was Friday and we'd both taken the day off work at no notice at all. Well, Nina had called in and told them she wasn't going to be in that day, which was cool because the Burrell do that very understanding thing for her and, like I keep saying (probably because I'm jealous), they give her a lot of leeway. I, on the other hand, had just pulled a good, old-fashioned sickie.

We'd driven all the way chatting about work really, expecting our visit to be more or less routine. I had accepted the stuff Nina had said in the pub. I wasn't expecting to find out very much more, just to finish the story off nicely, to tie up all our leads. To add in some kind of detail which we'd obviously missed. I was almost expecting it to be mundane. We weren't even really thinking about it. I was taking a turn at the driving and Nina was telling me the story of Sir William Burrell – I always like that. I mean, perhaps altruists are always of interest to the curatorial staff of a museum. The old man had been pretty canny – he'd picked up a Tang Dynasty figure for thirty-two pounds and ten shillings one year. Another time it was a self-portrait of Rembrandt for twelve and a half thousand pounds. He collected everything – stained glass to tableware, loom-woven sixteenth-century tapestries to royal memorabilia to relics from the tombs of the ancient Egyptians. So anyway, we chatted all the way and agreed to go for a late lunch after our appointment with Hamish Williams and I promised that when we did I'd stop going on about Scotty because apparently that's just what I was doing. All the time. And it was driving Nina nuts and making her do sick noises whenever I slipped up and did it again.

The Care Hotel was in an expensively cleaned, stone Victorian house which had obviously been converted for the purpose. There was a modern extension built all around one side of the place which seemed to stretch back much further than the original building, and all along one side there was a conservatory where old ladies were sitting up in comfortable chairs, looking out at the driveway. As we got out of the car Nina waved over at them, and they all looked rather bemused but, still, they waved back with their hands held up high above their heads.

'You realise they're going to worry all day about whether they know you or not, and who on earth you are,' I scolded her.

'I'm just being friendly,' Nina retorted. 'Besides, if they're that bad they'll forget me pretty quickly in any case.'

We walked across the gravel and rang the bell at the front door.

'I'll do all the talking,' said Nina.

She has this thing that I'm a really bad liar. Well, I suppose she's pretty well right. The couple of times we've had to tell whoppers to get us out of one scrape or another, I've always fluffed up. And they were kind of low-grade lies to tutors about late essays at college or to parents about how much the dress cost or how late the party actually went on. This was lying in a different league.

'Don't worry,' I hissed back at her, 'I won't say a thing.'

And then the nurse came to open the door. The hallway smelled strongly of air-freshener. It was a kind of offensive, lily of the valley smell, but it was better than what I had been expecting, which was that awful old lady smell of urine and talcum powder.

When Great-Auntie Petra took ill we all went to see her for the last time in the hospital. I was perhaps ten years old and the thing I remember most about it is the terrible smell of the place. It was a hospice ward, full of very, very old people, none of whom would leave the place alive. Auntie Petra wasn't really sure what was going on. She was fading. I tried to climb up on to the bed so that I could be next to her and give her a cuddle but I got told off. The visit seemed to go on for ages. After I'd tried to get up on to the bed, Simon read a story out loud to us all from his *Lost Warlords of Atlantis* book. Then everyone just sat around for a bit and the grown-ups made small talk. I'll never forget it, that day we went to see Great-Auntie Petra. It was about a fortnight later, I think, that she died, but Mum and Dad didn't tell us anything about it. They waited until we asked, several weeks later, how the old lady was getting on in the hospital and if we could go to visit her again. We were all having dinner in the kitchen. Mum had made a lasagne. There was an awkward kind of silence after I'd asked the question and I put down my fork, sensing that the reply was going to be difficult, that it might take some time to come, or at least to sink in.

'Great-Auntie Petra died,' my father said flatly. 'Two months ago.'

I remember feeling slightly confused. I was aware that it wasn't supposed to go like that. You were supposed to feel cosseted, you were supposed to cry. You were supposed to know straight away. People were supposed to comfort you.

'You should have told me. I would have liked to have gone to the funeral,' I pointed out in righteous, ten-year-old indignation, and I looked for my brother to back me up, but Simon didn't say anything, of course. He just accepted it. And I kept waiting, my eyes shining with fury. I felt like I'd been left out. It was horrible. There was another silence and then Dad laid down his fork too and took me on.

'You don't have to know about these things, Rachel,' he said as if I was just a nuisance. A pesky kid. 'You are a child. We're the grown-ups. We'll deal with it. Your mother and I.'

And that was supposed to be it. I remember lying in bed that night, trying to figure out which day it had happened, and kind of recalling seeing Mum bleary-eyed one time and her saying that she just had a cold. And Great-Aunt Petra was dead and was buried before we ever knew. It's hard to believe that story, I know. It's a difficult one to take in. When I told Nina she looked at me with her eyes wide, wide open as if I had made it up. But I didn't. That's exactly what happened. It's kind of a perfect example really of Mum and Dad and their cold and impregnable fortress of control and being in the hospice reminded me of it, I suppose. I shuddered.

The nurse led us up the stairway and along a corridor, while Nina chatted to her on the subject of Great-Uncle Hamish and I tried to come to terms with my own thoughts, until we all stopped together at a door, and the nurse knocked. A woman's voice called to come in, and then the nurse turned back towards us.

'You'll know Flora, of course,' she smiled, 'she would be, let me see, your great-aunt, wouldn't she? She visits most days around this time,' and before we could think of something to say, or just leg it down the corridor, the door was opened and we had walked into the room, caught completely on the hop. It must have been one of the Care Hotel's finest with a beautiful view of the gardens, and a high, corniced ceiling. There were lots of plants and then, sleeping in among them, old

Hamish Williams, pale under the white sheets of his varnished pine bed and an old lady in a purplish-grey tweed suit, with sparkling eyes to match, perched beside him on a high-backed chair, the sun streaming through the window behind her.

'I'll leave you now,' the nurse smiled and closed the door as she left.

I realised that Nina was about to come clean. She was taking a deep breath. I could hear her, as if time had stopped. I could feel her muscles tensing up. We had been rumbled before we had even started.

'I'm Flora Lachlan,' the old lady smiled as she got up. She had a soft, east coast, Highland accent and she moved very gracefully and with dignity. 'I shouldn't really be here. I told them that I was his first wife, you see. Well, his wife is dead now. I didn't think there was any harm. I like to visit him so much. I worked for him for years, you know. I was Hamish's secretary and his friend. Please don't tell them.'

'We're not supposed to be here, either,' I overtook Nina by a hair's breadth and moved forward to shake the old lady's hand. She seemed to sparkle even more as her smile widened. It was a mad sort of coincidence. Partners in crime.

'Who are you then?' she asked quizzically.

So we introduced ourselves and then we sat down, Nina on the edge of the bed and me in another chair which I pulled over from beside the old, empty fireplace.

I began to blurt out why we had come. About the bequest and how mysterious it seemed and how we had hoped that Hamish Williams might be able to help us. Flora shook her head slowly and her eyes became suddenly sad. 'Oh, I doubt it, dear. I mean, often he doesn't even know who I am. Every day for forty years I worked in his office. We were friends. More than that. I remember Molly Polinski, though. Oh, yes indeed.

Perhaps there is some way that I might be able to help you. What is it, exactly, that you want to know?'

We took Flora for lunch. It turned out that she went over to Juniper Green most days on the bus from her flat in Cluny Gardens. It was a long trail right across town from Morningside, but, she explained, she couldn't drive any more. Her eyesight wasn't up to it. I think Flora Lachlan is the prettiest old lady I have ever seen. We tend not to think of old people that way, but she was just so sweet. We only spent a couple of hours with her, but I don't think I've ever met anyone so lovely. She was just gorgeous. As we left Cherry Gates she peered out of the back window of the car and stared up at the house in the vague direction of Hamish Williams' room and then she laid her hands in her lap with a resigned and dignified sadness. We drove her back all the way over to Morningside and took her to the local tearoom for a late lunch. I suppose it must have been well after two o'clock by then. Flora and I found a table and settled down while Nina went up to the counter and bought milky coffees for us and some lentil soup, a double slice of coffee cake and a pot of Earl Grey tea for Flora. It was at that point that Flora started to glow. You could see it as she tucked in. You could see that she really enjoyed the feeling that we were looking after her. She had friends, I think. I don't think it was loneliness that I saw about her. No, definitely not, she was just really enjoying herself.

'Hamish was a wonderful man, you know,' she started. 'He was a very good lawyer, too. I went to work for him just after he opened up the firm. I was twenty-three, you see, and the war had only just started. Hamish was too old to be called up, but he did whatever he could for the war effort. And he gave us all in the office time off to be volunteers. I worked in the Red Cross twice a week, with the soldiers who had been sent home. The injured men. It was a time when people were close to reality, if you see what I mean. I often hear people say that. Not that nothing bad ever happened during the war. No, not that. But well, we knew we were all lucky to be alive. We knew what really mattered. Hamish was so public-spirited really. All through his life he was like that. Outgoing and generous. He's so changed now, so quiet, but I know that he's still in there, inside that brilliant mind.'

Flora nodded at a couple of old ladies she knew, who had come into the tearoom and taken a table on the opposite wall from ours. Beside the door.

'They'll think you are relations,' she smiled with a hint of pride at the thought and I reached out and touched her arm while Nina poured her a fresh cup of tea. Then she continued talking.

'Molly Savage, as she was then, was already one of Hamish's clients. She had been with him in his previous position and she moved her business with him to the new firm when he set it up. I always thought she was such an admirable woman. Very brave and very hard-working. During the war, you know, she moved out to Portobello and she took in three evacuees, I understand. From London. She was a great one for helping people. Right through her life. You don't always see that sort of kindness in a person and she gave away a lot of money, as I recall, to help the children in the Canongate where she had her shop. Hamish always dealt with that for her on a confidential basis. She never wanted anyone to know, but I suppose that it is all right to tell you that now. She's so long dead and, well, she must have had some feeling for you to leave you everything as she did. I'm sure you'll use the money wisely and in her spirit, Rachel.'

I nodded. 'I'll try,' I said. 'I haven't really done anything with any of it yet. You see, I'm not sure why she left it to me.'

And then there was a ghastly, dead silence.

'Don't you know?' Flora asked me, the disbelief coming through in her voice.

I shook my head, breathless. 'No,' I said. 'No.'

Flora stopped eating. She had finished about half of the soup and had moved on to her coffee cake but then she laid her fork down and paused before speaking.

'Oh, Rachel,' she said, 'I'm so sorry. I had no idea. It was her husband, you see. Mr Polinski. Well, I think she felt so guilty about him. Hamish was very perturbed about it. The kick seemed to go right out of her just shortly after the marriage. And then, when she found out about him. Oh dear. I mean, she was so generous to everyone. Such a nice lady. And he had taken advantage of her so badly. If she hadn't married him when she did then the Home Office would have sent him away. Back to Poland or wherever it was. The Communists were in charge there at that time, you know, and he'd told her that he would have been shot if they'd sent him back. She thought he was a war hero. Well, that is what everyone had thought. But it wasn't true, you see. He had fought in the Resistance for a while where he was from. But the Resistance in the Balkans, well, it was very different from the Resistance in France. They killed a lot of people. A lot of their own people. Hamish looked into it for her and, well, they were very, very cruel men. He heard stories, you know, that people said they would rather be caught by the Nazis than fall into the hands of the Resistance at that time. I can't remember the name they used. But, dear me, they shot a lot of people, you know. Quite unnecessarily. Hamish found photographs. Evidence. Men sawing other men's heads off. Awful things. I remember shedding tears. I'd never seen before . . . well . . . I think they call it ethnic cleansing now. Murderers. Hamish offered to get Molly a divorce from that man, but somehow, well, it is very difficult for young people like yourselves to understand, but divorce was a very difficult thing in those days. And somehow I think she found it hard to believe about him. Mr Polinski was so charismatic, you see. And we had all liked him, sad to say. I was quite ashamed of that. But he had seemed to be so very attractive. One minute he would be charming and well, the next time you heard of him he would have been rolling home drunk and scaring her half to death. But however bad you thought he might be for his drinking and all of that, well, you would never believe that he had been a collaborator with the Nazis. There now.'

'A collaborator?' I asked.

'Yes,' Flora sighed. 'He had worked in their records office, tracking people down. The last three years of the war he had done it. The Resistance in that part of the world had all but collapsed, you see, and, well, there was very great confusion. He had changed his allegiances although really, to be honest, he had only moved from one set of thugs to another. After the war there was even more confusion. The Russians moved in – Warsaw had fallen, you know. Tomasz Polinski had known he would find it hard under the Communists and then, somehow, he had got out and made his way over here. He had all the right papers, you see. Well, that had been part of his job, and they said that he must have been working on his escape plan for some time. Polish ex-servicemen were granted British citizenship, you know, for their bravery in the war. They had fought for us. Tomasz Polinski claimed his British citizenship, well, he claimed someone else's British citizenship. Probably some poor dead man who really did fight for his country. It was a terrible thing for a man to do, in a line of terrible things which he had done. He had murdered his own countrymen, spread terrible terror, and then switched sides and sent a lot of people to their deaths in the concentration camps.'

'Auschwitz, Treblinka and Majdanek,' I said, as if by rote, the names of the camps where three million ethnic Poles were killed. The names of the death camps the Nazis used in that part of Europe. And I started to cry. I get very emotional about it. I know too much not to. All my research into the Second World War and the atrocities of the Nazis. It's very hard to understand, to really get a handle on how many people Hitler killed, not only in the concentration camps but in total. In the killing leagues his regime has the highest body count of any dictator of the twentieth century by far. Pol Pot's regime accounts for two million deaths, Mao Zedong's regime was almost as bloody. Joseph Stalin's Soviet purges murdered twenty-five million. Hitler though, well, the Nazis, I suppose, rate the highest – I've heard some estimations as high as forty-seven million people. And the cruelty with which it was done, the callousness, is really beyond imagination. It was a true reign of terror. Most people separate themselves from imagining it. It's a normal response, I suppose, to think well, that's in the past, it's gone, and to sequester yourself from the horror of it through time. And then all those deaths, so much agony and terror becomes just another statistic consigned to history. You don't have to feel so much that way. It numbs you. But like I said before, my job, the way I think, is all about bringing history alive and for me, with the Second World War, because of my mother, it's a personal thing too. Reading the history books, watching the black-and-white footage of the time, well, when I was very young it was the only way I had of understanding her because she wouldn't talk about it. I saw some film a while back of the children who came out of Auschwitz – there were, I suppose, forty or so of them who survived and there is this moving picture of them, thin in their tiny striped suits marching out of the camp to freedom. I'll never forget their eyes. And knowing that my mother, in her own little blue-and-white striped suit was in Dachau at the moment that footage was shot. The camp hadn't been liberated then. She was there, she was alone, and Great-Auntie Petra wasn't even on her way. It made my blood boil that Tomasz Polinski got out of Poland and that he was never tried at Nuremberg.

I understood at last. It was a kind of terrible relief, but I had been right, I had known there was something extraordinary, some connection I had sensed and I felt so sorry for Molly Polinski, living with him, being deceived, marrying him. It's hard to imagine it, at a time when you stayed married no matter what, discovering something so awful, so chilling, so real. Because she had been alive through the war. It was real to her. There isn't a modern equivalent for us, in our cosseted, Western lives. In all our safety. There really isn't. And I understood then, at that moment, why she had left the money to me. It wasn't that he was a violent drunkard, or that they just didn't get on or something. It wasn't that at all. He was a murderer, he was evil, he was a deceiver and now I understood the mural on the ceiling in her bedroom. He had touched her with the same hands that had murdered God knows how many people and betrayed God knows how many more. He had lied his way into the country and taken her in so that he could stay. She was a moral kind of person, she'd have felt he ought to have been tried for his war crimes. Damn right he should have been, and somewhere among that she'd lost her way, I think. She hadn't publicly uncovered him for what he really was. Like a cuckold who doesn't want to see the truth.

Nina had her arm around my shoulder, and Flora was holding my hand quite tightly as the tears streamed right down my cheeks.

'There, there,' Flora tried to comfort me, but I was inconsolable.

'He shouldn't be buried on hallowed ground,' I murmured. 'He shouldn't be buried there. Next to her. That can't be what she would have wanted. It isn't right. Is it?'

Flora went into her handbag and found a paper handkerchief. 'Here,' she said, 'use this.'

I dried my eyes and blew my nose and took another sip of my coffee.

'Hamish went to Brazil, you know, to collect the bodies. He was very fond of Mrs Polinski and he felt very sorry for her. It was very shocking because when he got there they were so mutilated. It had been a terrible accident. He arranged for their remains to be shipped back to Leith and he arranged for the burials. Black marble gravestones, I remember.'

I nodded. 'We saw them,' I sniffed. 'We went to the graveyard.'

And then at last we knew.

We walked her across the main road and along Cluny Gardens to the doorway of her house where we said goodbye.

'Thank you,' I mumbled, as I reached out to hug her. 'I've been wondering what it was all about.'

'I'm so glad that I met you at the home,' Flora replied. 'Goodbye now, girls.'

Then we watched her go through the black iron gate and up her garden path and Nina took my arm and we walked together back over the main road to the car. We sat in the front and I leaned my head down on to the dashboard and held my hands over my eyes.

'Do you think that she knew about your mother?' Nina asked.

'I don't know. I suppose so,' I whispered.

Nina laid her hand gently on my back. 'What do you want to do?' she said.

I lifted myself upright again slowly. 'Can we go to

189

Morbrax?' I asked her. 'I think we ought to.'

And she started up the engine and pulled out into the steady stream of traffic which pulsed down Morningside Road. I thought that it was all over then. I thought of the trip out to Morbrax as some kind of a fitting end to it, but I didn't quite realise that I had such a temper. I was really going out there just as some kind of sign that I understood why she had done it. I thought that that weekend I was going to be able to tell my parents, to settle down to normality. To spend some quiet time with Scotty without any of the Ma Polinski story on my mind. I hadn't a clue that it was going to escalate.

Chapter Eighteen

By the time we were out in the countryside it was getting on for four o'clock, I suppose. Nina was driving and I was just staring ahead at the road thinking. I couldn't get it out of my mind. I'd thought once I knew what had been going on that I would settle, but the more I thought about it, the more furious I was. Old Mr Polinski had been a Nazi and in post-war Britain there wasn't really anything worse you could possibly have been. It was the lowest of the low and you could sink no further. And Molly Polinski, well, when she found out, she chose me to leave her money to and, like I had said to Nina, in my mind that meant that she must have known about my mother and the months she'd spent locked up and starving in Dachau. I mean, there aren't any coincidences in life like that, are there? That kind of thing just doesn't really happen. I was a Holocaust survivor's daughter and I suppose that I appealed to her because I was the daughter of an antiques dealer to boot and I was, perhaps inevitably, going to be cut out of the business. Maybe even when I was still in pigtails she could see how it was all going to happen because she knew how that little game worked. She'd nearly fallen victim to it herself. One way or another the whole thing made perfect sense to me then and I knew in my mind exactly why she'd left me the inheritance. The whole thing was sinking in slowly and I realised that it was a point of principle for her after all – an ethical kind of investment which she was making in me. She seemed to be a lady who knew about justice and who had a strong sense of what was right and what was wrong. The mural on the ceiling above her marital bed and the sundial kind of clicked into place then, too, as the sort of things which would stand the test of time until the day an antiques dealer's daughter would notice them and perhaps follow them up. A message from beyond the grave to let someone who would care know what had happened. Maybe a way, I realised, to take action without having to face the consequences. 'I'll never know,' I thought to myself, 'if she still loved him. I'll never know why she didn't do more herself. Expose him. I'll never know if she meant to leave me a letter as well.' She hadn't, after all, been expecting to die when she did.

As we got closer to the village, Nina speeded up. She was getting used to the road by then. I was so immersed in what had happened I couldn't think about anything elsc. I can't tell you what the weather was like or what other cars were on the road. I just remember feeling absolutely absorbed in her story, in the way that she must have felt. In what it had been like. The window beside me was open very slightly and the cool air suddenly made me shiver and then, as we rounded a corner, I raised my eyes as if I was waking up from a dream and I thought that I saw something flying towards us at speed. It was probably only a bird. A big white bird which flew right past the car. I was so emotional and it happened so quickly. Nina said she didn't notice anything. But I saw it go right past us winging along, and the face had such black, black eyes. I was jumpy, anyway, so I just screamed. Because it was so fluid, and also because it was so white, well, it looked just like a ghost and at the time, of course, that was what I was convinced I had seen. Nina made an emergency stop and then pulled over to the side of the road and put on the hazard lights.

'What is it? Are you OK?' she asked.

My hand was shaking violently as I pointed and I turned around in my seat to try to make out where it might have gone. It was like a spectre, a translucent spirit, a banshee as it swooped past me and in my fevered mind I was sure it was her, I was sure that it had her face. Nina slid her seat back, took her seat belt off and laid both her hands steadily on my shoulders to try to bring me back down to earth.

'I thought I saw something. I thought it was her.'

Nina guided me back around so I was sitting facing towards the front of the car again. Then she ferreted around in her handbag until she found a blue plastic bottle of still mineral water.

'Here,' she offered it over to me.

I took a sip or two and I felt a bit better. My lips were absolutely parched dry.

'You've some imagination,' she said.

I nodded.

'Still want to go to Morbrax?' she asked.

I nodded again. 'Definitely,' I replied.

I really needed to, you see. I wanted to go to Ma Polinski's place. I wanted to feel close to her. As we pulled off and drove the last five or ten minutes to the village I just kept thinking about how much she must have hated him. How angry she must have been at allowing herself to be taken in. At being so deceived. She must have felt very trapped and hated having to live with him and every time she looked at him only saw someone who was evil. A liar. A murderer. A coward. A traitor to his country. Someone very, very different from the way that Ma Polinski was. It was a marriage of anathema really. And she had felt things very strongly, Molly Polinski, you could see it from the records at the city council, the way she had spoken out about the things she really believed in. She was passionate about what she had thought was right and I felt very close to her for that reason. I suppose, the same as most people, I like to think that I'm that way myself. Passionate. Strong. And Ma Polinski, well, she kind of gave me something to look up to and I knew she had changed me. In those few weeks since the bequest I had changed a lot. Before, you see, I would have let more wash over me. I wouldn't have taken things into my own hands. I might have got lost the same way that she did. I might not have done anything about him.

Years and years ago, the summer I had left school, I was in London for a couple of weeks visiting a friend of my parents and I had gone into town to go shopping. I remember I was given this leaflet while I was walking down the Barkers side of Kensington High Street. It was a National Front leaflet all about how the Holocaust never really happened. It made me so angry when I read it. I was wandering along and I just got slower and slower as I took in the words and then I stopped in my tracks and turned back. I was only seventeen or so at the time, and I was too scared to go and argue with the guy who was giving the stuff out. I just didn't have the confidence to do it and I felt like such a coward because of that. But even if I couldn't take him on myself, well, I couldn't just let it go either. I might have been afraid and all that, but I was also livid with fury. Not just at the leaflet man but, I suppose, in part at myself as well, for not standing up for what I knew beyond question. I remember that feeling. I was ashamed of myself and furious with him at the same time, although I suppose that the main feeling I had was the anger. I couldn't quite believe it. Everything my mother had been through, all of her family who had been killed, that little scar on her arm which symbolised such a lot and then, here, forty years later, in London, was some smug, right-wing enthusiast who hadn't even been born during the war and he was handing out leaflets saying that none of it really happened because it suited his argument to cast doubt on what the Nazis did. Because it was unforgivable and he knew it, so he just disclaimed the whole thing. And me, I couldn't even bring myself to go up to the guy and tell him just how sick he really was. I did go up to a policeman though, further down the road near the tube station and I made a complaint. It really shocked me that there was nothing he could do. That the pamphleteer was within his legal rights.

'But, it's a lie,' I stuttered at the cop.

'Now we'd all be locked up for that, wouldn't we?' he said gravely. 'Sorry, love.'

And I had walked on without arguing with him either, without making the points I really wanted to make, just feeling betrayed and undefended. Feeling that it was unfair. Feeling that if someone wanted to put me in a concentration camp, that the policeman might not have helped me. In my mind it was tantamount to the same thing. I suppose that's something that I picked up from my mother. The fear that other people might not defend you, might not help you when you need them, so you just keep your head down and try not to make a fuss and not get into trouble. You accept things the way that they are.

On the drive into Morbrax in the car that afternoon I realised how much I had changed. I had grown up a lot since that day in London and I had made up my mind absolutely that this time I was going to come through for Molly Savage. At the very least, I decided, she shouldn't have been buried next to Tomasz Polinski. It was wrong, and on her behalf I had the unforgiving anger which comes from a sorry breach of justice – not

195

just that her husband had deceived her, but that he had complied with the Nazis, that he had worked in a Gestapo records office, and that he'd tracked people down for them. They had needed collaborators like him to make sure that people didn't get away, that those unfortunates deemed to be genetically weak didn't slip through the net. And, of course, in addition to the day-to-day torture and bloodshed, they had needed people like Tomasz Polinski for some of their more gruesome pursuits. They used twins, for example, in medical experiments. So when twins turned up they had to be transferred to the right doctor in the right death camp. The Nazis needed good record-keeping for that, among other things. When I say medical experiments, actually, it makes it sound like what they did was OK. It makes it all sound vaguely scientific. I read this book one time all about it. Well, I read half of the book because it was so sickening that I just couldn't finish it. When I got to the part where fluid was injected into someone's head until it exploded, well, I was way too squeamish to actually read on. But I wasn't squeamish any more. I was angry. Furious. And I was getting ready to do something about it this time. But then, of course, I didn't know what. The only thing that I knew, the only thing that I felt, was fury and it was directed at Tomasz Polinski as we pulled up in Morbrax. Molly Savage might not have had right done to her in life, I thought, but I was very determined that in death she should fare better.

We parked outside the house, but when I got out of the car I walked right over to the churchyard, trailing Nina behind me and when I got to the place around the side of the church where Tomasz Polinski was buried, I kicked his gravestone in disgust.

'He shouldn't be buried here, you know,' I said. 'It's not what she would have wanted.'

'What about what he wanted?' Nina asked in a

preliminary attempt to be the voice of reason, but I just ignored her and kicked the gravestone again. Harder this time. I've always had that blind spot about the Nazis. Even at college, when basically the archaeological line is that any dictator is as bad as another and where the Nazis left off the Russian Communists took over, I never quite bought it. I was involved, you see, so to me no oppressive regime was as bad as Hitler's. I think there's a pretty sound argument for that, actually. I think it's an argument I'm well placed to make but, like I said, I am involved. The fact that Tomasz Polinski was dead made no difference to me. It didn't mean that it was over. He didn't really have many rights as far as I was concerned. Dead or alive, he was below contempt.

'The bastard probably expected to outlive her. He probably thought he'd inherit everything. He shouldn't be buried here, Nina. We should have the grave moved.'

Nina leaned back on a moss-covered memorial stone behind her.

'Takes a long time, you know,' she said, working it out. 'But it's possible. You were effectively his heir too. It's a bit unusual, but why not? It's not like he was born here. It's not like he has living relatives who would object. Where do you want him to be interred?'

'Away from her,' I said. 'As far away as possible. Back in Edinburgh somewhere. And I'm going to research him, prove that he lied, prove that he collaborated with the Nazis and then make sure that it's published. He shouldn't rest in peace. It isn't right, Nina. People should know about him and what he did. People like that don't deserve, well, he shouldn't get away with it. Everyone should know.'

Nina walked over and crouched down in front of Ma Polinski's headstone. She reached out and touched the marble. 'Poor Molly,' she said. 'She didn't deserve the way it turned out, did she?'

'No. She didn't.'

'If you move him and you can prove that he lied to her, well, you'll have made it up to her, you know,' Nina smiled. 'And then you have to have the peaceful life that she never quite managed – you have to lay it to rest, Rachel.'

I shrugged my shoulders. 'Yeah, a good life. Lay it to rest. A life of doing the right thing,' I said. But I couldn't quite get my head around that concept. I was all fired up.

'Well, if anyone's up to the job,' Nina grinned at me, flicking her hair out of her face, 'then it's you.'

I reached out and pulled her close in towards me. 'Thanks,' I mumbled. 'Thanks a lot.'

'And I think you're quite right. He's got to go. He shouldn't be here. It isn't fitting. I mean, they weren't really man and wife now, were they? The whole thing was built on a lie. Maybe you should have him re-interred in a bigger cemetery – Mortonhall or Piershill or somewhere.'

'And her grave. I'm going to plant flowers here,' I decided.

'Yeah,' Nina said. 'That's nice.'

'Come on,' I took her hand and pulled her back down to the pathway. 'Let's do it now.' I suppose I was desperate to make some kind of a sign, some kind of a show of faith. I was desperate to do something. To get on with it. To make it all better.

As we walked over to the house I realised that the old place didn't hold any fears for me any more. I mean, I knew what the mural was about. A cry for help. A memorial. A reminder. And I also knew that once the remains of Tomasz Polinski were gone I would feel quite safe there. That she would rest in peace. I suppose I clicked then that I might keep the old place. We wandered around to the side gate and on to the back lawn where there were some old garden tools stacked up near the perimeter hedge. Then Nina and I carefully dug up some pansies which had been put in one of the flowerbeds and laid them into the wheelbarrow and Nina wheeled it back over the road and I dug them back into the ground again, though this time above her grave. It looked much better. We sat back to survey our handiwork, the burial mound dotted with velvety pansies, their gemstone colours standing out strongly against the lush springtime grass. Nina pushed her hair back off her face again.

'Hard work,' she commented. 'I'd forgotten.'

The tools were old and kind of heavy and it had been years since we had dug much – in the old days we were so used to wielding shovels that we wouldn't have even noticed the strain of planting a few flowers.

'Hard work, yeah,' I nodded happily, and I felt a lot better. I felt that there was something I could do to put the wrongs right, and I felt that we had made a start.

The dusk was coming on fast as we packed up the rusty shovel and garden fork into the wheelbarrow again and turned to go. But as we made our way around the side of the church and back on to the path there was a woman coming into the churchyard with a black Scottie dog at her heels. She looked kind of like the Scottie dog, very sturdy and wiry and bluff with pronounced eyebrows and she was carrying a set of old, heavy keys in her hand. They were obviously the keys to the church. You could just tell.

'Good evening,' she said, and she stopped to talk to us the way people in small country villages do, so I put the wheelbarrow down.

'What have you been up to?' she asked, and she smiled a big smile, so I told her about planting the flowers on Molly Savage's grave and she continued to beam at me the whole time I was talking. She was really friendly and really confident too. You just knew she'd lived there for ever and that she ran the Christian Ladies' Guild or something.

'Oh, the Polinskis,' she mumbled slowly, and as she pulled her fingers through her greying hair I noticed how rough her skin was and that she was all ruddy, and I figured to myself that her high colour must have come from spending lots of time outside and the dry patches on her hands and on her cheeks must have come from a combination of bad weather and hard work. She was a serious gardener. I had this sudden vision of her on her knees confidently weeding out a flowerbed. Then I decided that that was too frivolous. This lady was far more serious than that. She probably kept chickens.

'Are you related to the Polinskis?' she asked.

'Not exactly,' I shrugged my shoulders. 'But, well, I inherited. The old house is mine now.'

'Oh, it would be so wonderful for someone to move in,' she enthused. 'Over the years there has been lots of interest in buying that old place, you know. It's lain empty for too long.'

'I don't know if I will move in, actually,' I said, warming to her. 'I'm not sure yet. Did you know Molly Polinski?'

'Oh yes. Well, let me see, I moved here in 1968 when I first got married so I knew both of them for some years. I'm Trisha MacMillan by the way.'

We all shook hands, and Nina and I introduced ourselves. Trisha walked over on to the grass to peek at the graves, which were just visible once you got off the pathway. She complimented us on the pansies we'd planted and then, noticing that we had only dug them on to one of the burial mounds, asked us if we had a different variety of flower planned for the other.

'No, not really,' I replied.

'He was a great hoot, Mr Polinski,' Trisha continued, obviously oblivious to the coldness which had, quite naturally, crept into my voice. 'What fun. He used to get terribly drunk and chase cows around. He loved it here, you know. Absolutely loved it. Potty about the village. Said he never wanted to leave the place. Wrote articles for the local papers about the history of the area, you know. A keen local historian. You must come over to my place and look at them. I'll dig them out for you when I have a moment. I must have them somewhere. Let me see, oh, just come over whenever you like. Ring the bell at the door and just walk in. I live over there,' and she pointed over the road to a ramshackle-looking 1930s cottage further along the street.

'That would be great. Another day, perhaps. We've got to be getting along now. Nice to meet you, Trisha,' I said.

'Oh yes,' she smiled, 'very nice. Righto,' and she headed back up the path and disappeared into the porch of the church with a spring in her step and a dog at her heels. She was, of course, completely oblivious to the significance of what she'd told us. She was absolutely unaware that my heart had sunk right down in my chest and that I felt sick with anger.

'Shit,' Nina grimaced. 'Keen local historian. Shit.'

We made our way back over into Ma Polinski's garden. The sun was going down but the sunset wasn't too spectacular that evening. I've seen better there since.

'No sheriff will give you an exhumation order if he wanted to be buried there. If he loved the place and said he never wanted to leave,' Nina said. 'Nazi or no Nazi. It doesn't matter. You're not even a blood relative. You never even met him.'

I knew she was right. I mean, we were both pretty familiar with the custom and practice of digging up human remains on archaeological sites – you need a special licence for that. As far as exhumation of more recent remains goes, you need a sheriff's ruling and you need to give a reason in order to get it and have certificates – one from the cemetery authority and also one from the department of environmental health. Well, if Tomasz Polinski was known as a keen amateur historian in the area and had said that he wanted to be buried out at Morbrax, there was no way the local cemetery authority would have certified for an exhumation. There was just no way. We both knew it.

'Fuck,' I said. 'Fucking hell.'

'Maybe you should move her,' Nina suggested. 'I mean, you could say that you live in Edinburgh and you want to remove her body so you can be closer to visit the grave. That might work.'

I shook my head slowly. It didn't seem like that was fair. I mean, Molly belonged in Morbrax cemetery. She had lived in the village long before she had even heard of Tomasz Polinski. He was the interloper. It didn't seem right to move her out to Piershill or Mortonhall or somewhere. Not instead of him. It wouldn't have been right. Besides, her resting place had been specified in her will. I'd seen it myself at Mike Williams' office.

'No,' I said. 'No. That won't work and anyway she belongs here,' and I watched the last shadows slide off the plate at the side of the dislocated sundial as the light faded out of the sky at last. I perched on the edge of the garden bench while Nina lit up a cigarette and inhaled deeply. She thought it was over. She thought there was nothing else that we could do.

'We can be back in Glasgow in time for dinner,' she commented consulting her watch.

'No,' I said, 'we ought to stay here for a bit longer, Nina,' and I laid my hand lazily on the tip of the shovel which was protruding from the top of the wheelbarrow. And it was at that point that I really went kind of out of control.

Chapter Nineteen

You know how I feel about digging up bodies. I mean, in normal circumstances, well, it would never have entered my head. And I wouldn't have done it if it had been only for me. I mean, if it hadn't made any difference to anyone else. But I wanted to do right by Molly. And that was that. I couldn't see any other way out. Well, not a legal way.

'We should do it ourselves,' I said. 'We ought to.'

Nina protested a bit at first. It is a major offence to interfere with a dead body after all and well, given our backgrounds, we would hardly have been able to say that we didn't know that. I doubt that we would have got off lightly even though we had mitigating circumstances because when it came right down to it we knew exactly the seriousness of the crime. We were fully educated in that respect. Not that I'm sure of the last time anyone ever got done for it − it's not something people readily admit to on the Oprah Winfrey show or whatever. It's not something that people get banged up for terribly regularly. If you asked a policeman they probably wouldn't know the likely sentence you'd get for it because the last time there was a big case of bodysnatching, well, it was Burke and Hare, wasn't it? It's amazing how quickly you get practical, though. I mean, I disregarded the legal side of things very, very quickly to say nothing of my own moral reservations. My whole career had been formed and guided by the fact that I believed the dead should rest in peace. But Tomasz Polinski didn't deserve to and in the end it wasn't that I had a horror of the dead, more that I had a horror of the profane and he shouldn't have been buried where he was. It was the greater wrong, the greater profanity, I suppose. I didn't even have to think it through, the rights and the wrongs. Instead, there were all sorts of tiny details running through my mind. Small practical things. When Trisha MacMillan might be going to leave the church, for example, or when it might be safe to start digging up the soil, the thought of which presented other problems. The dilemmas you face when you are digging up bones. He'd been down there for twenty years, you see, and the soil in East Lothian is pretty sandy and the climate is pretty damp, so I figured he would be in the very advanced stages of decomposition. That was obviously good. I mean, the further gone he was the better. What was bad was that his coffin might also be decomposing so I decided we might well have to lift him out alone, without any of the wooden casing. Just his skeleton. His bones. There couldn't, I decided, be anything more than that left. There was another concern, though, in my mind. In the city, they tend to bury bodies in layers with the final layer a minimum of three feet from the surface of the ground to protect (if you'll excuse me saying so) against scavangers and carrion eaters, animals and birds. Out in the country, though, I figured, well, in a small place like Morbrax for a wealthy, local resident, it was more likely that Hamish Williams would have bought the entire burial plot and ensured that Molly and Tomasz would be the only incumbents, so to speak. I hoped it would be that way. It seemed most likely and that meant they'd probably be five feet down into the soil. Between that and six and a half feet, in any case. It was a long dig. But at least it had only just got dark, so we had plenty of time.

Nina's thought processes were way behind mine. I had already figured all of that out, and I was just addressing myself to what we ought to do with him once we had exhumed his remains, when the enormity of what I was planning to do sunk in and she piped up.

'Jesus, Rachel, it's a tiny wee village,' she protested. 'We'd never get away with it. I mean, there are houses fifty yards away.' And when she said that instead of 'Jesus, God, that's morally reprehensible', well, I knew she'd do it with me. I knew it. I think, though, she must have been kicking herself for giving out to me about not taking control of the situation those few days before in the park. Once I was committed, that was it and everything we did from then on in, well, I take responsibility for it and all I can do is thank Nina for going along with me. The moral responsibility is mine.

If we'd had any other profession, I mean, probably if we'd had any other profession except perhaps something medical, we would never have gone ahead. The social taboos are huge and the ignorance of the practicalities of death is massive. Most people nowadays have never even seen a dead body. We are separated from that by hospitals and funeral parlours and discretion. But Nina and I, well, we might have chosen not to make exhumation part of our day-to-day jobs, but we were both trained in it nonetheless. And we had both done it before. So we weren't constituted against it in the way most of the population would be. We knew how to do it and we knew what it was going to be like. It was just a procedure, that's all – something we could do to get something that we wanted. A bit spooky given the circumstances, but still something we'd done before.

'It's going to be dark,' I pointed out. 'The moon is only a sliver tonight. We can plant some flowers on top and that woman will think that we just came back to do that and that's why the ground is all turned over. There are small heather plants around the side of the house. We can use those.'

Nina cast her eyes down to the ground, took a last draw from her cigarette and stubbed it out under the heel of her pristine black Chelsea boot.

'And where do you propose to put him?' she asked me.

I thought for a moment. 'The museum,' I said, very definitely, feeling powerful that I had something so practical into which I could channel my anger. 'In the archive. I can catalogue him. We have lots of skeleton bones and we don't display them often. I'll catalogue him under something we have a lot of. He'll never be found.'

Nina crossed her arms.

'Fuck. We shouldn't do this,' she said. But she was too weak about it. I knew she didn't mean it. And we sneaked around the side of the house together and used a trowel to dig up the heather plants. Then we went inside the house and I rummaged around until I found some black bin liners which we could lay out over the ground so that there would be no trace of the mound of soil we'd make and, of course, so we'd have something to put his bones in once we'd hauled them out of the earth. Nina wandered back over the road and cased the site, checking that Trisha MacMillan had left the place and trying to figure out where the graves might be visible from. There was a detached house close by the church wall, but it was small and the only window to the side was glazed with opaque bathroom glass. Since it was spring the trees were in leaf and that afforded us quite a lot of protection from some of the higher houses further up on the other side of the road. To the back there was only farmland.

'Friday night in a tiny village like this – there isn't a

206

take-away here, there isn't even a pub. As long as we're quiet and we keep a watch out, I suppose it's about as safe as it gets. I just wish I'd brought my wellies, that's all,' Nina said, and I reached out for her hand.

'Thanks,' I whispered. 'Thanks for doing this with me.'

And we broke the surface of the soil and from that point on, I suppose, there was really no looking back and it was such hard work there wasn't time to be as afraid as perhaps would have been decent.

It took us a long time. Well, we had known that it would because, like I said before, we were out of the way of wielding a shovel. But at least the soil was more sandy than clay, which made it lighter to dig. At half past eight, we hit the remains of the coffin lid just over five feet down, but like I had expected it was more or less disintegrated. We had dug a deep trench about four feet long and three feet wide where we expected the body to be, figuring that once we found out which way his corpse had been positioned we would be able to dig along fairly easily to extract the extremities of the skeletal remains. Where we had come through we had all of the upper body, from the skull down to the middle of his thigh bone. In a graveyard in the pitch black of night, you'd have expected us to be scared. A few hours before I'd have expected it myself. I hadn't dug up remains since Shan Yat, remember, and you know what terrible things that had done to me. But I wasn't at all afraid. I was ecstatic and Nina, well, exhumation had never freaked her out – she'd just never really liked it much although once or twice when I'd been doing the digging she'd asked me a question, trying to keep the conversation going so it wouldn't be completely silent as well as dark and spooky and cold.

Down below the surface I touched the side of the earth where I knew Molly was interred and I felt really happy for her and I knew that we were doing just the right thing. Then I started to dig along towards his feet. Around nine o'clock it started to drizzle. I had been down in the hole since we'd found him, and Nina was standing over me, up on the surface. We'd been digging in fifteen-minute shifts originally, but I didn't want to stop and hand the shovel over now that we were so close to finishing it. Just as I felt the raindrops hit me, I uncovered the last of him, right down to the tips of his toes. I called out quietly to Nina who peered over at me. Our eyes had got over the dimness of the light and I could see just how streaked with mud we were and how wet. Our clothes were ruined.

'Rain,' Nina commented as she rubbed her hands together to try to keep warm. 'That's good. It'll wet the surface when we put the soil back in. It'll damp it down. Here, pass him up to me. Let's get on with it.'

Bone by bone I pulled him out of his resting place and Nina carefully laid him on to the black plastic bags she had made ready. I found a brass plaque with his name on it, which was still screwed to a rotting bit of wood just over his ribs. And on the pinkie finger of his left hand there was a signet ring. I couldn't see it properly in the light, I could only just make out that it was gold. I passed the grave goods up to Nina.

'Any bones missing?' I asked her, just like we'd been trained to check.

There was a moment's silence as she made sure.

'No, it's all here,' she mouthed down and I climbed right up out of the hole and began filling it in.

On an archaeological dig now, an operation like that could take days or even weeks. It's painstaking the amount of recording you have to do. Soil samples, photographs of the body *in situ*, the careful exhumation of each and every little bone. With Tomasz Polinski it took us all in all about three or four hours. We hadn't stood on ceremony. We planted the heather with our hands, carefully removed all the other evidence of the fact that we had been there and went back to the car in silence. Nina bundled the bag of bones into the boot and then we jumped into the front, keen to get out of Morbrax knowing that we were more likely to be caught, muddy-handed and guilty-looking, on the partially lit street than we had been in the dark sanctity of the graveyard. It took us just over an hour to get back to my place in Glasgow and all the long trip we didn't say a word to each other. We didn't talk at all in fact until we slammed my front door behind us and bundled the rubbish bag of his bones into the spare bedroom.

'Thank God that's over,' said Nina.

'Yeah,' I mumbled 'I'm all wet.' And then I went off to heat us up some Heinz Tomato Soup while Nina piled into the shower.

She didn't come into the kitchen for ages. Too long. I had dropped my clothes at my feet and washed my hands and face in the old Belfast sink, grabbing a tracksuit out of the tumble-dryer and pulling it over my limbs quickly, glad to be warm and dry at last. My arms were stiff from all the digging and my skin was numbed slightly with the cold so I began to go a bit pink all over as I slowly heated up. The soup smelled good and I was really hungry. Nina seemed to be taking ages. I sneaked a couple of spoonfuls from out of the saucepan and sat down at the kitchen table to wait, my knees curled up to my chest, hugged in closely. My legs were all stiff because I had been so damp and when that happens it takes you ages to warm up properly even after that first pinkish glow.

'It's over,' I thought smugly because then I thought that I knew everything, I knew all of her story and I knew what to do about it too. 'It's over.'

By the time it had been half an hour, I decided to go

and investigate what had happened to Nina. The shower had been off for a while so I went out into the hallway, with the intention of padding through to my bedroom to hurry her up. It was in my mind that she just didn't know what to wear, there being a conspicuous lack of black trouser suits in my wardrobe. But she wasn't in my bedroom, and as soon as I got into the hall I could see immediately that she was in the spare bedroom instead and that she was on her knees. With him. She was doing something but I couldn't see her hands because of the door. All I knew was that she was touching something on the floor and that she still had a towel wrapped around her and her hair was wet. The doorway into the hall was open and the light cut out a clean shape on the hall carpet, drawing me in.

'What are you up to?' I asked her before I saw.

And then I rushed in next to her because I could see it too. When you looked at them in the light it was obvious. The bones on the carpet didn't belong to a fifty-year-old man, they belonged to someone much, much younger. Someone still male, but only twenty-five perhaps. Maybe even a bit less. The bones showed signs of poor diet – we'd have had to have done tests to figure out just how poor, but this man had often been hungry. We couldn't tell much more than that from them. It's not really either of our subjects so we only know the basics. But, well, we didn't really have to know very much more. It wasn't him. It couldn't have been.

'Who the hell is this?' Nina muttered and then she put down the thigh bone she had been examining and scrambled around inside the black bag to try to find the little plaque which had been screwed to what remained of the coffin, but that didn't tell us anything either. *Tomasz Polinski*, it said, and the gold signet ring I'd picked off his finger, now I saw it properly, had the initials TP interwoven, engraved onto the plate of the ring.

'Fuck,' I said. 'Shit. He wasn't down there. He didn't die.'

Chapter Twenty

Nina and I sat up most of the night together in the living room after that. We gave up on the idea of eating, though I made some coffee which we sipped at kind of distractedly, telling ourselves that we ought to stay awake. At first, we considered that there were really only two possibilities. One – that Hamish Williams had mistakenly brought home the wrong burned and mangled body from Brazil. That there had been some kind of an international corpse mix-up. A mistake perhaps brought on by the difficulty of collecting bodies in English from officials who probably spoke only Portuguese. We didn't stick with that theory for long, however, because the fact that the poor kid was wearing a ring with Tomasz Polinski's initials on it pointed to the second possibility, which was that Tomasz Polinski had faked his own death in order to get away with murdering his wife. Signet rings are usually removed before burial, you see. This one had been left on the hand which meant that the dead man was probably wearing it when his body burned. When Tomasz Polinski had murdered him.

Polinski had been such an evil man, we had no doubts he'd done it. Every time we found something else out about him, it got worse. And killing Ma Polinski, Molly, his wife, well, he'd killed lots of people before. And worse. There was no reason why not. We'd even found him a motive. It fell into place so neatly – the missing treasure, the clues of the mural and the sundial attesting to Molly's suspicions, her desperation, her inability to take hold of the situation and save herself by exposing him. We'd stumbled on a murder, or rather, we had stumbled on two murders and now, we were going to have a hell of a time reporting them. I mean, what in God's name could we possibly say – 'Well, it just so happens that we were digging up the skeletal remains of Tomasz Polinski one evening when we discovered, quite by chance of course, that he had faked his own death.' We couldn't go to the authorities on the evidence that we had, that much was sure. And anyway, besides any of that, we weren't even really positive what the authorities might be able to do about it, although it did occur to us pretty quickly that Tomasz Polinski might still be alive. When we totted it up, in fact, we figured out that the old guy was probably only in his late seventies. It was quite possible that he was still holed up somewhere and, in fact, in some ways it was kind of likely – that necklace which had turned up in the auction sale in Geneva, for example, had to have come from somewhere. Perhaps the old man had been living off that stuff which went missing out of the safe for some time, selling it off piece by piece as discreetly as possible.

It was four in the morning when we finally decided to turn in. Nina piled into bed with me and we agreed to leave the hall light on. We were both a bit spooked.

'What are we going to do with that body?' she asked. The idea of cataloguing the bones in the museum had gone by the wayside. It lacked a certain respect about it. Fitting for Tomasz Polinski but not really appropriate, we decided, for his victim.

'I don't know,' I replied. 'I just don't know. But don't worry about it. We'll think of something. We'll lay him to rest somehow. Poor bugger.'

'And the Contessa di Gilberti,' Nina mumbled as she slipped into sleep. 'She's our only lead. I'll ring her tomorrow. *Domani.*'

But I didn't answer her because she was already breathing quite steadily beside me. I couldn't sleep myself. I lay still in the bed and I thought until the sun came up. It was a shitty cold day and it was raining. At seven I got up and opened the curtains and sat staring at the raindrops which battered against the window-pane and ran down the glass in plump, swollen streams. I scrambled around in Nina's pockets until I found her cigarettes and then I lit one up, and curled all around myself in the corner of the bedroom, just staring at the weather and thinking about it all as I sucked on the tip of the fag.

You find out a lot about yourself in a crisis. You find out just how self-reliant you are. How much you've grown since the last crisis you had. I have to say it kind of surprised me that I was so calm and, well, so competent. There was a stranger's skeleton in my spare bedroom for a start and that on its own should have been enough to induce a mild panic. But I was too busy. I had plans to make. And that skeleton was exactly where I decided to start. Calmly. Taking one step at a time. By nine o'clock, when Nina rolled over sleepily and mumbled something about breakfast, before she had even remembered what had happened the day before, I had already gone over the whole thing a few times in my mind and I thought that I knew what we were going to do. We were going to lay those bones to rest, find out as much as we could about where the necklace had come from, and then, by Christ, we were going to find that old man and we were going to have him charged. There were plenty of people who would help with that on account of his conduct during the war alone, never mind what he did to poor Molly Savage. We were about to embark on our career as Nazi hunters.

Moral vigilantes. Crusaders. An unexpected twist, but there you are. It was, as far as I could see, the only thing to do.

I had a quick shower and then we made some breakfast – a big pile of golden toast and a large pot of black coffee with a pan of warmed milk on the side. Nina regarded her little black trouser suit with dismay. The mud had all dried in and the jacket looked completely out of shape because wool does that in the rain and if you don't dry it properly it all goes to hell. Nina bit into her toast and a golden pool of butter and honey dripped right down her chin.

'God, that's good,' she said without taking her eyes off her clothes, which were laid out in a pile on the kitchen counter.

'We'll have to go shopping, underwritten by the Ma Polinski fund for well-dressed young ladies,' I smiled.

'Dry-cleaning?' Nina hazarded, but I shook my head.

'We could try it, I suppose,' I said, but we both knew that the black trouser suit was gone.

Once we'd eaten and sorted ourselves out with some clothes, I sat down on the bed and Nina leaned against the wardrobe with her arms crossed.

'OK. I have a plan,' I started. 'The first thing we have to do is bury those bones again.'

Nina didn't say anything, she just shifted uncomfortably in my jeans and glanced down at her boots, which we had managed to rescue but which, she knew, might not survive another mud assault. I have to say, I felt kind of uncomfortable about burying that skeleton again too. Exhumation. Re-interring. It was a bit like playing God. It's different normally because if you're a gravedigger, well, you have social rules and even laws on your side. It's your job. You're recognised for what you do. It is considered necessary and it is regulated. We were making up the rules ourselves, though, and deciding what we wanted to do, what we thought was best and it had, I suppose, kind of gone wrong. Digging up Tomasz Polinski's remains was one thing, digging up someone else, and then having to deal with it, was quite another. It wasn't a comfortable feeling for either of us, but we had to deal with it.

'Where do you think we ought to bury him?' Nina asked slowly.

'Well,' I said, 'the best idea I have, I mean, the only place that it might not arouse suspicions if he was found again later, is in a graveyard. I mean, he ought to be on hallowed ground of some sort, really, don't you think? And if he was exposed, by mistake, well . . .'

'No,' said Nina cutting in on me. 'No way. Once – maybe. It worked. We were lucky enough not to get caught. But twice? We would just be stupid to try it.'

She was right of course. The graveyard idea was crazy. It's just that if you think about it there aren't that many places you can get rid of a skeleton unless you own farmland or your own incinerator. And even if you do own the means, it's difficult to do it with any kind of respect, and I think we were both pretty set on the idea that it was important to inter the poor guy with some kind of gravity. It was, we knew, unlikely that we'd ever find out who he had been. A man who went missing in or near São Paulo in the week that Ma Polinski's car crashed and she died. There is only so much that official records can give you and the man had been ill fed which probably meant that he was poor. People disappear off the streets in South America all the time and it never gets reported. You've heard the stories. Everyone has.

'Look,' I said, 'I can't think of how else to do it. I can't.'

Nina shrugged her shoulders. 'Well,' she said, 'we want to take the minimum risk, there is no question of that. But he also ought to be somewhere that we can honour him privately. No gravestone, of course, nothing like that. But we owe him something. No one should be buried without some kind of ceremony, some kind of remembrance. Well, I don't think so, anyway. At first I thought maybe we ought to just chuck him in the archive like you'd planned. But that wouldn't be right for him. I mean, we ought to lay him to rest. Somewhere close by. Hallowed ground or not.'

I suppose that what we came up with may seem really, really strange but, well, it kind of made sense to us. Back in Edinburgh, there is this marshy ground up in the Queen's Park near Holyrood in the dip where the foot of Arthur's Seat meets the low incline at the bottom of Salisbury Crags, way away from the main road. We used to go climbing up there when we were at college. It's an amazing place all through the year, you can see the whole city if you go way up to the top and in the summer there are wild flowers and grasses and in the winter, when it snows, the air is really crisp and the lines of the hill make amazing shapes against the dark, cloudy sky. I have to say, it kind of has the feeling of a holy place. I mean, even though lots of people go there to climb up to the summit or to picnic on the lower slopes or just to walk their dogs, it doesn't really detract from the majesty of it.

'Arthur's Seat,' said Nina. 'It's our best bet. As soon as we can,' she shuddered. 'Tonight.'

And when I thought about it I knew it was just the right place really. Not only the best that we could do, but really the right place because we could visit there easily, both of us. Because it was open to the sky. Because they would never build on it. Ever.

There was a lot going through my mind that morning. It was pretty busy inside my head. Nina tried to ring the Contessa di Gilberti again but she drew a blank and I realised I was supposed to be in Edinburgh with Scotty. I had completely forgotten all about it, though when I rang him he was really nice about the whole thing and as Nina lolled restlessly in the living room, rolling her eyes, I told him that I needed a little bit of time and a little bit of space. We arranged to see each other the following weekend.

As I carefully packed up the bones into an old suitcase it kind of hit home that I had got Nina and I into a terrible mess. Things had gone really awry. The whole point of going out to Morbrax, of getting involved in the first place had been so that I could tell my parents about the money and, well, I had completely lost sight of that. I had got too caught up in the past. I had dug up more than I'd bargained for and in the process I'd lost sight of the one thing I should have known, the one place where my ghosts always seemed to lead me – back to my mother. I was shaking as I rolled the bones up in a tartan rug from the living room and then packed them away, trying to be as respectful and gentle with them as I could. When I glanced out into the hall I could see Nina sitting on the floor beside the telephone, just crouching there silently with her head in her hands. We were both pretty shaken – determined to sort the whole mess out for no other reason than then it would all be over. We were scared.

At midday we walked down the road and had lunch out at this local café at the end of the street. We never usually go there because, well, all they serve is toasted sandwiches and thick black tea. Nina sat on an orange plastic chair, spinning pennies on the Formica-topped table while we waited. Heads. Tails. Heads. Heads. Tails. I just stared, dry-eyed and exhausted. I hadn't slept in forty hours. I was looking for some kind of pattern to take my mind off things. Heads. Tails. Tails. Heads. I hardly tasted my sandwich when it came and I just gulped down my tea. Nina ate only half of hers and then she started smoking. A good six hours before she usually did. We were feeling pretty low. That afternoon we both slept again. Nina on the sofa in the living room and me curled up, exhausted in my bed. At five o'clock I woke up and splashed my face with cold water and pulled on some clothes. Then I got down my atlas and looked up Forte dei Marmi, where the Contessa was staying. Nina had rung and from the short, curt conversation with the Contessa's housemaid had gathered that she wasn't going back to Florence for another couple of weeks and would be staying on in her villa beside the sea. Forte dei Marmi was a tiny place on the north-western coast of Italy. The writing on the map was so small that it took me ages to find it. When I finally did, I measured the distance between there and Florence and then, on a map of the same scale, between Glasgow and Edinburgh. 'About an hour,' I thought. 'As long as there's motorway.' And I stared at the map taking in the whole area – above the village were the Carrara mountains, famous for their marble quarries and in the bay below the settlement were a sprinkling of tiny islands. It was just a seaside town by the look of things. A holiday place. Then I flicked over the pages until I found Lvov just over the Polish–Ukrainian border, but still on the Ukrainian side. He couldn't go back there, I thought to myself. There was just no way. He was a murderer. People would remember him. He would be known. Still, I stared for a while at the map, familiarising myself with it. Like lots of border towns in Eastern Europe, Lvov had seen some action. It had been part of the Austrian Empire until that fell, but it had been over half Polish until 1945 when the Polish border had been pushed back two hundred miles or so and the Nazis had wiped out three million of the country's population. From then until Glasnost, the town had been under Russian jurisdiction. People have long memories in places like that. Divisions run lifelong and they run deep. Lvov has three cathedrals and, I thought to myself, that, if nothing else, is the sign of a divided city. I decided that Tomasz Polinski couldn't have gone back there. He'd have to have been crazy to try it. I flicked half-heartedly through the pages looking for some kind of idea, some kind of guidance, but the Contessa was our best chance. And I think then I realised that with just one lead or two we might open up a trail, and once we'd done that, well, maybe we could get some help. There are whole organisations dedicated to tracking down ex-Nazis. With just a lead or two, something positive, we could say that we suspected he hadn't died because of the missing jewellery and that then we'd turned up some positive clues. I think that made me feel better. The idea that we'd have company in our search – other people who'd be behind us. As for going back to Edinburgh, well, that didn't even occur to me. Once you set out on the road I was travelling, there wasn't really any turning back. Scotty was going to have to wait.

At six, Nina wandered through and lay down on the end of the bed – an innocent travelling companion who'd got enmeshed in something which wasn't really her business. I knew that I needed her, but also knew that as soon as I could I'd have to let her go. The best either of us could do was to get on with it.

'What are you doing next week?' I asked her. 'Got any leave due?'

She turned over and held her head in her hands. 'I could do with a holiday,' she said.

'We'll go out to the airport tomorrow,' I told her. 'Any flight to Italy will do.'

Chapter Twenty-One

We chose the marshland. It was the messiest place, of course, the most difficult place too but we thought long and hard and that's where we chose in the end. It seemed to be the safest idea. We saw to it that we were kitted out properly with long green wellington boots and waterproof dungarees which had regularly seen active service in our excavation days. We looked a bit like fishermen really, taking the rug swaddled bones out of the boot and making our way across the scrubland and uphill away from the main road. We had weighted them down with quarry stones before we left Glasgow and it took a while for us to carry the bundle over to the marshy ground that we had in mind. When we finally got there, Nina said a few words before we started to bury him.

'We don't know who you are,' she said reverently as we stood with our heads bowed on either side of the bundle just off the narrow track we had followed up to the bog. It was dark up the hill and we'd brought torches but we didn't want to use them. Other folk walk over there at night and even though it was two in the morning we knew that we had to be careful. 'You had a great wrong done to you,' Nina continued, 'and we just hope that you can rest in peace now, knowing that we will do our best to find out what happened to the man who perpetrated that wrong, and that we will do our best to bring him or his memory to justice.' We observed a moment's silence and then waded out a few feet into the boggy ground until the mud was nearly up to the top of the rubber boots and then we let go of the bundle. It sank slowly into the muddy depths and I helped it on its way with a pole, the handle of an old broom which we had brought with us from the flat. When we had both tried, but neither of us could feel where it was any more, we waded back out on to the dry land.

'Do you think that they'll ever find him?' Nina worried.

People occasionally have found the most astonishing things up on that hill. The most famous find ever was a dozen or so miniature coffins with crudely made, tiny dolls inside. There was an outcry when that happened, that some eighteenth-century Edinburgh witch had buried the effigies to jinx her victims but well, professionally, I think that some kid had made them. Children play games based, largely, on what they see around them, and 150 years ago it would have been a rare child who hadn't buried at least some of his or her friends and relations. The witch thing is a better story though, and the public of course had loved it.

'I doubt they'll find him there,' I sighed, because really we couldn't be sure. All we could do was make educated guesses. 'There isn't any reason to drain the ground,' I carried on, 'and he's too far down in the mud for a dog to get at the bones. We can come back. Every year. This day every year. In memoriam.'

'May ninth,' Nina said and then, after a couple of moments just to kind of take that in, we walked back towards the main road through the park. It was freezing cold because the night was so clear and we smiled at the state of each other as we came back towards the orange street lights of the wide sweep of road and lashed our muddy overclothes into the waiting bags in the boot of the car.

At ten, later that same morning, we caught the first flight to Pisa out of Glasgow. Two clean, well-dressed girls in dark glasses carrying smart leather suitcases. Nobody knows, I remember thinking. No one suspects a thing. And there we were – drinking mineral waters and espressos in the departure lounge, testing Christian Dior mascara with cashmere in Duty Free, and having two sly last cigarettes before we boarded the plane. Two friends going on holiday together, just having fun. You'd never have guessed what was really binding us together.

Whenever I travel anywhere, it always astounds me that people in Scotland don't ever really click just how cold the place is. I mean, people don't recognise that it's warmer in London than it is at home. Despite the odd bit of rain we thought we'd had a pretty bloody great run of weather in May last year. People were predicting a humdinger of a summer, though it never came. When Nina and I got off the plane in Pisa and walked down the staircase to the tarmac you knew you'd arrived somewhere with truly great weather. The place was just baked through and I realised yet again that nearly everywhere has better weather than Scotland. In Italy it had been summer-hot for weeks already and as we walked, dreamlike, away from the plane it was like sinking into a warm, smooth bath. The air was virtually liquid. We peeled off our cardigans and stretched out our arms, luxuriating in it.

'Home,' Nina murmured, because, well, she's liable to do that kind of thing.

We walked over to the terminal building and picked up our bags and then made our way straight through the European Union Duty Free Entry Zone and out of the arrivals gate at the other side. The place was really busy even though it was the middle of Sunday afternoon. Queues of holidaymakers were lining up to go into the departure lounge, checked one by one by a laconic security guard with an enormous side-arm holstered in a leather pouch on his big, black belt. Way to our left we could see the queue for coffees. People were clamouring up at the bar. Nina called over one of the taxi drivers who were hovering at the glass doors ahead of us and negotiated a decent fare for the trip over to the coast and then the guy took our bags and we followed him outside. As we relaxed in the back seat of his white air-conditioned Mercedes he hit the dual carriageway at ninety miles an hour and we drove into Forte dei Marmi in forty-five minutes flat, past the sandy-earthed farms and the gnarled old olive trees spread out here and there in the wake of the blue-white misty mountains high behind them.

'The best hotel. Expensive. Private. Small.' Nina instructed the driver and he dithered around for a bit before dropping us off at the Lido.

'This little town is bigger than I thought,' I said as we climbed the curved stone steps up to the Victorian, arched entrance hallway and Nina dealt with the doe-eyed clerk at reception. She got us a twin-bedded room which I secured with a flourish of my credit card, secure in the knowledge that the vast majority of the money Mike Williams had sent was still languishing in my account. We did go upstairs but we only dropped our cases there and opened the green shutters, gasping at the diamond-sparkling ocean beyond the bottom of the Lido's high-hedged, private gardens. Then we took the old, rattly lift back down to the ground floor and Nina ordered us a couple of stiff drinks and some pasta out on the red clay-tiled terrace to the back of the building. There were high-backed, canvas chairs and wooden tables set out there in the shade and we sipped on Campari and sodas under the thick, white canopy as we waited. The place was deserted, apart from two freckled, short-haired little girls playing hide-and-seek in a copse of trees, far away at the bottom of the sloping, sprinkler-strewn lawn.

'She's not in the phone book,' Nina said. 'I've checked.'

When the food arrived we lashed into it. It was really our first square meal in a couple of days of coffees and sandwiches of one sort or another. By the time we'd eaten our fill it was nearly five o'clock and the red-faced holidaymakers who had spent a leisurely Sunday afternoon on the beach were making their way up through the gardens back to the cool, marble-floored comfort of the hotel. They nodded peremptorily in our direction as we sat back in our seats, thinking. Finding the Contessa was kind of a tough one. I mean the police, for example, wouldn't have helped us. Neither would anywhere with official records – the library or any of the offices which supply utilities. They have strict rules about handing out people's addresses or phone numbers in places like that. Bribing officials, well, whatever you read about in the tabloids, it isn't easy and it can get you banged up in a local jail. So anyway, we had to find other people who would have the number or the address but wouldn't, perhaps, be so strict about withholding them. If the place had been smaller, then it would have been easier. As a rule, in really tiny places people tend to be more open – like Trisha MacMillan had been out at Morbrax. Forte dei Marmi was a bit too big for that, though. We weren't going to just bump into someone in the street who would tell us what we wanted to know whenever we asked. It wasn't a place where everyone knew everyone else. It was a holiday town.

'We should go into the centre tonight,' I said. 'We should go wherever the shops are, because anyone who is staying here for a month has to get their food and stuff somewhere.'

Nina nodded at me. It would be, at least, a good place to start and we both wanted just to get on with it. Then we headed inside.

We bathed. We changed. We told them we'd be out for dinner. It's odd – I mean, I almost felt like I was really on my holidays and maybe that's because I had some time to reflect on the bizarre turn of events of the previous two days. And also to realise that well, to be honest, things were not, by any means, becoming less strange. It was so obviously a place where people came to get away from it all, not a place where people came to face things down and sort them out. And I thought to myself, 'He could be here, in this sleepy little town. He could be right here and neither of us would know.' Ex-Nazis, whenever they are found and charged, are always so innocuous. You see it on the news – those nice old men whose neighbours say they never bothered anyone. Before we left the hotel that evening we wandered down to the sandy private beach and sat on the deserted, blue canvas chairs in silence, watching the sun meld into the violent orange streaks on the horizon. Nina signed her name in the sand and I splashed my hands in the ocean and smelled the salt on my skin.

'Italy,' Nina murmured. 'Just the job.'

It felt fantastic. We sat there for quite a while. I was thinking so deeply that it was almost meditation.

'When we find him I'm going to tell him about Mum,' I said eventually. 'Even if he knows already. I'm going to tell him.'

'You save it for court,' Nina smiled. 'We'll take him to court. Wherever he is. We'll find him all right and if we can't take him to court where we find him, then somehow we'll move him somewhere we can.'

And as we walked back up the beach we linked arms. I've always thought it was crazy that after Nuremberg no international criminal code was established to help prosecute ex-Nazis or, for that matter, any perpetrator of dictatorship. You're dependent on domestic prosecution procedures for that, so if your ex-Nazi is, say, in Syria, like Brunner was, then he doesn't get prosecuted for his crimes. Even the War Crimes Commission can't touch him.

'We have to find him first,' Nina said, pushing me lightly on the arm.

I guess she can read my mind.

It was, I suppose, about twenty minutes' walk from the Lido to get to the piazza at the town centre. About a mile or so. Children, freewheeling on pushbikes, squealed as they passed us, their mothers behind them, panting to keep up as they raced towards the piazza where, it turned out, there was an idyllic little fair every evening with dodgem cars and a carousel and little ponies pulling traps which trotted to order around a small, tarmacked track. It was very smart, though. Well, it was northern Italy of course so well, it kind of had to be smart. The world was out for a pre-dinner cocktail or a post-dinner ice cream. And the world was well dressed. The crowd outside the open-fronted pizzeria scrambled to buy single slices as they came out of the huge ovens and the air was scented with baking rosemary and oregano. Apart from the pizzeria though, and the restaurants of course, the food shops were closed. So we marked out where they were, and which ones looked best, to try to save us time the next day. Then we strolled along like kids in a toy shop, staring at the window displays in the smart clothes shops and the high-heeled, impractical shoes tottering on display racks next to patterned silk scarves and shiny, well-crafted handbags and discreet, gold-buckled belts.

'Beats the hell out of Brighton,' Nina laughed, and we stopped off and bought ice-cream cones and sat eating them on an old wooden bench beside an ancient, carved stone water fountain where, as we licked, we watched a bright-eyed gypsy couple singing, begging around the tables at the café opposite us, each one holding a sleeping child in their arms. It was too, too perfect.

We decided to walk back along the seafront and as we made our way down towards the beach we could see the town pier lit up with multicoloured lights, so we just carried on and strolled along that and listened to the ocean washing up against the huge pillars which supported the wooden walkway. A gang of teenage boys were daring each other to dive off the end and into the water. A couple of old men were fishing. We wandered lazily along, staring out to sea, and then, when we got to the end and turned round we could see the whole of the little town because it was all lit up, and from the low vantage point of the beach you could make out houses right back to where the incline began to steepen on the road up to the motorway.

'How do you find someone in and among all of that?' I said nodding my head towards the expanse of lights.

'We'll do it,' Nina assured me. 'Never fear. We always do what we say we'll do.'

And well, after the few days which had gone before, I could hardly disagree with her. It looked like she was right and we always did. Then we walked in silence down to the shore and made our way back along the bay towards the Lido's private beach, holding our shoes on one finger and kicking in and out of the spray as we wandered along looking out to sea at the inky night-time sky.

I slept so well that night that I don't think I even dreamed. It was just like slipping into a warm, comforting blackness and hiding there. I suppose I needed the rest quite badly. Nina woke me up in the morning, I could vaguely hear her in the shower as I opened my eyes and took stock of the room. There was a tray of breakfast things down on the little table at the bottom of my bed and one of the windows was open and the sunlight was streaming in. I sat up for a moment and then fell back down again on to the pillows and stretched right out, luxuriating in the warmth as sleep fell away from me and I gradually came to my senses. I could feel the sand in between my toes from the night before and I flexed them, stretching out between the cool, white cotton sheets.

'Monday morning,' I thought. 'Must be in Italy.'

Then Nina came back into the bedroom.

'That shower is something else,' she grinned. 'I don't think I've ever been this clean in my life.' And she picked up a pastry off the tray and nibbled on it as she opened the wardrobe door and pulled out a white dress and a pair of tan sandals with ankle straps.

'You owe me an outfit,' she snarled, eyeing the dress with disdain.

'I'd say we are in the right place for that,' I replied, and helped myself to a snack from the tray as I sloped off to try out the shower.

It was ten by the time we were clean, dressed and fed. We fished our sunglasses out of our handbags and set off once more for the town centre. I don't know if we would have got anywhere in the food shops. I mean, I don't see why it wouldn't have worked, but in the end, we didn't need to even go that far. We hadn't noticed it the night before, but there was an office just on that main road, a lawyer's office with a sign outside that said Marco di Gilberti. Nina picked it up first, of course. I mean, I was too busy trying to catch the streaming sunlight full on my face. Nina is much cooler about all of that and luckily she was looking up, but not at the sunshine. We were walking past this little row of local shops which had beach toys and flip-flops out on the pavement in big baskets and then Nina grabbed my arm and showed me the sign on the office on the first floor.

Di Gilberti. It's hardly a common name. Let's put it this way, it's not the equivalent of Smith, Jones or Green. I couldn't believe we'd walked right past it the night before.

'Fuck,' Nina smiled. 'It has to be, doesn't it?' And she pulled me across the pavement, through the glass doorway and up the pale, marble steps.

'I'll do the talking,' she said, though this time that was kind of unnecessary because, well, my Italian is pretty limited, let's face it. I'd have been hard pushed to say anything which anyone else would readily understand. Usually, though, I can pick up the odd word here and there when someone else is speaking, but I was too nervous that morning to be able to really concentrate so, in fact, I'm still not completely sure what the hell Nina actually said to the receptionist once we got in there. I mean, I know that she talked about the auction sale in Geneva where Simon had picked up the necklet, that much I could make out, and she mentioned the necklace and did lots of expansive hand gestures which showed how great she thought it was, but what her story was, and how she got the phone number out of the poor girl, well, all I know was that it worked. Marco di Gilberti was the Contessa's son as it turned out and he wasn't in, but the receptionist gladly gave us his mother's home number. She even offered to let us use the office telephone, proferring the receiver to us and getting us a free line. I shuddered in the now unaccustomed coolness and let Nina do the talking while I surveyed the black and white architectural prints framed up on the walls and stared almost disbelievingly at the receptionist's perfect manicure. Nina just took the number when it was offered and then she smiled effusively, stuck it in her handbag declining the kind offer of the telephone with a few words which I didn't understand. Then, finally, she said goodbye and pulled me out behind her with a graceful kind of sweep. She was developing a peculiarly Italian kind of style. Very Sophia Loren. Outside we walked the rest of the block before we really spoke to each other. Nina pulled the number out of her handbag and waved it in front of me.

'Home number,' she squealed. 'We found her. We did it!'

'You did it,' I said. 'Well done. Let's find a phone.'

We couldn't quite believe it had been that easy although, later, when we thought about it, it was a stroke of luck and all that but Forte dei Marmi is a pretty small place. Not hamlet-tiny but, still, at the village end of the town scale. And well, as it turned out, getting the Contessa di Gilberti's ex-directory home number was easier than trying to use an Italian public telephone. They're not hot on instructions at the Italian telephone service. We had to try three or four different boxes before we figured out that the phonecard we'd bought would only work if we ripped the corner off it. But then, when we did get through, and the Contessa finally came to the phone, Nina did the job once again, admirably. This time she said that we were from the museum, that we had been at the sale in Geneva and we were very interested in buying anything else she might have of note and, in fact, finding out any more that she could tell us about the carved amethyst necklet which she had entered into the auction a couple of weeks before. I think, myself, that Nina was too cheesy. She went on about how it was an incredible item of great social value and hammed it up good style about its historical significance but perhaps she didn't overdo it too much because, after all, it worked. The Contessa invited us over that afternoon. Nina wrote down the address on my arm and when she hung up we both just stared at it.

'It's up past the hotel,' she said, 'the posh end of

231

town.' To the north of the main drag, fashionably out of the way, there were larger houses with big, plush green gardens. Rumour has it, because before we went up there we asked, that Giorgio Armani hangs out there for a few weeks every summer in a fabulous, marble-clad hideaway. One way or another it was the Contessa's end of town, though we figured that she must have been a bit of a fallen aristocrat, selling off a piece of jewellery like that instead of gifting it to some niece or other, or just keeping it locked away in the family vault.

We had most of the day still to while away, of course. We weren't due there until after four o'clock and even counting how long it took us to make our phonecard work, we still had five and a half hours, so we did what it was only sensible to do. We had to distract ourselves somehow and Nazi hunters or not, well, we're only human. So we walked on into town and we went shopping for a while in those fabulous shops until everything closed for lunch at one. I didn't really get into it myself, but I suppose we had to pass the time somehow. My mind kept on wandering, though, back halfway across Europe, back to Edinburgh, as I paid for everything absent-mindedly with my card. We hauled our trawl all the way back to the Lido where we unpacked it in the bedroom, trying on the clothes again and again in assorted combinations and still I was a thousand miles away with Ma Polinski or maybe, more accurately, with my mother. Looking close into her big, scared blue eyes, the way I'd always imagined her when she first came to Scotland.

'Wow, we look sorted. *Bellissima*,' Nina said, admiring us in the mirror. And well, I couldn't help but agree. We changed, of course, and then we plotted over a late lunch down at the boardwalk restaurant on the Lido's private beach. Even the wind was warm. I could feel myself soaking up the heat, basking in it, all my bones relaxing after the biting chill of the Scottish springtime with its odd day of what we think of as sunshine. Nina and I broke bread together and ate away slowly at what we had served up for ourselves from the seafood buffet which was spread out on a long, linen-draped table set up on the way in. I didn't have much appetite and neither did she but we picked here and there. Around us, rich, older couples were sipping on their lunchtime wine, luxuriating in the laziness of the place. Actually, I think Nina and I were the only people under forty there. We talked quietly, huddled together, figuring things out, biding our time. Talking about how to get the Contessa to tell us where she got the necklace from. And finally agreeing with each other on the details we would be looking for, the names and places of people she might have met. 'Weird,' said Nina, 'we're talking like we're on to a sure thing. A definite lead or something.' And I had to agree with her. The Contessa might not, after all, be able to tell us anything. She might have bought the necklace at a market stall or through an anonymous intermediary. She might not even remember. She might, we hazarded a guess, be some dreadful old alcoholic, selling off her things, little by little to finance her habit. A mad old lady in decline, hopefully not so far gone that she would get truculent on us when she realised just how much we needed her. I suppose in a way what I was really hoping for was someone colourful but still someone who would be open to giving us the information we needed. It seemed so magical really. I knew that it might not work out like that but, well, whatever the Contessa turned out to be like, I suppose what strikes me now about that afternoon is that we were so optimistic. I know that it hadn't really occurred to me that the whole journey to Italy might have led us nowhere at all, that we might not find out anything. That's positive thinking for you. That's it in action. I was expecting a pretty high baseline of information, in fact I was expecting to find out everything I wanted to know, so if it had occurred to me that we might not be able to find out anything, well, I just put it to the back of my mind and as far as I was concerned, it was a definite thing that we'd find him. To me, it was certain that we'd track him down, take him to court and win a conviction. Strange, that. I wasn't about to count on failure. It's almost as if I willed it to go as well as it did. Nina and I, we were kind of on a roll and after all our hushed calculations over lunch, by quarter to four we were very clear in our minds what we were looking for. We were ready and we had reception call us a cab.

Chapter Twenty-Two

The Contessa was no down-and-out. She wasn't an alcoholic. She wasn't the least bit desperate. She was, in fact, exactly how people without money imagine people with it. Everything around her was terribly, terribly expensive and she was very prim and totally in control. When we pulled up at the villa, which was enormous, and we were allowed in through the security entrance, there was a convertible red Ferrari outside in the driveway as well as an old black Daimler stowed away to the side of the house in an open garage. The villa itself was three storeys high and just covered in ivy and some other kind of creeper which bloomed with very pale pink flowers here and there. There were stone steps leading up to the front door, which was opened by a butler as we approached it. The hallway was cool after the baking heat of the afternoon, and it was bordered by a mass of white lilies in elongated vases every yard or so, and gilded, eighteenth-century, marble-topped side tables. It was extremely grand and I think we both felt a bit humbled. A bit small. The Contessa herself awaited us in a conservatory to the rear of the palazzo. The butler said something or other in Italian to us and Nina and I dutifully followed him through a couple of reception rooms, this time lined on either side with great lengths of distressed antique mirror encased in beautiful, carved, wooden frames. I watched us as we passed. It was as if we floated through those rooms and out, into the leafy, light glasshouse, its green doors open on to the garden. The plants inside were tropical and huge. They grew out of heavy, old, terracotta pots like a little jungle. In the middle of it all, the Contessa was wearing a straw hat with an enormous brim which cast a shadow over her face and right down her chiffon, red summer dress. She was in her late sixties and as she extended her hand towards us, you could see how well groomed she was and how well preserved. Her nails were immaculate, painted with red varnish, and she wore rings on nearly every finger, which is something only the elderly can get away with. She was very confident, very secure in herself and quite graceful. She paused very beautifully and then motioned to us to sit down. Then another butler arrived out of nowhere with a tray of tea and little lemon biscuits with thin icing on top and a sprinkling of finely-chopped fresh mint. I could smell it as I sat down and the tray went past me.

Nina made small talk while the tea was poured, explaining that I couldn't speak Italian, and commenting on how lovely it was to be in Italy at that time of year, when it was so cold at home. She said that we had been sent by the museum and passed the Contessa her business card. The Contessa smiled and signalled to the butler to leave us alone and once he was gone, she sat back in her seat and asked something about the carved amethyst necklace, the whole reason why we were there. I could pick out the odd word of what Nina said to her in reply, something about the King Farouk sale. The Contessa pursed her lips. She hadn't known the provenance of the piece, obviously. She had been relying solely on the auction house for that.

'Where did you buy it?' Nina asked, as if casually.

'It is a family piece,' the Contessa replied. 'A family piece.'

'I see,' Nina said, a little taken aback.

I stopped breathing. I looked around myself carefully. A family piece. It felt as if it was too close. As if he might be nearby. There were tiny shivers pulsing up my spine at the very thought of it.

The Contessa picked up a little brass bell in the shape of a lady from a sidetable to her left and she rang it. I could see that instead of a brass ball on a length of chain inside the bow of the bell, that there were two little brass legs, the feet of which dangled down just below the hem of the metal skirt. Everything, even the tiniest details of that visit, has stayed with me. The slightly humid heat of the old greenhouse on the back of my neck, the itching in my fingers as I waited to see what was going to happen. When the butler came back into the room he was carrying a tray with a black leather box on it. He laid it down beside the Contessa and she opened the lid as he silently disappeared again.

'These things,' she said, 'belonged to my brother-in-law.'

Nina passed the box over to me, and I fished around inside my bag for my eyeglass and then looked to see what was inside. They were Ma Polinski's things, or what was left of them. I knew it as soon as I opened the lid. An eclectic mixture but all in such fine quality. A Georgian diamond collet; a Chinese carved jade head-dress; a sixteenth-century Dutch handpainted fan; an ornately worked baby's coral and silver soother; a heavy, three-carat sapphire single-stone ring. I didn't need to know the provenance of any of it, I could see because each one was such a good example of pieces of that kind and it flooded back to me – the details of the pieces my father had described to me. The items he'd seen himself so long ago. And here they were. They had been her things. I just knew it and I bit my lip hard as I examined them, piece by piece. I was determined not to cry while the Contessa was looking at me. It would have blown the whole thing.

'They're hers,' I breathed, and Nina bowed her head. 'Ask her what happened to him,' I whispered, and my voice sounded kind of tight, but it didn't break. Nina passed on the question and the Contessa told her, without even looking at me, that her brother-in-law was dead. He had died the year before, outliving her sister by only a few months.

'I'm sorry,' I heard Nina say, but I heard it from a distance. It was as if I was dreaming. 'These items,' Nina carried on, 'were last known to be in Scotland in the early 1970s. How did your brother-in-law come by them?'

'Oh, they had been in his family for some years. Passed on to him. He had never, to my knowledge, visited Scotland.'

'Really? Was he Italian?' Nina pushed her.

The Contessa shook her head. 'No. He was Polish,' she said.

And then, of course, we knew for sure, though by that time it felt like I was floating.

'We must buy them,' I said to Nina. 'We have to take them home.'

And I heard her ask the Contessa about the box, and mention something about the collection at the museum. The Contessa shrugged her shoulders. She picked up her cup and saucer delicately and sipped on the tea. I thought to myself that she was going to play hard to get. She would hold out for a good price. It didn't bother me though – I'd have paid every penny that I had to get those things back. I think it just bemused me a bit, really. Nina was more on the ball than I was. She carried on although, I suppose, the Contessa must have thought that she was only making small talk.

'We would also be very interested to see any

photographs that you have of your brother-in-law,' Nina said. 'The provenance of such pieces can make a marked difference to the value.'

The Contessa put down her drink very definitely.

'He lived in Florence with my sister,' she said. 'They were very happy together for many years.' And she rang the bell again and asked the butler to bring her a photograph album.

It felt like he was gone for a long time, that butler. We sat there in silence with the leather box laid out on the table in front of us and we sipped politely on our tea and nibbled on the crisp little biscuits. I had to hold myself back from touching the jewellery. It had been hers. At last, the butler arrived with the album of photographs and the Contessa opened it up and began to point out a rather old, rather gruff-looking man who still combed his hair back as if he was younger and far smoother looking. It was, without a doubt, Tomasz Polinski, although she called him Josef Swick. There were photographs of him with the Contessa's sister and they were both laughing outside, with the shadow of some great tree cast over them. Then there were photographs of them out to dinner, with the Contessa, who was herself with another man. Her husband, we presumed, although we didn't ask. Family photos he didn't deserve, I thought. He'd moved straight from murdering Molly Savage on to another wealthy woman. He must have been so charming. Just like those men charged with war crimes whose neighbours say they wouldn't hurt a fly. I bit my lip and hoped the fury I was feeling, the despair and the turmoil too, weren't showing in my eyes, and thank God for Nina because I couldn't have just politely carried on. If I'd opened my mouth to speak God knows what I would have said. Certainly not what Nina managed to get out, anyway.

'The artefacts you have,' she continued with a smile

as the photograph album was placed to the side of the Contessa's chair, 'we will need to work on their provenance. But they are definitely items from the same collection and we are very, very interested in purchasing them to bring back to Scotland.'

The Contessa nodded. 'I will have my agent look at them. You can agree a fair price with him,' she said. 'I have no need of them. Museum pieces,' she mused with a smile and then it was time for us to go. And I wanted to scream. I wanted my voice to reverberate round the high, elegant ceilings. I wanted to purge the place of his memory somehow. The cool spring evenings he'd probably spent there, the empty botttles of wine, the plates cleared away by the discreet, competent staff. Bastard. But I stood right behind Nina and I even managed to smile as she said,'That's great. Thank you. We'll be in touch.'

And the Contessa nodded politely. We didn't tell her then. Of course we couldn't. We didn't know how she might have reacted and well, we wanted the contents of that jewellery box more than we wanted to enlighten her. She shook our hands in turn – a firm handshake really for such an elderly lady who'd been taken in all of her life.

And well, in effect, it was all agreed. Everything bar the money, and that was hardly going to be a problem now, was it? And the poor old lady, she didn't have a clue.

Chapter Twenty-Three

That night in Italy I slept badly. I think that's because he was finally, really, dead. The next morning Nina and I decided to spend a day in Pisa before we left, although when we got there we discovered that we weren't allowed to go up the leaning tower which had, of course, been our intention. It was closed for renovations. The guide told us it had been closed for ages. It didn't matter, I suppose. Actually, come to think of it, it kind of fitted in with the way that we both felt. In the end, we just wandered around the base of it, looking at all the scaffolding and engineering machinery which was holding the old monument up. Propping up a bit of history which wanted to just fall. I can't say it was really a pleasant sight. It gave me a kind of weird feeling and I didn't want to hang around. I suppose I wondered if that was what I was doing myself – caring so much about something which was so long gone that I was only propping it up. Then we took a bus into the city and stayed there all day and I was kind of restless because I knew that apart from the arrangements which had to be made, the details of the purchase, my next move, well my only move was to speak to Mum and Dad and finally come clean, and I was scared, but I was ready to do it. And, well, I knew I had to do it alone in the end, and I was just itching to get on.

In the evening, we caught the last flight back to

Glasgow and when we got in we took a cab back into town. We were kind of dazed, kind of completely unaware of the stormy weather which was swirling all around us. The sudden chill of the air. It was the middle of May. The start of what was supposed to be the summer. Mike Williams was going to see to the purchase of the contents of the Contessa's leather box. I had seen to that straight away back in Forte dei Marmi, the morning after we had met the Contessa. I had rung him as soon as I had woken up and I had told him that I didn't need to have the things valued – I knew more or less what they were worth. What they were worth financially at any rate – three hundred thousand or so, I reckoned. The jade was pretty good quality, you see. Well, it all was, but the jade was kind of special and it bumped the price up quite a bit. But that didn't matter. It's not like I'm short of money. It's not like I wasn't prepared to pay a bit over the odds. They were my things and I wanted them back. If I'd been able to prove they were stolen I'd have called in the police, but as it was I gave the lawyer my valuation and then I told him to go as high as he had to.

Back in Glasgow I dropped Nina off at her place and kissed her cheek as we said goodbye in the back of the cab.

'Back to work tomorrow,' she said, and I didn't say anything about the idea which was running through my head. I didn't tell her that everything had changed. I just nodded.

'I'm going to transfer you some money,' I told her.

'You don't have to.'

'I know. I want to, though,' I mumbled kind of uncomfortably and she hugged me and got out of the car. She never even asked me how much it was going to be. It was weird being without her. Watching her grab her little suitcase and disappear inside the door of the tenement after the last few days and everything that we'd done together with hardly a minute apart. It felt very odd. I had the driver wait until I saw the light go on in her living room. My best friend, Nina Fabrizzi, who had been the best friend anyone could have asked for. Look how far she'd gone. Look what she'd done just for me. She was amazing. But it still wasn't over. There were things to do which Nina couldn't help with. There were things I had to say to my parents which I could only sort out on my own. It was an instinct then, that was all. I worked on instinct alone from that point on, I think, really because I didn't have anyone to convince other than myself. But I knew it was going to be difficult and that nonetheless I had to do the right thing. I was sure of it. Maybe because I'd come to trust that knot in the pit of my stomach, that instinctive fear of change that Mum and Dad had instilled in me so carefully. But things were going to change. So much had changed already.

Back at my own place I wandered around the empty rooms with the lights out. It had been a bit of a come-down, in some ways, to have death resolve the problem with Tomasz Polinski when I was ready to take action myself. Direct action. I had been ready to launch a campaign, to make a case and then prove it. Ready to go to court. Ever since we had known that he hadn't died in the car crash. Ever since that night when Nina had been in the spare bedroom examining the bones, well, I had been all fired up and though some of it had seemed like a dream, I had been determined all the way through that he'd lose his name. Seeing those photographs of Tomasz Polinski, and meeting the Contessa, well, at one point I had almost stopped breathing. It had been intense – I couldn't really have hoped for more – but, still, the outcome wasn't what I had been expecting. I had been spoiling for a dramatic climax, an unmasking, an arrest, and in the end all I got was a smartly dressed old lady who obviously didn't have a clue and a few old photographs. It didn't seem enough to bring back to my mother. I knew then that I would research him, of course, I knew that I'd find out everything there was to find. Well, in the end, that's exactly what I have done. I've made well sure that it has all been recorded for posterity. But that was just paperwork in the end. The memory of a dead man set to rights. It didn't seem enough when I'd thought I was going to get to actually do something. When I thought I was going to get to confront him. Bring him to justice in the domestic courts. Tell him face to face about how he and men like him have overshadowed the lives of people they've never met. How my own life has been muddied. How I have lost so much time trying to figure things out which ought never to have been there. Even now, after all the work I've done on it – all the forms I filled in, the searches, contacting every museum with records and permanent exhibitions on the subject, even passing information on to the few agencies who deal with ex-Nazis – well, none of that was the same as a face to face meeting with the old bastard. None of that was the same as making him stand trial. I still wish that I'd had the opportunity. And that evening last year, when I was finally home again, well, after a while of just wandering around my flat, like a stranger, I sank on to my bed and stared up at the ceiling, watching the reflection of the car headlights from the main road playing along the cornice of the room. I lay there for a long time until the cars became less frequent and then it was so quiet I could hear the footsteps of the odd drunk, stumbling along the pavement on his way home.

It must have been very late when I finally fell asleep because it was late when I woke up. Nearly eleven. My mind had been working all night and when I opened my eyes I had a kind of purpose about me again. That instinct thing was kicking in. I pulled on some clothes and banged the door behind me, my own footsteps echoing down the tenement hallway as I made my way out into the street and walked the short distance to work. It felt like I had grown up overnight and, well, I'd made some decisions and that day I knew that I was going in to work at the museum for the last time. When I got there I nodded at the security guard and, well, he didn't even ask to see my ID, as I walked through the door. I just wandered into the building and took the lift up to the third floor. To my boss's office. To resign.

Bob Morris is a dear old guy, really. Passionate about the public's right to education and also rather an expert on the Golden Age of Steam. A kind of academic train-spotter, I suppose. When the Government finally passed that bill which guaranteed free public access to all museums, Bob threw a big drinks party. He didn't do that on his birthday. He hadn't even done that when he got married. The museum was everything to him, and he really believed in it. When I knocked on his door he opened it himself and I swept into his dusty, bright office and sat down before he'd even made it back to his chair.

'I need to take some time off,' I said. 'I might not be back.'

'You all right, Rachel?' he asked. He looked kind of taken aback. I mean, I don't suppose anyone ever goes to see him like that unless it is an emergency. So he was on his toes. And well, Bob has great integrity so he was concerned, I guess, about doing the right thing by me and making sure that I was OK. He'd shaken Dad's hand, after all. He needn't have worried.

'I'm fine, Bob,' I said. 'But I have to sort my head out a bit. I'm sorry. I'm supposed to give you notice.'

Bob Morris took off his glasses and peered at me. His eyes were very green. It was something that I had never noticed before, his sharp green eyes. They reminded me of Scotty. I wonder if he saw how intent I was, as if I'd got a whole new purpose about me, which, I suppose, I had.

'Well,' he said, 'if you have to go you'd better go then.'

I gave him a quick rundown of where I had got to on the plains people exhibit. I apologised without really explaining and then I left. I wouldn't have been able to do that if it hadn't been for the money. But God, I did need to do it, you know. I really needed to. Everyone always says that they won't give up their job. You ask any lottery winner on the night they find out. You ask anyone. But I'd realised, you see, that I had to go. I'd realised that having all that money does change your life. I'd realised I had to just accept it like Nina had said in the park that day. I'd realised a whole load of shit. I might love the past, all those stories, the history of it, but I didn't want to work there any more. However much I loved my job and, yeah, I did love that job. But at that point it was clear to me I had other things to do. She hadn't only given me the money, you see. She'd endowed me with something far more valuable. A vocation. A passion. Something which had grabbed hold of my soul.

Back at my flat I packed up all of my stuff and wrote a letter to the landlord. A month's notice. And I enclosed a cheque, of course. And then I got a cab to the station and took the first train to Edinburgh to face it all. I landed on Scotty's doorstep around five that afternoon. He wasn't at home. He was working, but I just sat there like it was where I belonged until he finally showed up around seven. I suppose I had learned a thing or two about determination and I wanted to see him first, before anything else. I'd wanted to see him for days, of course, and my heart just sang when he kissed me. He kissed me a lot, pushing me up against the door frame at the entrance to the flat.

'I tried to ring,' he started, but I put my fingers up to his lips.

'I've been away,' I said, 'but now I'm back.'

'I missed you, Rachel,' he breathed. He has such soft lips that I got a bit carried away. It was really good to see him again. Sometimes you just know when something is right because it feels so good. We sat up in the flat for ages with our arms around each other and it felt like I had come home. I had done what I had had to do and I'd made it back. That night I was proud of myself as I told Scotty what had happened from beginning to end and Scotty just listened, gently and still. I was proud of the fact that I hadn't been scared of what needed to be done. That I'd faced my fears and trusted my gut instinct. That I hadn't crawled back to Edinburgh to my nice, safe love affair. That I'd made it as far as I had, even though there was still quite a way to go, even though I was still afraid. I knew I had to prove everything we'd assumed about Tomasz Polinski. First though, I had to prove something to myself. I had to sort things out with my mum and dad. I had to tell them what had happened and I had to come clean. In my mind, once I'd done all of that, I knew I would be able to lay Molly Savage to rest once and for all.

'Can I stay here?' I asked Scotty. 'I don't want to room over at Simon's.'

'Sure,' Scotty smiled. 'You can stay with me for as long as you like. Just remind me never, ever to get on the wrong side of you. A woman who'll disinter a skeleton and then re-inter it 'cos she got it wrong. Wow. You're some girl, Rachel,' and he stroked my hair and kissed me again before we fell asleep together on top of the bed just before midnight.

Chapter Twenty-Four

I thought I was going to have an aneurysm as I pushed open the gate at Mum and Dad's place the next morning. My heart was pounding like crazy and my hands were clammy and they were shaking like mad. I had known I was scared, I had known it was a big deal, I just hadn't realised exactly how scared I was. It took me a few seconds to actually manage to get my key into the Yale lock on the front door. I was like one of those little kids who can't put the square peg into the square hole. I just couldn't make it fit. I took a couple of deep breaths and focused and then, before I really had time to think about it again and get nervous, I got the door open and called out to see where Mum and Dad were. My mother's voice echoed up from the kitchen and I slammed the front door behind me and padded down the hallway.

'Rachel,' she grinned, putting down her cooking utensils as I came into the kitchen, and giving me a big hug. 'What are you doing home, darling?'

'Oh, Mum,' I said, 'it's really good to see you,' and she smelled of vegetable soup as I pressed my nose into her shoulder. And then when I surfaced I asked 'Where's Dad?'

'Gone to London,' Mum replied. 'Went to a sale. He'll be back tonight probably, or maybe tomorrow. Here, let me put the kettle on. Why aren't you at work?'

I leaned against the kitchen table. I'd worked myself up into a near frenzy to get the nerve together to come to see them at all, and the old man wasn't even at home. I thought for a second and then I took a deep breath. I couldn't put it off any longer.

'I have something to tell you, Mum. Something has happened.'

Mum didn't even turn round from the work surface. She was putting out a couple of mugs and sorting out the coffee.

'Mmm?' she asked absent-mindedly.

'I came into some money. Big money. A bequest. I quit my job yesterday, Mum.'

Mum turned round slowly. The kettle was boiling behind her and there was a big cloud of steam billowing up right behind her head.

'Money?' she asked.

'Yes,' I nodded. 'Lots of money. It came from Molly Savage. You know, Ma Polinski. She left me eight million pounds. I only just found out.'

I had been expecting it to be a bit uncomfortable for Mum and Dad, the great providers, to be told that they didn't have to bother any more. I'd expected Mum to be upset when I told her about Tomasz Polinski, about why I thought the old lady had left the money to me. Nonetheless, I was expecting her to congratulate me even if there was an undercurrent there that both of them would feel excluded, ousted from their position. I had thought they'd be proud of me, especially when they found out what I'd done. That's what I was prepared for. I hadn't expected anything quite so dramatic as Mum sinking to the floor. I hadn't expected her to actually vomit as she pulled herself up and dashed over to the sink. I hadn't expected her to go as pale as she did. To look quite so thin. And I had only told her about the money. I hadn't got any of the real story out.

'How?' she mouthed, wide eyed. 'How could she?'

'Mum.' I started over towards her and I tried to put my hand on her arm. 'Mum,' I said again.

But my mother pulled away from me. She backed right up against the fridge.

'What is it?' I asked her gently. 'What's wrong?'

And then, as if it was in slow motion, I saw my mother gain control of herself again. I saw the drawbridge to her castle raised, and a calm kind of coldness welling up in her clear blue eyes as she retreated from me, gathering her emotions close to her again, fading away. Putting herself back in control. Just like she always did.

'I'm sorry, Rachel,' she said. 'I didn't expect that. I was shocked. It's wonderful news, darling. Congratulations.'

'Don't do that, Mum,' I began. I was losing my temper. 'Don't you dare do that to me. You've always done that. You tell me what happened there. You tell me,' I shouted.

Mum kept her composure. 'I was just a little bit shocked, dear. That's all. Why don't you sit down?' and she made a move to go back over to the kettle and make the coffee. She didn't get all the way over there, though. I couldn't let her. I caught her halfway across the kitchen and I held her tight right in front of me. It was the spookiest thing I've ever seen. The coldness of it.

'Mum,' I said, 'you never tell me anything. You and Dad operate like some kind of Secret Service. Now you either tell me what happened there, or I will walk out of this house and I will not come back. Ever.'

Mum's eyes were hard. The lady was not for turning. 'You go then,' she spat. 'What do you know? Go on, you silly little girl.'

'Why aren't you ever just honest with me?' I said, and I began to cry.

My mother was quivering. Not with sadness or with pity. Not the soft-shouldered tremor of someone who might cry, who might crack. Not the way that I was shaking. But with the rigid jawed movement of someone who was furious.

'What do you know?' she shouted. 'We protected you all of your life. What do you know? You are soft and spoiled, Rachel. You're an academic. A theorist. All airy-fairy. You haven't a clue about real life. You don't know anything.'

'If I don't know it's because you won't tell me anything. Why is everything such a big secret? You're the one who is afraid, Mum. Look at yourself. Look how scared you are. You can't even be honest with your own daughter.'

It was a stupid argument really, I suppose. But one we had been needing to have for a long time. Twenty-five years or thereabouts. Usually my mother had my father to come in when things looked like they might lead to some kind of confrontation. Usually things never got anywhere near as far as that because my parents formed a kind of unassailable alliance. They headed anything like that off long before there was any danger of it actually getting as far as being said. They always knew best.

'Just tell me, Mum,' I pleaded. 'Please.'

'You haven't a clue,' she snorted. 'You don't know what you're asking.' And she began to cry without moving a single muscle in her ashen face. The tears just rolled down her cheeks.

'Her husband was a Nazi, you know,' my mother said eventually. 'He was a Nazi.'

And I nodded and I told her everything that I knew, everything that I'd found out.

'I'll prove it,' I swore to her. 'I'll prove it and I'll make sure everyone knows,' and at first, you know, because she'd spent her whole life trying to forget, her whole life in denial, I think the thought of that really horrified her.

Chapter Twenty-Five

I stayed with Mum all afternoon. I think it was the closest I'd ever been to her since the womb. Really. We didn't eat all day. We didn't move. We just talked and talked and talked. And it all came out bit by bit as the morning wore away and the afternoon rolled on and the evening came upon us and the room became dark and we were still sitting together, talking. Mum told me about Dachau. Finally. At last, somehow because of what happened, she found the words. She remembered lying on a wooden bunk, five people deep, with her mother. She remembered her mother stroking her patchy hair, holding her close, using a nail to carve their names on the bedpost. Most people had expected to die. Most people did.

'We'll go like two little butterflies, we'll fly off and leave the cocoon behind,' my grandmother had said. It had been so cold, so miserable, so filthy. At the end, the Germans had marched inmates from Auschwitz and some of the other camps back to Dachau as they retreated from the Allies. Dachau had become very overcrowded. There was no food at the end. None at all and death was everywhere.

'I don't know why they had to torture us. If they wanted to kill us, they could have just killed us. But they didn't. They humiliated us. They starved us. They wanted to watch us suffering. They wanted to watch families scream for each other in the night. They wanted to make us give up. My mother gave up,' Mum said. 'She gave up for both of us. She expected us both to die.'

'What happened?' I pressed her, gently. I had waited all of my life to know.

'They had taken my father away and my brothers. I had two brothers,' my mother said. 'You'd have had two uncles if they had lived. I heard that they had done experiments on my father. There was a doctor there, Dr Rascher. He conducted hypothermia experiments. They had wanted to know what their soldiers could endure on the Russian front, just how far they could push their own people. So he froze my father to death. Just to see how long it would take. I don't know what happened to my younger brother. But the other one, Oskar, he survived for a long time. He was clever. He made himself useful on the work parties and he was strong. I heard that he had died, though, a month or two before the liberation. They speeded up, you know, when they realised that they were going to lose the war. They worked more quickly. That was when they took Mama away. I wasn't with her when they did it. I didn't say goodbye. They took her away and they killed her. But they left me behind. There had been a typhoid epidemic. I fought for my food. I stole. I was so tiny. I used to hide when there were inspections. I lived for three months like that. Aunt Petra and I worked it out. We tried to make out the dates. Three months. It wasn't necessarily the good people who survived, Rachel. It was the people who fought. The people who stole. It was the only way to get through. There is so much I can't really remember, Rachel. I was so small and I had nimble fingers and I was determined to live. After the Americans arrived there were soldiers and nurses. They fed us. There were people who died, you know, because they ate too much too quickly. The Allies brought oil and bread and people had waited so long for food, they were so starving that they would just eat and eat and then their bodies couldn't cope with it and they died. In the end Aunt Petra came. She took me home with her. She smelled just like my mother. I remember smelling her. She smelled just the same.'

I had known all about Dachau before. I'd tried to find out everything that I could about what had happened to my mother. About what it had been like. She had been in the camp for nine months and it was amazing that she had survived at all. The last nine months were the worst and Mum, well, she was only five years old. There was overcrowding and disease and virtually no food. People were living on tiny amounts of water in which a butcher had previously boiled sausages. That was it. That was all there was. It lasted for weeks on end and some days there wasn't even a cup of sausage water. Some days there was no food at all. Dachau was grim. When the Americans arrived in April 1945, there were fifty wagons on a railway siding piled high with starved, unburied bodies. The stench had been unbelievable. They had just been left to rot. Towards the second half of the war, in 1942, the Nazis had built a gas oven at Dachau but no one has ever been able to prove if they used it or not. Even after the war, during the Nuremberg trials, it was never proved. The camp had been primarily a work camp for the armament industry. It had been set up in 1933, long before the war started. When the liberation came there were a handful of people who had survived since the beginning. They had been tortured and starved for twelve years. I can't even imagine that. If I think about what I was doing twelve years ago, how old I was, and then I imagine if all that time instead of living my life here in cosy, middle-class Scotland, I had been starved and beaten. I think I'd have given up. I'd have wanted to die. I suppose Mum was kind of right. I didn't have a clue.

And I cried alongside my mother. I mourned properly for the first time. I was able to because I knew what I was grieving for. My grandparents had died along with my uncles. I had been cheated out of my family – the love of my relations who had been murdered and that of my cousins who were never born. All the people I might have known. They'd killed all that along with my mother's right to a normal life. It wasn't that I hadn't known about the murders, about how they starved people so that they would be so weak they would be cheap and easy to kill, about the medical experiments they'd done with hypothermia and atmospheric pressure and malaria. I'd read all of that. I'd informed myself. But it's different when you transpose the words on the page into your own life. It's different hearing that someone died as a result of Dr Rascher's medical experiments from knowing that that person was your grandfather. I think I cried more than my mother, in fact. Not only because of what she was telling me, but because she had finally found the words and I knew that the drawbridge was down then and it was down for good.

'This isn't the history I wanted to give you. I wanted to give you better,' she whispered.

'Oh, Mum,' I sobbed, 'I'm sorry.'

She rocked me for a long time and I felt very relieved. Very loved, really. She held me in her arms until it was dark, in fact. Until we heard the front door open and my father come into the hallway. I heard him put down his case and call out. Mum sprang to her feet and walked out to greet him. I stayed put. He felt very alien, very far away.

'Rachel's here,' I heard my mother say. 'She's in the kitchen.'

'What's wrong?' my father asked.

'Nothing,' said Mum. 'Nothing at all.' She was

turning the lights on in the hallway and in the kitchen too as she came back into the room.

'I made soup,' she said. 'Rachel, would you like some soup?'

I was hungry. I hadn't eaten since breakfast and now that the lights were on I could see the clock. It was half past eight. 'Yes please,' I nodded. 'Soup.'

'What are you doing home?' Dad asked jovially. 'What's going on?'

It was kind of a seminal moment. I think Mum was holding her breath.

'I told Rachel everything, Charlie,' she said, and there was absolute silence again although this time it was uncomfortable. I felt like then I knew their secret, which was crazy because, of course, it was my secret too. My secret history. It was part of where I had come from. But still I felt guilty. I'd burst a bubble after all. Dad couldn't believe it.

'What?' he snapped, and when he turned towards me I saw the kind of anger in his eyes that Simon had exploded into that morning at Scotty's and I was scared but I knew I had to face it down.

'I'm moving back to Edinburgh, Dad,' I said.

'Back home,' he commented. 'Good.'

'Molly Polinski left me all her money. Her lawyer has held it in trust since she died.'

Dad closed his eyes and when he opened them he wouldn't look directly at me, he just stared, fixedly at my mother.

'Blood money,' he murmured. 'Guilt money. She will rot in hell for that. The coward. He had told her everything and she did nothing. She could have proved it. She could have made it stick that time.'

'Dad,' I said, cutting in, 'he killed her. It wasn't an accident. He made her die.'

And I began to tell him, I began to explain her

desperation, her ineptitude, her terror. The mural on the ceiling of her bedroom, the ghost I thought I'd seen on my way out to Morbrax the last time I was there, the leather box in the Contessa's safe which proved that Tomasz Polinski had made off with her fortune.

'I think she left the money to me to make it right,' I said. 'I think she knew somehow that I'd look for the reasons, that I'd find him if he was still alive, that I'd do the things she didn't have the courage to. And Dad, I will. I'll prove it.'

'It's too late,' Dad said. 'The last time I saw her I said so. It's too late. Proof is all we've got but even that isn't enough. They're dead now. They died. Millions of people. City upon city. Nothing anyone can prove will bring them back. There is no justice for that. Tomasz Polinski should have been shot. They all should have been shot.'

And I think that is really the strangest thing of all. My mother, who seemed to understand and seemed to forgive, was the one who'd been there. And my father, who'd lived his whole life safe in Blighty, was the one who couldn't bear it. Mum moved across the kitchen, lightly, and I saw in her face the bright eyes of the child she had once been. The survivor.

'Charlie,' she breathed, and she wrapped her arms around him. 'There was nothing else you could have done. They were gone. They never came back.'

And I realised that I'd succeeded there, where my father had failed. Tomasz Polinski was probably the only Nazi he'd ever come into contact with, the only time in his life when he could have done something practical to someone who had, in conscience, perpetrated those wrongs upon my mother for which we all suffered. And he had failed. Tomasz Polinski had got away and that's why Dad was avoiding my eyes. He was ashamed of himself. My father, who hadn't done anything wrong, was wracked with guilt.

'Dad,' I started, 'I found him. He didn't get away with what he did and Ma Polinski died for what she did wrong.'

And my father reached out towards me and pulled me in and we stood there for ages, the three of us, in the kitchen. And I knew that it was over, that the secrets were well and truly out.

Late that night I walked back into town from the Grange. As I left the house, I fixed my hat in front of the hall mirror and I noticed that there was a new light in my eyes. I don't know if it was all the crying or what. I don't think so. There were a million things going through my head, running in a list. Things that I had to do before I would be able to really enjoy Molly's millions. You have to sleep soundly and burgeoning piles of money won't lull you. As I closed my parents' front door behind me, that list of things was scrolling through my mind. Now, though, I think I've worked my way through most of it. Molly's treasures are safely stowed away in my name in one of the Chubb safes in the basement of my brother's shop. We ended up paying a bit over the odds for them, but who cares? Mike Williams was almost glad about it. I even let him set up a direct debit into my account so that I'd have money to live on while I was doing the other things I had to do. Probably most importantly, Tomasz Polinski's memory is well and truly set to rights. I've proved now that he was a Nazi beyond any doubt. It took a long time, but I did it in the end. Ten months. He wasn't just a collaborator, you know, he wore a Nazi uniform. He'd covered his trail well. It took a lot of work, but people like that, well, once someone as determined as I am is on their case, someone with a vocation, a passion for uncovering them for what they are, well, no amount of false papers and fake files can hide them. The Contessa was appalled. After the papers had been published, once the truth was out, she rang Nina one afternoon and told her that she'd had all his old clothes burned in a big pile in her garden and that she'd had his grave-stone removed. And that kind of gratified me, I have to say.

It's been a busy year. Scotty and I have moved out to Morbrax now. Together. That one really freaked Simon out at first, but slowly and surely he's come to terms with it and he drives out some Sundays and the boys play golf. Once or twice he's even stayed overnight and we've all sat up late together by the fireside, talking. Mum and Dad had to tell him too, of course. They told him everything. Simon, though, has a system of draw-bridges of his own and in the end, instead of being open to it, he's really retreated a little bit. He's really backed off and I suppose I've let him, we all have, because you can't make someone be open, you can't make them want to know. Not everyone's constituted the same way. Still, we've had a chance to talk a little bit and even if it hasn't helped him (and you never can tell) it's certainly helped me.

I love it out here in the country. I bought some old furniture for the house, and in between Scotty's own work he's been doing the old place up. Now it's over I don't know quite what I'm going to do next. I haven't decided yet. There are a couple of jobs going at the National Museum of Scotland, what with the new extension and everything, but really, I'm not sure that's what I want to do any more. I've been thinking about going back into the field now that I've broken my desperate fear of exhumation. I'm going to decide this summer. And I suppose I'm half hoping I'll come across another case which needs unravelling. Another Nazi. Nina's still at the Burrell, of course. She bought a great little flat in Partick. And this year on the ninth of May we hiked up Arthur's Seat and lit a candle together beside the marshland, just like we said we would. Once in a while we still go for a big slap-up dinner at Rogano's.

'Do you think we'll ever get sick of this?' she asks me from the luxury of the booth that we always insist on sitting in.

And I just laugh and tell her that she's the best friend that anyone has ever had, which I believe to be the truth. And well, Molly's laid to rest now and it's over. But all that was a million miles away the evening that I walked back to Scotty's place from the Grange. When it was out at last with Mum and Dad and I finally knew for sure.

It was after eleven o'clock when I got back to the Grassmarket. I remember Scotty was sitting on his bed reading a book when I came up the stairs. I had run part of the way. I was quite freaked out, of course, because it takes a long time to come to terms with the kind of stuff that I'd just found out. But God, I was ecstatic. Really. I felt like I had sorted out so much. Got so much out of my system. Scotty had given me a key so I didn't even knock, I just opened the door and belted up the stairs.

'Ever thought about moving to the country?' I asked him as I burst into the room.

'Yeah,' he said, 'what have you got in mind?'

We didn't talk that much, though. Not that night. I was tired of talking and nothing we said was ever going to be able to match up to the emotional intensity of the rest of the day. I draped myself around him and kissed his neck. 'Dunno,' I mumbled, 'just a thought.' And we fell back down on to the mattress. That night, Scotty and I made love. It was our first time together, and I remember feeling really nervous as we grappled with each other to see who got to go on top. I'd give you two guesses as to who made it, but well, you know me pretty well by now, so you'll probably only need one.

**If you enjoyed MA POLINSKI'S POCKETS,
read on for an extract from Sara Sheridan's first
novel, TRUTH OR DARE . . .**

'Something is really wrong here,' I said, and then we heard the key turning in the lock.

There isn't a lot of storage in mews flats – most originally had a big hayloft, but David Curran's, like most of the mews flats in London, had been converted. If we hadn't panicked we would probably have made it out of the back window again, but, well to be frank, we did panic. Before David made it up the stairs, though, I had thrust the photo album back into the vacant space on the shelf and we had both dived across the hallway and into the wardrobe in the bedroom. This was not an ideal place to be located. It being late at night, he was almost certainly sure to come into the bedroom fairly soon. He was pretty sure to want to take off his clothes and hang them up. The wardrobe was fairly large, but also fairly full and didn't readily accommodate two normal-sized girls. If he turned on the light and opened the door, he'd probably see us. I can't honestly say that I was scared, but I didn't really want to get caught in the guy's wardrobe with my friend.

'One of us should go under the bed,' I whispered.

'You,' mouthed Becka.

Some wild adventurer. I could hear David in the living-room, so I gingerly pushed open the wardrobe door, sneaked across the carpet and rolled under the bed. There wasn't a lot of room – it was a low sort of a bed. Luckily it was a double, so if he lay down, as long as I stayed wherever he wasn't, I would still be able to breathe. I figured that once he was asleep we could sneak out. These are the sort of things that I was thinking about, when he did come into the bedroom. My heart was hammering. You can't imagine how annoyed I felt when he took off his tie and threw it on the floor. Perhaps the wardrobe would have been safe after all. No. No. He opened the wardrobe door and took out a coat hanger for his jacket. Quite right. It was a very expensive jacket. Then there was a little unexplained pause. The kind of pause which shouldn't really have been there.

'What the hell?' he said, and extricated Becka from between his perfectly laundered shirts.

'Oh my God,' said Becka. 'I can't explain this. I can't even think of anything to explain this.'

There was no point in lying when you could tell the truth. The closer it was to the truth the less there was to get caught out on. I willed plausible replies in her direction to little avail. There was a silence.

Social death in a banker's bedroom. I just closed my eyes and offered a silent prayer. I think he was just so shocked that he let her go. I heard her footsteps hammering down the stairs and the bang at the front door. Then there was this silence and he came and sat on the edge of the bed, picked up the phone and dialled a number.

'Conor,' he said, 'what the fuck is going on?'

ALSO AVAILABLE IN ARROW

ALL ARROW BOOKS ARE AVAILABLE THROUGH MAIL ORDER OR FROM YOUR LOCAL BOOKSHOP AND NEWSAGENT.

PLEASE SEND CHEQUE, EUROCHEQUE, POSTAL ORDER (STERLING ONLY), ACCESS, VISA, MASTERCARD, DINERS CARD, SWITCH OR AMEX.

EXPIRY DATE .... SIGNATURE ....

PLEASE ALLOW 75 PENCE PER BOOK FOR POST AND PACKING U.K.

OVERSEAS CUSTOMERS PLEASE ALLOW £1.00 PER COPY FOR POST AND PACKING.

ALL ORDERS TO:

ARROW BOOKS, BOOKS BY POST, TBS LIMITED, THE BOOK SERVICE, COLCHESTER ROAD, FRATING GREEN, COLCHESTER, ESSEX CO7 7DW.

TELEPHONE: (01206) 256 000
FAX: (01206) 255 914

NAME ....

ADDRESS..

....

Please allow 28 days for delivery. Please tick box if you do not wish to receive any additional information ☐

Prices and availability subject to change without notice.